# WILL HENRY

## AUTHOR'S NOTE

This is an accounting, straightforward if sometimes sinister, of the "Robin Hood of the little Blue." The real Jesse James will always remain part man, part myth. He lived that way, he died that way. It was the way he himself planned it and wanted it. But it is time for a long, hard look at Dr. Samuel's pale-eyed stepson—a look which peers beyond the popular fictions and stares flatly at the unpalatable facts. Jesse James was, and in all truth, an incredibly wicked man.

By that token, readers from the home-state counties of Clay and Jackson—native sons, like the undersigned, of the Missouri heartland of the legend—will now be warned that what follows is not another testimonial to the spotless memory of the sainted "Mr. Howard." Neither is it a further chanting of the threadbare recessional against the villainy of "the dirty little coward" who shot him, and thus, for two generations of weeping hero worshippers, "laid poor Jesse in his grave."

This is, basically, a true bill of indictment returned against the persistently misrepresented life of a cold-blooded murderer.

*W.H.*
*Jackson County*
*1954*

**Henry Wilson Allen** wrote under both the Clay Fisher and Will Henry bylines and was a five-time winner of the Golden Spur Award from the Western Writers of America. Under both bylines he is well known for the historical aspects of his Western fiction. He was born in Kansas City, Missouri. His early work was in short-subject departments with various Hollywood studios, and he was working at MGM when his first Western novel, *No Survivors* (1950), was published. While numerous Western authors before Allen provided sympathetic and intelligent portraits of Indian characters, Allen from the start set out to characterize Indians in such a way as to make their viewpoints an integral part of his stories. *Red Blizzard* (1951) was his first Western novel under the Clay Fisher byline and remains one of his best. Some of Allen's images of Indians are of the romantic variety, but his theme often is the failure of the American-frontier experience and the romance is used to treat his tragic themes with sympathy and humanity. On the whole, the Will Henry novels tend to be based more deeply on actual historical events, whereas in the Clay Fisher titles he was more intent on a story filled with action that moves rapidly. However, this dichotomy can be misleading since *MacKenna's Gold* (1963), a Will Henry Western about gold seekers, reads as much as one of the finest Clay Fisher titles, *The Tall Men* (1954). Both of these novels also served as the basis for memorable Western motion pictures. Allen was always experimental and *The Day Fort Larking Fell* (1968) is an excellent example of a comedic Western, a tradition as old as Mark Twain. His novels—*I, Tom Horn* (1975), *San Juan Hill, Death Of A Legend*, and *From Where The Sun Now Stands* (1960) in particular—remain imperishable classics of Western fiction. Over a dozen films have been made based on his work and both *The Day Fort Larking Fell* and *The Bear Paw Horses* are currently in development. At his best, he was a gripping teller of stories peopled with interesting characters true to the time and to the land.

"I am but a solitary horseman of the plains, born a century too late and far away," Allen once wrote about himself. He felt out of joint with his time and what alone may ultimately unify his work is the vividness of his imagination, the tremendous emotion with which he invested his characters and fashioned his Western stories. At his best, he could weave an almost incomparable spell that can involve a reader deeply in his narratives, informed always by his profound empathy with so many of the casualties of the historical process.

# WILL HENRY

## JESSE JAMES
## DEATH OF A LEGEND

**LEISURE BOOKS**  **NEW YORK CITY**

A LEISURE BOOK®

February 1996

Published by special arrangement with
Golden West Literary Agency.

Dorchester Publishing Co., Inc.
276 Fifth Avenue
New York, NY 10001

Printed in the United States of America.

# JESSE JAMES
# DEATH OF A LEGEND

# DAYBREAK

# Chapter One

*Centerville*

It was the 27th of May, 1856. As far as the eye might reach across the coiling creeks and loamy bottomlands of Old Missouri, spring lay everywhere upon the land. Everywhere, perhaps, save in the hearts and minds of the two small boys lingering in the warming dust of Centerville's Pleasant Grove schoolyard.

The elder of the boys, a square-shouldered lad of thirteen, spat uneasily into the dirt. "Dingus," he said to his companion, "what you reckon has happened to Bud? I bet he's tooken another hiding from Old Colonel."

The smaller boy, clearly his brother, did not answer at once. He was no more than eight years old, and poorly grown for that age. His pale blue eyes appeared weak and watery and he blinked them with a nervous constancy bordering on affliction. When at last he nodded, his voice was as thin and quick as the blink of his strange eyes.

"Bud will show up," was all he said.

"Well, supposing he don't?" challenged the other. "You meaning to go on through with it, anyways?"

Dingus looked at him. "Ma wants that nigger back, and we know where he is," he said. He said it as if it was the last word on the subject. The older boy, impressed, was not quite convinced.

"Uncle Eben's no good anyhow you look at him," he objected. "He aint worth a mouthful of ashes and you know it. Cuss it all, Dingus, it aint nowhere near like Ma couldn't buy another twice as good!"

"It aint," agreed Dingus shortly. "But he's *ours*."

"Yeah," the other grudged, "I reckon that's so. All the same I'd feel a heap better if Bud would come along. It's getting late."

"You losing your sand, Buck?"

There was a touch of impulsive anger in the smaller boy's question. Surprisingly, the older lad deferred to it.

"Hell no, Dingus. It's just that them thieving Jayhawkers is sort of worked up right now, what with old John Brown having pulled off that raid only the other day, and all. Maybe we'd ought to wait a week or so."

"We done waited three days now!" snapped Dingus. "We wait any longer and Old Man Pettis will have Uncle Eben undergrounded clean to Ioway!"

Buck grimaced unhappily, tried from another direction. "Ma will hide you, certain, when she learns you swiped the gun again."

Dingus blinked rapidly. "She aint going to learn, you hear me, Buck?" With the shrill question his small hand tightened on the butt of the big Walker Colt revolver protruding from his frayed waistband. Buck backed hurriedly away from him, looked anxiously up the road, and then nodded his clear relief.

"Well, anyways, yonder comes Bud. He can settle it."

"Aint nothing to settle," announced Dingus flatly. While he stared his brother down with the statement, their tardy companion padded up through the dust to join them.

Bud was outwardly cut from a different bolt of cloth than either of his two friends. He was a tall boy, a head taller than Buck though a full year younger. Where the adolescent youth will generally be a gawkish caricature of the man to come, Bud was already peculiarly handsome. He walked like a young lion—large of bone, big of paw, loose of joint and still, to be sure, a little awkward in his growing strength. But conscious, withal, of that strength and managing instinctively to move and speak with impressive control of it.

11

He came up to Buck and Dingus now, grinning broadly. "Let's cut," he greeted them. "We aint no more than just time, providing we step lively."

Buck and Dingus followed him, saving their breath for the more important work ahead. They shortly left the schoolhouse road, angling down through the brush toward the Little Blue. Coming out on that stream's heavily wooded course, they moved westward along its south bank, heading for its confluence with the Missouri, trotting single-file and as tirelessly as three young foxes out on the first spring hunt.

There was little in their appearances or attitudes to suggest the desperate nature of their mission. The fact remained that three small boys, accompanied only by a rusted Colt's revolver, were intending to swim the Big Muddy in spring flood, cross into enemy Kansas and free a Negro field hand liberated but seventy-two hours earlier in the opening slave raid of Old Missouri's "dark and bloody" Border War.

Sam Pettis was a widower of known short temper and fire-eating abolitionist sentiments. As the boys lay hidden in the river cottonwoods, two among them, at least, were entertaining reasonable doubts.

"Dadburn it, Ding"—it was the soft-voiced Bud objecting—"it aint going to work as slick as you let on. What about that damn dog, yonder?"

"Yeah, Ding!" Buck's agreement was fervent. "Maybe, like you say, Uncle Ebe's bound to be locked up in that smokehouse over there. And maybe, like you say, it shouldn't be no great chore to creep in and turn him loose. But, hang it all, not with that cussed Redbone hound stretched out across the doorstep of it!"

Dingus rubbed his turned-up nose, blinked his pale eyes. "Don't fret none about the dog," he ordered quickly. "I'll take care of him. You two just cut in across that corn patch and turn old Ebe loose, like I say. You hear?"

"Supposing Ebe puts up a fuss and don't want to come?" queried the practical Bud.

Dingus struggled to work the big revolver free of his sagging waistband and handed it to him.

"He won't put up no fuss," he said quietly.

Bud's grin was as warm as it was quick. "You're a ringtail wonder, Ding. You always got more ideas than a Pawnee Injun's got grayback body lice. Only trouble is, sometimes them ideas is just that."

"Is just what?" demanded his young comrade, blinking more rapidly now. Even at eight, Dingus had a limited capacity for jokes.

"Lousy," shrugged Bud, the good-natured if less than accomplished humorist of the trio.

"You're real funny, aint you?" said Dingus unsmilingly. "You watch yourself, you hear?"

Bud looked down on the smaller lad. He towered over him. He would have made two of him with enough left over for a fair start toward a third. Yet, in the end, he only grinned again.

"Sure, Ding," he agreed quickly. "You'd best shag now. Sun's dropping powerful fast."

They watched as Dingus darted down the near edge of the cornfield, around the melon patch and along the rail fence leading to the distant road and Old Man Pettis's front gate. Only when he was well out of earshot did Bud turn to the worried Buck and nod soberly. "Now, we got to be careful like Ding says, Buck. Whatever we do, we mustn't shoot the damn nigger. Not lest he starts laughing."

Dingus hitched up his galluses, spat into the dust of Old Sam's front yard. As he started for the front stoop his whistle and the willow switch he had picked up en route were going full blast.

The change in his attitude since leaving his companions was startling. He could not have presented a more appealing picture of the wide-eyed, wandering, barefoot boy. The nervous blink of his eyes, accented when he was angered or upset, was entirely gone. The thin face, normally about as pleasant as that of a weanling ferret, was beaming beneath a bucktoothed smile that would have disintegrated the heart of a limestone headmarker. When his reaching foot struck the first plank of the weathered stoop, his high-pitched, "Hello, in there! Anybody to home?" sang out with an innocence and purity unequaled.

# Death Of A Legend

Out back by the smokehouse, the Redbone hound missed a snore, pulled his head up out of the dust, cleared the crusted flies from around his nostrils with a suspicious "whoof!" Presently, he got up, stretched, yawned, trotted around the house.

On the front stoop Dingus waited, hearing the approach of the hound and hearing the stir of the old man moving inside the house. Shortly, Sam Pettis came out. He listened to Dingus's polite "Please, sir, can I have a drink of your well?" stared at him a minute, then grumped, "Hell's fire, it's right in front of you, boy. Aint nobody stopping you that I can see."

"Oh, please, sir," Dingus changed subjects nervously, "could you put that dog up?"

The ancient Redbone had shuffled around the corner of the house, leaned wearily against the roof-post of the stoop to rest up from his long journey. Regaining his breath, he woofed quarter-heartedly at the visiting ragamuffin, collapsed back into the dirt, crawled under the stoop with a grateful sigh.

"Old Hickory won't bother you none," said Pettis. "He aint got but four teeth left in his head, is half blind and caint hear a shotgun six feet away. Only thing he's got left that's any account is his nose."

"Oh, thank you, sir! I was bit by a Redbone once. They're powerful biters. My! Aint he a grand dog though? And see how he minds you. I sure am beholden to you, Mr. Pettis!"

Dingus's gratitude was not alone well done, but a little overdone. Old Sam Pettis's eyes narrowed.

"How come you to know my name, boy?"

He moved toward Dingus with the question, what was supposed to be a fetching smile uncovering his few tobacco-rotted teeth. Dingus was not in the market for any fetching smiles. He backed away a bit faster than somewhat. Then, just as the old man was reaching for him, a saving, earsplintering noise came ripping into the quiet from the direction of the forgotten smokehouse.

"What in the tarnal hell was that!" roared Old Sam.

Dingus could have named the noise for him. But he didn't bother. As the old man ran past him to get a clear view of the backyard, he was saving all his breath for a run and jump over the front picket fence. For what the fiery old Kansas abolitionist was glaring at was the barefooted flight across his young cornfield of a reliberated Missouri slave and two Clay County farm boys. Not to mention an old Colt's revolver which was banging happily away at the heels of the terrified Negro.

The booming black-powder explosions were enough to raise the dead—or the almost dead. Old Hickory, the Redbone hound, came stumbling out from under the stoop, shaking his old head and baying distractedly. At the same time, Sam Pettis dove for his front door and the double-barreled 12-gauge shotgun hanging over his living-room mantel. And Dingus cleared the picket fence and took off up the road like a stomped-out cottontail.

Old Hickory ran three times around in a circle, blundered out the front gate, peered up the road with his rheumy eyes, bayed once after the fleeing Dingus, galloped back into the yard, ran gallantly into the corner-post of the stoop, fell down, got back up, shook himself, dropped resignedly to his haunches and began scratching.

Minutes later, he was displaying his sole remaining talent. Cursed on by his enraged master, he quartered briefly around the empty smokehouse, took off, baying dolorously, across the still settling dust of the cornfield. As Sam Pettis had said—Old Hickory still had a nose.

Dingus, circling far east of the cornfield, saw the old man and the hound move across the mounded rows of the corn patch. He saw, too, the bounce of the May sun off the twin barrels of the 12-gauge. And heard, as well, the bawling notes of the dog's voice. Somewhere ahead, Bud and Buck and Uncle Eben were already lost in the welcome tangle of the bottom willows. But no boy born of hound-dog country needed to be told that, given time, and not much time, Old Hickory and Sam Pettis would come up to them. Nor did he need to be told what might happen then.

It was a day and time when if a boy would undertake a man's work he could expect to be paid off at a man's wage.

He himself could cut and drift. The hound was not running his track. But that was not the plan, and when Dingus made a plan, nobody, not he nor anybody else, fooled around with that plan. He had said they would join back up at the slough north of Old Pettis's place, and that is what they would do. Dingus would be there. The others had better be there, too. They were.

When he popped out of the brush, scratched and torn and flushed with panting, he found them waiting for him. And even as they talked, the belling of the old Redbone drew nearer and nearer.

"Now what the hell we going to do, Ding?" It was Bud doing the asking. "We dassn't stick here and we dassn't cut and run. Ebe's turned his cussed ankle and caint do no more than gimp along."

Bud wasn't frightened, nor flustered. But Buck, chiming anxiously in, was both. "Oh Lord, Dingus, you've got us into one, this time! We got to do something and do it fast. That old fool will *shoot*! We caint just covey-up here and leave him wing away at us!"

His eight-year-old brother stared at him. He shifted his glance, including Bud in the level cold of the look. "Now, you two simmer off," he advised them. "We aint got a blessed thing to fret about excepting that ganted-up old hound. First thing we do is take care of him. He's a quarter mile up on Old Pettis. We'll just leave him come along up to us."

"Doan you do it, Marse Ding!" Uncle Eben, torn between old family loyalties and new freedoms as yet untasted, made the suggestion with bug-eyed fervor. "You boys jes' skeedaddle on out'n hyar and leave Ol' Ebe handle dat houn' dawg. Now, you lemme do dat foh you, Marse Ding!"

Dingus moved quickly toward Bud. Before the latter could guess his intent, his hand had slipped the big Walker Colt from the other boy's waistband and jammed it into the pleading Uncle Eben's face.

"Now, Uncle," he said quietly, "you just keep up your infernal blubbering and I'll blow your damn black head off."

The freed slave lost his pure Kentucky color.

"Lawd, Lawd! Doan you leave him do it, Marse Bud. Doan you leave him, now!"

Dingus turned his back on the old Negro as Bud stepped forward, frowning. "Don't give me none of your sass, Bud," he warned. "I aint going to harm the old ninny none." With the abrupt dismissal, he pushed the gun into his trouser tops, waved toward the farther brush. "Yonder comes the dog. Now, you do as I say."

Seconds later, Old Hickory came up to them. He stopped twenty feet away and bawled four times in a row, letting Pettis know he had the game treed. Then he dropped his bony rear into the bottom loam and began to scratch. His job was done.

"Take that rope you brung along and snub him to yonder sapling," Dingus ordered Bud quickly. "Snub him good and short."

Thinking his companion meant simply to tie the old dog up and run for it, Bud nodded and grinned. He moved forward, gave a low whistle, clapped his hands encouragingly. Old Hickory looked up, stopped scratching. Presently, his tail began to club the ground in slow friendship. He got up and met the advancing boy halfway, tail still wagging.

Bud slipped the rope around his neck and led him uncomplainingly down the slough toward the cottonwood indicated by Dingus, who followed him. And behind Dingus came Buck, thoughtfully helping the limping Uncle Eben down the steep bank. They could all hear Old Pettis thrashing through the willows above them, cursing and hollering-up his missing dog with every step.

Old Hickory lifted his head to answer but Bud cuffed him playfully alongside the muzzle. "Here, you. None of that, now. You just hold still till we get you trussed up here. Then you can try and yammer all you dang please."

Dingus moved forward.

"You got him tied short like I said?" he asked easily.

"Shucks!" grinned Bud. "He couldn't scrootch

around far enough to fetch himself a bite in the behind! He's snubbed for sure. Let's mosey along."

"Get out of my way," said Dingus.

The other boy moved unthinkingly aside. As he did, Dingus stepped past him. Bud's mouth dropped in shocked disbelief. "Here now, for cripe's sake, Dingus!" he cried. "You caint actually mean to—"

"*Shut up!*" snapped his pale-eyed companion, and holding the big Colt with both small hands he shoved it into the side of the old dog's head and pulled the trigger. "Now let the son of a bitch holler if he's a mind to." He nodded softly to Bud. "Let's go."

White-faced, Bud dropped his head. He did not answer him. He did not want to look at Dingus and he did not want to look at Old Hickory. He felt sick in the pit of his stomach and only wanted to go back in the trees a piece and vomit. Coming up through the willows, Buck and Uncle Eben stopped in turn and looked down at Dingus, and on past him to what he had done.

"I said let's go," repeated the latter, his voice still quiet.

And with the words he turned away, ramming the still-smoking revolver hard and sure into his trousers' waistband.

Mr. Hurlburt Peabody heaved his daily vast sigh of relief and closed the Pleasant Grove schoolhouse doors from the inside. He leaned against them a minute, praying in silence that Providence would soon send him some more rewarding labor than that of Centerville schoolmaster.

While he awaited the Lord's answer, however, each day, no matter how dismal, had its own peculiar rewards. Mr. Peabody was, withal, a sanguine man. In his moments of rare relief, such as the present one, he did not hesitate to count his blessings. This day, those blessings had been three in number, and three in the order of their classroom nicknames, to wit: "Bud," "Buck," and "Dingus."

Any day which saw those three failing to appear in school was one to be thankfully recorded. With full gratitude, now, the weary headmaster made his way to his desk and took up his attendance book. He heaved the worn volume open, reached for his pen and ink. As his hand swept down the listings of his Clay County charges, Mr. Peabody shook his head in scholarly reservation.

Ah, indeed, he thought, what's in a name? Those three names for present instance, now. Such nice names they were. Such fine, Christian names. Names with the true Anglo-Saxon ring of quality folk to them. And yet—

Mr. Peabody entered his notations of absence behind each of the three names, one thing entirely settled in his mind. As promising as those names might appear upon the enrollment records of the Pleasant Grove District School, no good was bound to come of the three small boys who bore them. That much was absolutely certain.

Mr. Hurlburt Peabody may have had his limitations as a man. Perhaps even as a savant. But there was one qualification he possessed with a vengeance. He was a hell of a prophet.

His day had been a hard one and Mr. Peabody was weary unto collapse. He left his desk and his schoolhouse in uncustomary disarray, pausing only long enough to blow upon and adjust his pince-nez and to reach his round beaver hat from its cloakroom peg. He was gone, then, leaving the last shaft of the late sun peering in through the broken panes of the west window.

The slim ray wandered idly across his desk top, lingered on the abandoned pen, moved on to stop and pry inquisitively at the still open attendance book. And at the three names so recently tolled off in Mr. Peabody's precise hand.

As the headmaster had paused to note, they were fine, Christian names.

*"Younger, Thomas Coleman."*
*"James, Alexander Franklin."*

Then, as innocent, upright and Christian as any of them:

*"James, Jesse Woodson."*

# Chapter Two

*Salem Church*

Thus began, and passed, the years of the Border War. It was in February of the fifth spring following the boys' liberation of Uncle Eben that the first rocket from Fort Moultrie ran up into the southern night and exploded over Fort Sumter. The echo of Confederate cannonfire released by its fiery signal carried growlingly across the land.

Frank James, coming a full eighteen and no longer the mild-mannered "Buck" of the boyhood years, enlisted in the rebel Missouri State Guard. Cole Younger, now seventeen and a man grown, hesitated between his loyal desire to join up and his bounden duty to stay at home and work the land. In the end he listened to his mother, staying on at the family farm near Harrisonville in Cass County.

Up at Centerville in Clay County, Dingus, now rising fourteen, underwent the same struggle but with less cause. The situation had not yet deteriorated to the point of enlisting little better than thirteen-year-olds. He, like Cole, stayed on the land, that land being the Centerville farm of his new stepfather, Dr. Reuben Samuel.

Dr. Samuel was a quiet, well-educated medical doctor to whom Dingus looked with great respect. He was, in fact, the first real father the boy had known; his natural parent and his mother's first husband, the Reverend Robert James, an ordained minister, had abandoned his family to disappear in the California gold rush of '49.

The first weeks of the war were strangely quiet in the border country. Then, three weeks after the South's first smashing victory at Bull Run, Sterling Price and his Missouri Guard clashed at Wilson Creek with the first regular Union troops to penetrate the area. Frank, a boot corporal in Price's irregular cavalry, distinguished himself in the victorious action and was granted a thirty-day furlough. He was ahorse and headed homeward before the ink on his pass was decently dry.

If the five years of the Border War from 1856 to 1861 had been Dingus's cradle, the two from 1861 to 1863 were Jesse's crucible. They marked in swift fact the end of Dingus and the beginning of Jesse James.

On his return from Wilson Creek, Frank became the idol of his clansmen in general and of young Dingus in particular. Shortly, reports of the latter's boastful accounts of Frank's rebel exploits arrived in the Union town of Liberty. As promptly, the commander of the Union state militia garrison saw his duty. Within the hour his men were riding. Before daylight of August 15, Frank was considering the freedoms of Confederate speech from within the limestone walls of Liberty's Union lockup.

Throughout the years to come, the political connections of the James family in Missouri were to play a behind-scenes part in the progressive outlawry of Frank and Jesse. The beginning situation of the Liberty lockup proved typical. Shortly before noon of the 15th, the garrison commander received telegraphed instructions from his area corps commander to the following unhappy effect: State Senator Erasmus R. Cole, firstly a loyal blood-cousin of Jesse's mother and only secondly a lip-service Union man, had made official protest to the arrest. The Senator deplored the Liberty officer's rash action, personally guaranteed the future loyalty of young James, and demanded his immediate release on parole.

Frank went free before the day was up, solely on his own signature to an oath of loyalty to the Union.

This naïve document was no sooner signed than violated. Some time during the week of August 20, 1861, Frank slipped his Union parole to vanish into the nameless ranks of Charley Quantrill's Confederate guerrillas. It became at once inevitable that the fourteen-year-old Jesse would attempt to follow him.

The favorite tale is that of the serious-minded, Bible-quoting Frank, prevailing upon his younger brother to return to the Samuel farm and "stay by his faithful mother's side." The simple fact is that Quantrill himself laughed the baby-faced candidate out of the bandit camp, hastening his exit with a well-placed cavalry boot and the derisive promise to "cut off his ears and pin them to his backside," should he again pester into men's business.

Through the fall and early winter Quantrill's raiders murdered and looted along the Kansas border. In swift retaliation, Jennison's Kansas Red Legs struck back. By July of the following summer, the guerrilla stage was set for Jesse's entrance. In that month the Jayhawkers, under "Shawnee" Harker, invaded Harrisonville, putting the town to the torch. Leveled among its ashes was old Colonel Younger's famed livery stable. Within thirty days the Colonel himself was found murdered upon a lonely road near Independence. Mrs. Younger and the children fled Harrisonville, seeking refuge on the family farm. They fled in vain. That winter the Jayhawkers, again under Harker, returned and destroyed the farm. It was too much for young Cole. In desperation he went over to the guerrillas of George Todd, the second in growing fame among the leaders of the Missouri irregulars.

On November 14 Cole and Todd, with four other guerrillas, trapped Harker in a Kansas City saloon. The latter, with five of his men, was playing poker at a back table. Cole and his followers, disguised as Federal cavalrymen, entered the room at 11:00 P.M. Outside, his clumsy uniform coat turned high against the sting of the wet November snow, a pale-eyed, blinking boy held their nervous horses in instant readiness.

Approaching the table, Cole waited politely until Harker glanced up, then asked quietly, "Excuse me, sir. Are you Mr. Harker?"

"I am," grunted the other. "Who might be asking?"

"Cole Younger," replied the soft-voiced Union soldier, and whipped out two pistols and shot the Red Leg leader dead in his chair.

Before his companions could move, Todd and his four henchmen were blazing away. In as many seconds the entire six of the Jayhawk gamblers lay spread in death around their last game. Cole Younger, the second of the boyhood trio of Bud and Buck and Dingus to gain this distinction, was embarked, full-blooded, on the outlaw trail.

And Jesse James had held his horse!

The following month a party of Federal militia, still on the trail of the vanished Cole, swept down on the Samuel place shortly before dusk. Angered at failing to find the wanted man in hiding there, they seized Dr. Samuel with the announced intention of jailing him as a Southern sympathizer.

When the ex-Mrs. Robert James, a gaunt, fierce-eyed woman well fitted by harsh nature and training to be the mother of outlaws, sprang to his defense she was roughly handled. Dingus, literally weeping with rage, leaped at the jeering troopers. He was knocked down and, on the orders of the young lieutenant commanding the search party, held and flogged unmercifully. The rest is threadbare legend. The detachment at once departed, taking Dr. Samuel only far enough down the road to string him up to the nearest tree. Dingus and his mother, trailing them, cut him down in time and he survived to become the physician in constant, shadowy attendance to the future wounds of his savage stepsons. Fact or folktale, it could not have altered the result. With the mistreatment of his beloved mother, and with his own brutal flogging, Dingus James, like Cole Younger before him, had had enough. Within the year a more evil name began to be heard along the border: *Jesse James*!

In rough-voiced council before the patched remnant of a Union dog-tent sat the fabulous

William F. "Bloody Bill" Anderson, fresh from his major part in the recent Confederate guerrilla sacking and burning of Lawrence, Kansas. Flanking him squatted eight of his chief lieutenants. Confronting the uncertain tempers of this tough group stood an understandably awkward Cole Younger.

"Here, now, my young bucko," Anderson was growling at Cole, "you aiming to tell us you got a friend that's only just turned sixteen, what's fitten to ride with the likes of us? Why, I aint even decided to leave you join up yet, let alone no wetnose friend of yourn. What's his name now, Younger? Speak up fast, you hear."

Cole was beginning to wish he had stayed with George Todd, instead of falling for this wild idea of Dingus's about bracing Bloody Bill right in his Piney Ridge hideout, and in the middle of the night to boot! Todd was a pure mean one, but this Anderson, with his voice that sounded like it was coming up out of a bear's bowels, was enough to untemper a bobcat.

He toed an errant ember back into the firebed, kept his head down.

"Dingus James," he said at last, uncomfortably.

*"Dingus James!"*

Cole winced. A body would have thought, from the way Anderson roared it, that he had been arrow-shot square through his broad behind. "Goddamn you, boy. I wouldn't let that flicker-eyed runt foller me far enough out in the

30

woods to make water! Why, Frank himself says he's crazy as a turpentined cat. That puny squirt couldn't get into no camp of mine with a pass from General Price himself!"

*"Oh, couldn't he, now?"*

In startled response to the thin, high-pitched query, the eyes of the outlaw circle swept past Bloody Bill to the entrance of the tent behind him. Nobody, Anderson included, said a word. To a man they simply sat and stared.

And with good reason.

Somehow, while his friend Cole had been stalling for him, the despised subject of Bloody Bill's outburst had got past the guerrilla pickets and into their leader's tent. He was standing insolently now in its ragged entrance.

At sixteen, Jesse stood not over five feet six, including the considerable uplift of his Union jackboots. He wore hickory homespun britches under a cavalry-issue overcoat. A black slouch hat, its brim riding his jug-handle ears, and the belted-on sag of an old Walker Colt completed his attire. His face, pale and receding of chin, his eyes weak and watery as always, together with the shoulder-long tumble of his dark hair, gave him that peculiarly girlish appearance which was to be remarked so frequently by his future comrades-in-arms—and was to figure so prominently in what followed now.

Overcoming their original astonishment at the boy's being able to penetrate their midst undetected, the guerrillas, still heady over their successes at Lawrence, broke out in a coarse round of backhouse humor, the total of which was charged to the account of the newcomer's comic-opera appearance.

A rare, high time was had by all—up to a point.

That point was shortly made by the unsmiling Jesse.

"Comes the time you're done with your jackass laughing," he suggested quietly, "I got some business to give you. That is, providing you've got the guts to go after it."

The laughter stopped. Bloody Bill heaved himself up off his haunches, moved in on Jesse.

"You got a big mouth, boy. Lemme tell you a few things you shouldn't leave come out of it."

He was a huge brute, black-bearded, pin-small of eye, shading six feet in height, broad and shapeless as a two-hundred-pound powder canister. He towered menacingly over the slender youth, a guerrilla giant threatening a tender child.

He didn't get far with his loud-voiced lecture. Jesse cut him off with an unqualified sneer, together with a quick blink of his blue eyes and some thin-lipped advice. "I don't scare worth a damn, mister," he said, "so you may as well leave off sweating yourself."

He said it, Cole thought, like he said most everything. Like he wasn't asking any questions nor expecting any answers, but like he was giving an order. And looking to see it hopped to.

The effrontery paid off.

Anderson stepped back. Took a second look at the boy and saw a couple of things he had missed in his first inspection. He grunted thoughtfully and dropped his booming basso accordingly.

"Go ahead, young'un," he grudged. "Take your cut at it. I allow we had you wrong."

"I allow you did," was Jesse's sole concession.

Having made it, he briefly laid out the harsh details of his plan. It was a calculated plot of brutal vengeance against a certain Lieutenant Ferris P. Smith of the Liberty garrison, the unlucky young officer who had commanded the Blue patrol the day of Dr. Samuel's "hanging." As he went along, Anderson's growing grin of admiration was picked up and passed around the charmed circle of his high command. By the time the wolfish jury had heard all the evidence, its verdict was unanimous: Cole Younger's friend was in.

Jesse James, last of the Centerville trinity to receive the accolade, was an accepted guerrilla.

It was a rainy summer afternoon, unseasonably cold and blustery. The date: Friday, August 24, 1863.

The gingham dress of the young girl guiding the fine black horse down the Independence road pressed wetly against her slender form. The garment, clearly its wearer's Sunday best, covered the contours of the girl's graceful seat in the sidesaddle, revealing only the toes of the

33

dainty boots peeping out beneath its frilly hem.

Shortly she came to the house she sought, a drab two-storied affair of red brick set well back in the woods from the main road. She reined the black away from the thoroughfare, halted him in front of the silent building. With pretty hesitation, she tilted her bonnet brim, nervously called out her presence. Presently the door swung open to show a painted slattern in a pink silk dressing gown. This was "Big Mary" Binistrone, a madam of the old school and one plainly out of sorts at being disturbed before business hours.

But the moment Madam Binistrone's shadowed eyes alighted upon the tender years and willowy sex of her visitor all signs of irritation vanished. "Why, dearie! Do come in! Now whatever in the blessed world could have brought you to see poor old Aunt Mary?"

Her caller explained, in a fetchingly shy voice, that she was one Betsy Marie Burris, from down yonder along the Mill Creek road, and that she could not possibly tarry to come in. She must away and back to her unhappy home. She had come only to determine if she might not upon happy occasion hope to elude her Puritan parents and visit with the dear young soldier boys who came so regularly from the nearby garrison to Madam Mary's?

The plea touched the good madam—particularly when it was revealed that poor Betsy had several girl chums who were likewise afire with the need of solacing the loneliness of the Union lads from Liberty.

The assignation was generously set for that same evening.

In the flustered act of departing, shy Betsy awkwardly mentioned a certain dashing young Lieutenant Ferris Smith, who had taken her eye and heart. Would it be too much to hope that this handsome youth was among Madam's friends?

With the hasty assurance that Lieutenant Smith was indeed among that fortunate number, poor Betsy Burris turned her fine-limbed saddler and departed. Big Mary shut the door and shuffled back to bed, not troubling to watch her new recruit decently down the lane. It was immediately the better for the latter and swiftly the worse for Big Mary, that she did not.

Fifty yards from Madam Binistrone's front door, a vagrant gust of the August bluster squalled across the rainpools of the muddy road. It whirled about the cantering black, flaring up the skirts of its demure rider. With a backflung glance, and an ungirlish snarl, the cursing "Betsy" slowed her mount and smoothed the offending garment.

The profanity appeared singularly justified.

What had under Big Mary's careless glance passed for the dainty toe of a parlor slipper was a clay-smeared Union jackboot. And what had appeared to be nothing more sinister than the proper stays of a whalebone corselet was the belted girth of a low-holstered Walker Colt.

Some time before midnight Jesse, bereft of Betsy's gingham and giggles, led his "girl chums" down upon Madam Binistrone's recreation hall. In swift silence the guerrillas surrounded the house. At the last moment a difference of opinion developed between Billy Gregg, Anderson's chief subaltern, and "sweet Betsy Burris."

The former insisted that Bloody Bill's orders to seize the celebrating officers as hostages for use in bargaining some of the guerrilla-kin out of the Liberty lockup be carried out. Jesse as vehemently demanded a full-scale, no-quarter assault. For a time it seemed the effort of the sentimental mission might be wasted on the midnight air. But Dingus James, as Cole had so many times ruefully noted, could always be trusted to bullhead his own ideas through.

In the present case, Jesse seized the carbine of his nearest fellow. The next instant the weapon's butt was shattering the glass of the handiest window and Bloody Bill's newest enlistment was leaping through the shattered panes.

He lit on his feet inside, his eyes blinking furiously to adjust to the dazzle of the lamplight. With outlaw luck, he had picked the right room. Across from him, laughing and drinking around a rough pine table, lounged the select officer

group privileged to await the arrival of Betsy
Burris and her Mill Creek virgins.

Lieutenant Ferris Smith had only time to
push away from the table, drop his tumbler of
forty-rod and cry out, "What in the name of God
*is* this?"

His answer was three .44-caliber Walker Colt
slugs beneath the heart, their spread no greater
than that of the small hand which fired them.
He was dead before his body slumped forward
into the litter of cigar stubs and spilled whiskey
beneath the table.

In the seconds which followed, the other
guerrillas, accepting Jesse's shots as the signal
for the attack, poured through the side and rear
windows of the house. It was a complete surprise and a grisly massacre. When it was done,
twelve Union soldiers lay dead or dying on the
crude pine planking of Big Mary's sordid bor-
dello.

The name of Billy Gregg, the man who nom-
inally led the guerrilla murderers, has long been
forgotten, as have been the names of Lieutenant
Smith and his fellow officers. Only one name is
remembered today—and seldom with the real
significance of its connection to the Independence raid.

*Jesse James had seized his first command.*

He was never to forget the thrill which surged
through him that night. Nor was he ever to re-
linquish that first realization of his strange

power over other men as wild and wicked as himself.

Riding with Gregg at the head of their followers back toward Anderson's Piney Ridge hideout, the young guerrilla's thin mouth twisted with the vicious pleasure of his thinking. From now on, by God, he would lead! Even if he had yet for a tedious while to appear to follow such as Anderson, Todd and Quantrill, simply in the routine learning of the profession. He would one day, *and soon*, lead them all. A body could lay to that as sure as sin was no longer for sale back at Big Mary's!

The day, indeed, came soon.

On August 27, seventy-two hours after the Independence raid, General Ewing, the Union area commander, issued his notorious General Order No. 11, requiring every resident of Cass, Clay, Jackson, Bates and parts of Vernon counties to come at once into the Union lines or places of military fortification, or be henceforward treated as outlaws.

There was no mercy in the demand. In enforcing it the Federal troops looted at will. For three weeks the quarantined counties were in a state of shock under the open rape of their human and property rights. Then shadowy riders began to pound the outer roads. Backwoods doors were opened a wary crack, the whispered word was passed, the nameless horsemen galloped on.

"Set tight. Be ready. Stay out of sight. Charley Quantrill is riding again!"

The generic phrase meant not alone Quantrill but of course Anderson, Todd, Maddox, Shepherd, Poole and the whole galaxy of the guerrilla confederacy. And it was soon to include a new name.

Jesse James broke the counterattack.

Early in the frosty twilight of October 3, with Cole and two other guerrillas, he swept down upon a Federal picket post north of Wellington, Missouri. Of the eight troopers who held the post, none survived. Cole, in retelling the event, generously insisted on crediting Jesse with four of the kills, and the blinking-eyed youth's reputation was delivered, full-formed.

He gave it no chance to die aborning. Two days later, this time sided only by Cole and brother Frank, he ambushed a company of eighty Federals along the Lexington road near Salem Church. The murderous crossfire of the partisans "left twenty bluebellies lying in the dirt down by the church."

It was not enough.

The third week after that saw Jesse, progressing in command now, riding with George Todd at the head of thirty guerrillas. Flanking him as he trailed the fabled Todd, "a man of iron who would have a go at a circular saw," were the omnipresent Cole and Frank. On Shawnee Town Road, they ambushed a Union wagon train of nineteen ambulances loaded with replacement infantry. Sixty Federal troopers died in that wild half hour. Of the number, twenty were forcibly held, hale and wounded alike, while their throats were cut. It was literally a hog butchery, an act without military parallel. Yet, still, it was nowhere near the end of the guerrilla brutality.

Within the year another name of outrage was to be added to those of Wellington, Salem Church and Shawnee Town Road. This name would reach far beyond the borders of infamy set in the preceding slaughters and, even above Lawrence, this name will still cause a Missourian to hawk and spit bitterly, as though to clear the shameful taste of its sound from his remembering mouth—*Centralia*!

# Chapter Three

*Centralia*

At the Samuel farmhouse only the dim light of the coal-oil lamp in the parlor window smoked and shifted against the seep of the wind through the crudely glazed panes. By the lamplight Mrs. Zerelda Samuel sat gaunt and upright in her ladderback rocker, framed squarely against the window, the picture of a good woman deep in her pious study of the family Bible. Across from her, as carefully staged before the window, Dr. Samuel nodded over his copy of the weekly Osceola *Democrat*.

Under the innocence of this scene it was interesting to note that the quick hammer of hoofbeats approaching along the Kansas City wagon road brought a stiffening of backs and exchange of sharp looks between the couple, eased only when the parlor door subsequently opened and Frank looked in to nod and drawl, "It's all right, Ma. That's the last of them."

The gray-haired falcon in the rocker returned the nod with a curt, "Mind you now, Frank! You boys take care out there in the barn. And see that Jesse hurries it up. He shouldn't have had them to meet here in the first place."

"Sure, Ma," said Frank quickly. "Remember, if anybody happens along the road, have Doc wave the back room lamp like Dingus said. You hear now?"

"All right, son, see you hurry it up," repeated the once widow James, and returned to her slow lip-reading of the First Book of Samuel, xxii, 2: "*And every one that was in distress, and every one that was in debt, and every one that was discontented, gathered themselves unto him; and he became a captain over them. . . .*"

The Samuel barn stood dark under the drive of the wind and the seeking fingers of the rain. No light shone beyond its weathered doors, no sound carried past its hewn log walls. Yet the long horse-shed abutting on its rear was crowded with a baker's dozen of the finest thoroughbreds in Old Missouri, and any Union commander west of the Mississippi would have given away three grades of rank to have had a listening post within the darkness of that shed.

"All right, by God!" big George Todd was saying. "We're all agreed then?"

His answer was a wash of quick nods from

the assembled guerrilla captains, and he concluded jubilantly, "It's sandbag poker, boys! We'll rake in the biggest raise of bluebellies yet. By Christ, it's table stakes and I say we're calling them sky-high this time!"

"It's penny ante," said Jesse James, stepping from his place in the shadows beyond the main group, "and I say you're calling them dirt-low."

Todd whirled at once from the frayed Missouri map he and the others had been studying. Anderson and the remainder of the guerrilla command turned more slowly. "Maybe," said George Todd, thick-voiced and watching Jesse's pistol hand, "you'd best call that again, *real slow*."

Jesse blinked at him a moment, then turned his back on him. He moved to the makeshift map table, bent over its grimy chart, his pale face expressionless in the yellow light of the solitary lantern suspended above it. "You all step up here a minute," he said softly. "I'll show you something."

The outlaw leaders edged nervously in around him, each of them in uneasy turn feeling the sudden touch of that power over other men which was growing so swiftly in Jesse. Only the faces of Cole Younger and Frank James were left relatively undisturbed by the reflection of that power. It was not new to them; they had felt it long ago. They even had a name for it—Old Hickory—and a sight and a sound to remember that name by: the muffled burst of a black-powder cartridge, and the splash of a poor brute's skull striking the smooth bark of a bottomland cottonwood.

As the guerrillas listened, spellbound, Jesse's slim finger leapt back and forth across the map, his high voice rattling his corrections on the previously approved plan of attack, sharp as volleyed musketfire. When he had concluded, Anderson was the first to find words for his admiration.

"Son of a bitch!" shouted Bloody Bill, smashing his bear's paw of a fist down upon the packing-box table. "You've done it again, Dingus! Now, boy, we'll just up and fetch it off like you say. It'll be the God-awfullest slaughter of Yanks yet seed in these parts. And that by somewhat, I say!"

"It'll be twenty-dollar poker, leastways," agreed his star pupil, unabashed, "and I'll call the first pot."

"You'll what?" challenged Todd, glaring at him.

"*I'll lead the main bunch that takes the train at the depot.*" Jesse said it short and he said it flat. Strangely, not a man among twelve of the most desperate west of St. Louis made a move to deny him.

Five minutes later, the last of the clay-smeared horses in the outer shed had vanished back into the wind and the rain. In the dark stillness of the barn, only the stale smoke of many cigars and short cob pipes lingered to argue the matter with the coal-oil stink of the blown-out lantern.

The youthful soldier aboard the North Missouri's train No. 66 was surely not eighteen. The freshness of his skin, its lack of beard, the tousle of his blond hair all bore clear witness to that. A Howard County boy, he wore the uniform of the Sixth Missouri Guards, and was not nearly so interested in the approaching stop as were his coach companions. He had, after all, seen Centralia many times.

But as the train slowed now, his blue eyes suddenly narrowed at the milling rank of horsemen blocking the station house. "Hold on, for the luvva Gawd!" he gasped aloud, his frightened glance fastening on the slender, gun-belted youth sidestepping the fine black horse along the depot platform. "*Jesus Christ, it's Jesse James!*"

Ten minutes after his startled cry, the boy was kneeling alongside the North Missouri's track facing the morning sun and his Maker. Flanking him were the other Union soldiers taken off the train at gunpoint by the rebel-yelling guerrillas. Down the long line of kneeling prisoners Jesse, Frank, George Todd and Bloody Bill Anderson moved methodically. When the last of their Colts had barked its heavy echo across the meadow beyond the tracks, the toll of Federal dead stood at seventy-five—every last Union soldier found aboard the

North Missouri's train No. 66.

With the grisly execution done, the guerrillas gathered in an orderly column of fours and rode unhurriedly out of town. When the last of them was gone, the dazed citizens of Centralia gathered to stare at the soldier dead. Shortly, still moving in stunned silence, the townfolk produced mattocks, spades and shovels. Within the hour, the last of the pitiful windrow of trooper bodies was spaded under, buried without memory of name or rank in a common, open grave.

Five miles south of Centralia, riding ramrod-straight with Frank at the rear of the retreating guerrilla column, Jesse looked for Cole. Presently he saw him, jogging his bay, head down and alone, some distance ahead.

Cole glanced up as Jesse eased the black down to match the jog-trot of the bay. "And where were you when we lined up them blue-belly bastards?" demanded the latter belligerently. "I didn't see no Younger lead being put to use."

Cole stared back at him, saw that he was blinking rapidly. Dingus was really mad about it; he wasn't just horsing now.

Somewhere in the back of his adventurous mind, Cole Younger had a line. As long as he followed Jesse, and he followed him to the last, he never stepped across it. He had known about that line since barefoot boyhood. He knew, now, that it would cut between him and Dingus James until the last horse was shot out from under either one of them.

When the throats were cut on Shawnee Town road, Cole had turned away. When the kneeling troopers had just now slumped into the gravel of the North Missouri's right-of-way, his Colt had been cold in its holster. He had always accounted for his fair share along with the others, that was certain. But he had never shot a defenseless human being—man, woman, or child.

And he had never killed a dog.

"Sometimes, Dingus," he said at last, and softly, "I just get plain damn sick to my belly."

In guerrilla as in any warfare, the first mistake is apt to prove the last. Up to Centralia the outlaw campaign had been a signal success. Now, the North was at last aroused. Blue patrols rode the back-country lanes around the clock. As usual, the guerrillas vanished. And, as usual, awaited their chance to regather and strike again. The chance did not come. The Union pressure became intolerable. A year of desultory skirmishing passed with no single outlaw victory. By the fall of 1864 the raiders were forced to the last resort—attaching themselves to some unit of the regular Confederate Army. The unit they chose was the Missouri Corps of General Sterling Price.

But the star of the South was paling. Jesse, second now only to Todd, Anderson and Quantrill in the guerrilla command, led his followers into Price's regiment late in September. Riding with the regular cavalry of fabled fellow-Missourian, Jo Shelby, he was in time to see George Todd killed leading a charge in the October raid on Independence. The following month he saw the bearded head of Bloody Bill Anderson speared upon a telegraph pole in Missouri City, where he fell in a raid designed to cover Price's retreat to the south.

Only Quantrill now remained between Jesse and undisputed leadership of the Missouri irregulars. Then, early in November, at White River, Arkansas, Quantrill, too, passed from the scene.

The guerrillas, following Shelby and Price in their desperate attempt to cut their way through to Texas, got only as far as the Arkansas town. There Quantrill proposed to abandon the regulars and strike for Kentucky, a nearer and dearer sanctuary where many of the guerrillas expected to find waiting kinfolk and well-prepared hideouts. Jesse flatly refused the defection. Quantrill departed with his followers that same evening. His brief ride into the land of the blue grass, with its swift oblivion under the guns of the Union guerrillas of Edward Terrill in Spencer County, Kentucky, is schoolboy history in the Border States.

Jesse was left in sole command of the once mighty Missouri Raiders. But what a command!

Todd and Anderson were dead, Quantrill deserted. Frank had gone with Quantrill, and so had Jim Younger, Cole's dour older brother. Cole, himself, sickened by Centralia and evidencing the only documentable loyalty to the South of any of the outlaw band, save for Frank's bobtailed tour with Price's original command of State Guards, had enlisted in the regular Confederate Army and been transferred to Louisiana. Of the fading hierarchy of border irregulars, only Jesse and a hard core of Todd's and Anderson's faithful remained.

Four days later, riding advance guard for the fleeing Price, Jesse and his Missourians met an old enemy—and the course of history altered again.

The guerrilla horsemen were galloping through Cane Hill, in the Cherokee Nation. They were uneasy. The tiny frontier town was too empty. Too quiet. Something was in the wind, they knew. Too late, they realized that the wind lay behind them. What came with that wind, blowing suddenly upon their startled rears, was a long column of Blue troops from Jennison's Fifteenth Kansas Cavalry.

Cut off from Price, the guerrillas fought wickedly and with momentary success. Jesse pursued and killed Captain Emmett Gross, the column's commander and, as his victim knelt defenseless and in agonized pleading for recognition of the cloth he wore, blew out the brains of the regimental chaplain, the Reverend U. P. Gradner. In the confusion which ensued, he was able to lead his followers into the temporary safety of the broken hills flanking the scene of the action.

But the trap was closing.

The following day, in attempting to leave the hills and rejoin Price, the harried raiders were sighted by a scout band of seventy-five Federal Cherokees.

In the resulting clash, a running action which continued until late afternoon, fifty-two of the Indian cavalry were slain. But the fight swept many miles to the west of Price's line of retreat. The alarm lit by the previous day's fight with Jennison's Fifteenth ran like a grass fire from one border of the Indian Nation to the other. With dawn of the 24th, Jim Cummins and Dick Maddox returned from a scout to report no less than five Federal patrols of company strength between them and Price's bogged-down command. They were isolated. One direction alone beckoned—the same direction which since frontier time immemorial had called to the outlaw weary and oppressed.

At a hand-gallop, Jesse swung his hunted riders south for Texas and the border.

In March, 1865, Texas was literally the "lone star" remaining in the battle flag of the Confederacy.

Before the month was out, the fugitive Missourians, driven by that nostalgia for their hardwood forests and creek-watered bottomlands which was later to characterize their odysseys, began the long journey home. With Jesse at the time was the ragtag remnant of his dwindling command—fifteen gaunt, hopeless men. Crossing the Missouri border a week later, they were ambushed by a waiting Federal patrol. Again, Jesse killed the Union commander, but when his followers had skimmed the fence rails to scatter and find safety in their beloved woodlands, their number was less by four.

The thirty days which followed saw six more of the guerrillas trapped and killed in clashes with the relentless Blue patrols. The word was out that Jesse James had come home. No single hour was granted him or his companions in which to rest or receive the blessings of that return.

At month's end, Jesse was down to his last, long-gamble plan: he would leave his remaining followers where they were hiding at the Carroll County farm of his great-uncle, Jesse Stevens, and make one final effort to break through the Union patrols swarming between him and his Clay County home—and between him and his single, surviving hope for asylum and advice: his gaunt-faced mother, Zerelda Samuel.

His instructions to the others were brief but detailed with the usual care. His followers were to wait twenty-four hours, then follow him into the home county, one by one. He gave each a different route and departure time, warned all to be at the Samuel farm before midnight of the next day. At that time and place they would hold their last meeting, make their final decision.

His own route was typically direct. In a Mother Hubbard cloak and big-brimmed Sunday bonnet borrowed from his great-aunt, he drove the Stevenses' fast Morgan mare and springbed sulky into the Union headquarters town of Liberty in broad daylight. There, he put the mare up in one cousin's livery stable, sauntered down the main street to a second cousin's woodyard, walked in through the front-office door, and disappeared.

An hour later, with the afternoon sun standing four o'clock low in the west, a high-piled wagonload of hickory cordwood pulled out of the yard under a bill of lading for Centerville and the empty woodshed of Dr. Reuben Samuel. The heavy draft horses which drew the wagon were held on their jingling trot by a sixteen-year-old lad whose name, for the Union record, was Hibbard Woodson—but whose mother's maiden name, not for that record, had been *James*.

Shortly before ten o'clock that night, the cordwood was properly stacked in the Samuel shed and Jesse, dirty and haggard and limping with the stiffness of his jolting hours in the packing box beneath the logs in his cousin's wagon, was pacing the closely curtained lamplight of the Samuel sitting room.

In her rocker by the window, omnipresent Bible in lap, stern frown following the caged-lion restlessness of her pale-eyed son, sat Zerelda

# Death Of A Legend

Samuel. Outside the house, Dr. Samuel smoked his pipe in the gusty spring darkness of the front stoop, and watched the starlit, southwestward stretch of the Kansas City wagon road. Up that same road, a quarter mile in the opposite direction, young Hibb Woodson crouched in the jack oaks, head cocked warily for first sight or sound of an approach from the northeast.

Back in the sitting room, Zerelda Samuel put her Bible aside, spoke her mind, hard and sharp.

"Boy!" she commanded. "Set down and let up on your walking around. You're not going to stomp yourself out of this trouble."

Jesse stopped pacing and looked at her. If you took his own narrow face and fierce-crazy eyes, handsomed them up considerably and added some length and iron grayness to his dark brown hair, you would have his mother. All that was in him of strength and cunning had come from Zerelda Cole. But there was also that in her which had not come down to him. She demonstrated that quality now, as she watched him and waited.

"Ma," he said at last, breaking nervously under the steady regard, "what's a man to do? Where's he to turn? They've got me rode down to my last five men. They clearly mean to give me no chance."

Still, she waited before she spoke. Mother of outlaws she might be, and loyal to the last drop of blood common to her and her dangerous son.

But where her mind was as tough and suspicious as Jesse's, it was without that wild unsteadiness and utter lack of morality which seemed to twist his. Above anything on earth—above Frank, above self, above husband, home, or fireside, or even treasured Confederate cause—she might love this watery-eyed, homely, second son of hers. Yet, in the end, there was that difference in them, that deep sense of the right and the wrong, as set forward in the laws of the Old Testament, which abided within her. And which had told her, since Centralia, that Jesse was no longer on the side of the South, *nor of the Lord*.

She looked at him now, her fierce eyes dark with the hurt and the sorrow of the reckoning.

"You've only one chance, Jesse," she told him softly.

From the shadowed day of Centralia, she had not again called him Dingus. To her mother's mind, intensely loyal as it always remained, the boy had somehow died on that murderous afternoon, and the man been created in the bloodstained image of that death.

"One chance, boy," she repeated grimly. "And it is a chance they will not give you, but which you will have to take for yourself."

"Say what you mean, Ma." He moved toward her with the weary appeal, standing by her rocker, letting his slim hand fall gently to her shoulder. "I'm way too tired, heart and body and soul, to do any more guessing about anything. It's why I came home to you, Ma. If you won't help me—" He broke off the words despairingly as she stood up, facing him.

She touched him, in turn, on the shoulder, and said it with the simple quiet of inner certainty:

"I will help you, son. But only if you will help yourself—only if you will agree to come in."

"*Come in!*" He stepped back from her as though she had slapped him in the face. "You caint mean that, Ma! Not for me to give myself up to the Federals?"

"Nevertheless, I do mean it, Jesse," she replied firmly. "It's the only way. It's the right way. And I say you will do it."

"But I caint! You can see that! Why, Jesus Christ, they'd—"

"*Jesse Woodson! Not in this house!*" Her eyes blazed and she raised her hand in real anger, as if she meant to strike him for the blasphemy.

He dropped his glance, humbly, muttering the quick apology with awkward, small-boy sincerity. "I'm sorry, Ma. I didn't mean that. Just forgot, I reckon. But it's crazy, you hear? I caint surrender to the Union troops. They're shooting on sight. You know that."

"It can be arranged, given time." She clipped the words off meaningly. "And you know *that*."

"No, Ma," he shook his head slowly. "Not no more, it caint. The war's made it all different. Our kin are all as scared and scattered as us. Who's there left among them that would dare to help Dingus James, even if they was able?"

"Boy!" She moved back into him, seizing his arms and holding him fiercely as he started to turn away with the bitter shrug. *There's me*!

"Now *you* listen, you hear?" Her harsh voice dropped, a softness coming into it that was strangely foreign to the lean strength of her face. "The war's over, boy. It caint last another month. If you don't come in now, you never will. God gives us one chance, Jesse, and no more. He's telling me this is your chance, and your last chance. I'm saying you will give yourself up, and you will do it. Do you hear me, Jesse?"

"I'm listening, Ma," he said hopelessly. "But I don't hear you. There's no chance left for me."

"You will come in when I say." It was not a question, but a command. "For they will kill you if you don't."

He knew that without being told. He knew, as well, that they would kill him anyway. But there was no use saying that to her and he was suddenly too thought-out and brain-weary to move another foot or fight another yard. "All right, Ma," he said quietly. "We'll try it your way. The boys will be here tomorrow night. I'll leave it up to them, and promise to put it to them like you say.

"Meantime"—his high voice picked up in the thin, brittle way it always did when it came time to rattle the orders—"you and Dad keep a sharp lookout. I'll bed down in the barn with the horses. Have Hibb saddle my sockfoot bay mare and stand a guard outside. I aint slept in four days and caint stay awake no longer."

"Then sleep easy, boy." His mother nodded with calm assurance. "For the Lord will show the way."

Jesse paused in the doorway, haggard face twisting in the brief shadow of a tired smile. "Likely, He'll send somebody along to point it out for me, too, I suppose," he suggested cynically.

"He moves in mysterious ways," was all Zerelda Samuel said. But Jesse did not hear her. The outer door and the waiting darkness of the barn-lot had closed behind him, and he was gone.

Twenty-four hours later, at 10:00 P.M. of April 1, unwittingly antedating General Lee and that other, grimmer gathering by seven short days, he called his five survivors to their last meeting in the familiar, close-watched gloom of the Samuel barn. The council of war lasted, in all, twenty terse minutes. The bitter terms of its defeated findings were equally succinct: unconditional surrender.

Jesse James had found his Appomattox a week before history and General U. S. Grant brought theirs to Robert E. Lee and the lost cause of the Confederacy.

Hell's narrow highway is cobbled with the good intentions of bad men, and many a decision is more easily taken than implemented. The first week passed. The cornered outlaws found no way to come in safely. Nor did the good Lord in his infinite wisdom, despite Zerelda Samuel's faith in that wisdom, show up to point the way for them to do so. Nor did He send anyone to point that way. The candle had burned too long from both ends.

It had to come to the middle now, and the light was going out.

They were men with prices on their heads, prices of which the medium of instant exchange was: "Shoot on sight and bring the body in for identification afterward." It was not so simple, no mere matter of riding into the nearest Union command post and announcing, "All right, we give up. The game is over."

The day after Appomattox word of Grant's general amnesty swept the land. For twenty-four hours the hearts of Jesse's men took sudden hope. Then came the grim postscript. The pardons of Nashville and Appomattox were not for the known guerrilla followers of Quantrill, Todd or Anderson. In Missouri the exception was taken as a mandate to hunt down these sons of the South. Throughout the counties of Clay and Jackson guerrilla bodies swung in the spring wind from the gnarled limbs of a hundred oaks and sycamores along the back roads. The farms and homes of the Confederacy's outlaw sympathizers were burned to their fieldstone bases. Vengeance was the sweeter for its long time in coming.

Jesse and his men took to the limestone caves along the Big and Little Blues, never sleeping two nights in the same lair, never making a fire against the evening sky, never passing abroad in daylight, never unsaddling a sweated horse or unbooting a weary, stirrup-swollen foot.

The second week wore on. Its fifth day came and passed.

Shortly before midnight of the 13th, Jesse came upright upon his lathered horse blanket. He listened a moment, rose and padded silently around his sleeping fellows toward the cave's entrance. Outside, he cocked his head downward to the blackness of the Big Blue's bottomlands.

This time he heard it clearly. Its sound sent a prickle of nerve ends running up his spine. Pursing his thin lips, he answered it, his heart so strangely glad within him that its thickening hammer constricted his throat. He waited, swallowing hard, his trapped mind not daring to believe it could be *him*. The small hand which had not lost its steadiness in cutting throats on Shawnee Town Road nor in blowing brains out along the North Missouri's right-of-way beyond Centralia trembled uncertainly now as the low-pitched call of the bob-white came again from the Big Blue's midnight bottomlands.

Seconds later that same small hand was enclosed in one twice its size, and for a fleeting, naked moment Jesse James was once more Dingus.

*"Cole! God Amighty, it's Old Cole!"*

It was all he could say, or think of to say. As it unfailingly had since they were boys, the slow-drawling shadow had arisen from the outer shades of despair to stand beside him, to take him by the hand and tell him that, no matter whence he came or whither he went, so long as Cole Younger lived to follow him he had one man to call him friend, one man to share the emptiness of the dark and lonesome road ahead.

In his lifetime, few men knew even the face of Jesse James. Cole alone knew his heart. His long arm came quickly around the narrow shoulders, his words dropping in that slow, half-smiled way they always did. "Well, now, that shines, Dingus. A man dearly loves to be remembered by his friends!"

Jesse broke away from the embrace awkwardly. The moment of meeting, together with whatever twisted meaning it may have had for him in its first unguarded seconds, was gone. The illusion of the small boy reaching in the dark for the larger, stronger hand faded under the returned thinness of the high voice.

"Anybody with you? How'd you find us? Where you been at? Where'd you come from?" The dry rattle of the questions at once reestablished the old pattern of leader to follower.

"Well, now, Ding," grinned Cole, "I come from Alabama. But not with no damn banjo on my knee, you can lay! I was mustered out in Montgomery, rode the cars three days, made it in afoot from Jeff City. I got the lay of the land and a horse from your ma. Now how about you and your boys?"

"We're done," said Jesse glumly. "I got Jim Cummins and four others with me, asleep in the cave yonder. We been trying to come in but the Feds won't leave us do it."

"Yeah, I heard," muttered Cole. "It's partly why I come."

"I allow you can go right along back!" snapped Jesse. "We aint dragging you into this. You're clean; you was a regular. You got amnesty."

"I got some, I reckon," shrugged his companion. "Such as it is, I aim to use it, too. You hear me, Ding?"

Jesse sensed more meaning than lay in the calm words themselves. "I hear you," he grunted. "But you aint making sense. Don't put off on me now, Cole. There aint nothing you can do for us."

"I allow there is."

"You're like Buck. Always long on allowing. What you getting at?"

"What I just said. Using my amnesty—*for you*."

"I aint never cottoned to your funny streak. You got something to say, get it said."

"You really got your britches down around your ankles, aint you, Ding?" The slow grin broke again. "Well, boy, this time old Uncle Cole is going to pull them up for you. See you don't forget it." He paused, the smile broadening. "You have the boys at your ma's place tomorrow night, ready to ride. Don't give me none of your sass, neither."

"Goddamn it, you lay off pushing me, you hear, Cole?" In the darkness Cole could not see the blink but he knew it was going full blast. He quit grinning, sobered his soft drawl.

"I got it set for you to come in, you damn fool. With Major Rogers, the Union provost marshal at Lexington. He's kinfolk way back somewheres on Pa's side. You be at your ma's place like I said."

He paused again before turning away, his final suggestion coming slow-worded.

"That is if you want to go in astride your saddle rather than acrost it, you be there. . . ."

# Chapter Four

*Lexington*

Jesse looked at the sign over the door of the frame shack next to McClellan's harness works. The boards of it were sap-green, its new paint not even set up yet. Still, a man could read it.

*Headquarters Union Provost Marshal—Maj. J. B. Rogers, Fifth Corps Area.*

He swung the black up to the hitching rail. Cole eased his dappled bay alongside him. The others followed in silent suit: big George Shepherd, slight, diffident Jim Cummins, scowling Billy Gregg, boisterous Oll Shepherd, quiet, dangerous Clell Miller.

The straggle of the crowd was already beginning to clot the plank walks on either side of the provost marshal's office. Jesse eyed them contemptuously, ignoring alike hostile Northern

stare and covert Southern wink of encourage-
ment. His thin voice carried penetratingly in the
morning quiet.

"Mind the horses, Billy. Oll, tend the door.
Hold them nosy ninnies clear of it. George, you
and the others come along."

Gregg and Shepherd nodded wordless re-
plies, understanding the orders and their intent
precisely as they understood the man who gave
them. Even in surrender, Jesse James was taking no chances. Should anything go wrong inside, or anything funny outside, some new
widows were due to be made.

Jesse came down off the black without further word. Cole, Jim Cummins, George Shepherd and Clell Miller followed him. The door of
Major Rogers's office closed behind them.

The crowd, pressing forward to cram and
peer at the shade-drawn windows, moved uneasily back as the swaggering Oll loosened his
big pistols in their leathers and spat calculat-
ingly into the Main Street mud.

"Fine morning for a curious cat to get himself
killed," he drawled to the unsmiling Gregg.

The onlookers tittered uncertainly, and lost
some of their interest in Major Rogers's windows. Billy Gregg nodded silently. Just as silently he hunched his right shoulder, slipping
the carbine strap and letting the weapon come
to rest across the pommel of his saddle. The
good townfolk abandoned the remainder of
their interest in the windows.

The minutes passed. Gregg scowled. Oll Shepherd spat. The crowd murmured awkwardly and stood well back. Presently the office door opened. Jesse came out, tailed by the others.

"All right," he said to Oll. "Let's go. We got what we came after."

It was that simple. Cole had done his work well. Once more the hidden political power of the James and Younger families in western Missouri had functioned smoothly. In five minutes, and in the face of a standing government order to shoot them on sight, the last and worst of the guerrillas had made their peace with the Union and were riding, scot-free, back up the middle of Main Street. Until the conditions of surrender-on-demand set forth in their paroles might be called into effect, or until they might meanwhile be brought to civil trial, they were as privileged to their share of "equal rights" as any of their fellow Missourians in the dumbstruck crowd behind them.

"By God, Jess, you done it again!" George Shepherd was feeling a jubilation natural to any reprieved murderer. The last houses of Lexington were falling behind. Ahead lay only the open road and the good, solid chances of a trial which would undoubtedly be held before a jury of highly sympathetic Clay or Jackson county kinfolk. The rain had broken away. The morning sun was warm and clean on a man's back. Things were looking up for the "last of the James boys."

Withal, Jesse failed to fall heir to his followers' optimism.

"I don't like it," he growled, casting a quick look back toward the town. "I don't like it a damn bit. Something's wrong as hell about the whole blamed mess. You mark what I say. We aint home yet."

"Aw, come off it, Dingus!" Cole was the sole member of the gang who still used the familiar address. The rest, except Frank, had taken to the newer sobriquet, "Jess." Frank, as fitted the growing seriousness of his nature, had begun, before the parting of ways at White City, to call his famous young brother by the full and formal "Jesse."

"You heard the Major," Cole continued. "It's a regular parole he give us. There aint nothing can go wrong with it—it's all official and such like. I swear, you're getting jumpier than a sore-tailed sheep! We're out on bail and we'll beat any trial they can throw at us in this country, hands down. You'll see, Ding. Now you just forget it, you hear!"

"I hear," said Jesse, not returning the big rider's grin. "But I caint forget it. He's still a Yankee, Goddamn it!"

"You'd suspicion your own ma, providing your back was turnt to her!" boomed Oll Shepherd. "Brace up, Jess. We're out of the woods, son of a bitch if we aint!"

"Let's leave off chawing the fat," muttered Jim Cummins nervously. His normally mild manner was not in evidence, and his wary glance joined Jesse's in scanning the roadway behind them. "I side with Jess. Something bad wrong will yet come of this whole cussed doings. I lay it will."

"Bushway!" laughed Cole. "You and Dingus are both so goosed-up you caint set your saddles straight. Oll's right. Dry day or damp, all dawgs smell wet to Ding. We aint heading into no trouble whatever, saving what we lay up for ourselves."

In a way, Cole's breezy prognosis was correct. The trouble they were heading into was "laid up" for them, all right. It was laid up on both sides of the Lexington Road, not four hundred yards from where Cole's bold laugh upset the stillness of Old Missouri's warming April air.

Jesse saw them first.

To an eye trained in such things, the blink of a morning sun ray off of the moving steel of a rifle barrel screened in deep brush can be as illuminating as a rocket flare over an entire regiment in the wide open.

*"Federals!"*

The side-mouthed hiss of the single word straightened the backs and swung the eyes of his six followers. "We got one chance, boys." The continuance of the thin voice was marked by a tightening of seasoned hands on shortened reins, and nothing else. The pace of the long-limbed thoroughbreds did not alter so much as the stretch of a fetlock. The narrowed eyes of their riders held as carefully away from the brush ahead as though it held nothing but the noisy jay who was currently scolding the hidden invaders of his privacy. *"We ride through!"*

Jesse's terminal words were superfluous. Each of the men beside him knew the course as well as he did. Settling themselves in their saddles, they steadied their horses. With the undirected skill born of long practice they gradually opened the distance between their mounts as they rode down on the ambush.

A hundred yards. Seventy-five. Fifty. Forty. Twenty-five—

Jesse's black threw up his slender muzzle, pricked his trim ears. The muffled expulsion of the air clearing the suspicious flare of his nostrils was the signal.

"Now!" yelled Jesse.

As the cruel spur jammed, shank-deep, into his tensing haunch, the black leaped down the middle of the road. The other six horsemen broke in all directions, a literal covey of equine quail bursting outward along every point of the woodland compass. The belated hammer of the hidden troopers' rifle fire sprayed harmlessly as bird shot into the heavy timber. In the space of the first soldier volley, every last one of Jesse's men made it cleanly away.

The frustrated troopers, an eight-man Union cavalry patrol, blundered their horses out upon the road. Frantically, they swung them in pursuit of the sole target still visible—Jesse and his hard-running black, racing southward down the open track of the Lexington Road.

Looking over his shoulder at the clumsy labors of the cavalry mounts, Jesse grimaced acidly. He pulled the black in, easing him off to a disdainful hand-gallop. He could hold this gait all day, and gain a yard a minute on such cut-plugs as those back yonder.

Sixty seconds later he was kneeing the black around an abrupt turn in the road, past the last of the heavy brush, into the clean, free sweep of the meadowland beyond. And dead into the advancing fronts of two troops of Union cavalry.

With that queer detachment which inhabits the minds of desperate men, he recorded the military composition of the enemy even as he threw the black clear of the road and sent him skimming the left-hand fence rails—one troop of the Second Wisconsin, regulars, and one troop of Johnson County militia.

The column proper never broke ranks. Two sergeants, well mounted and flanking the lead troop of regulars, drove their horses over the fence almost on top of the flying black. Jesse saw his situation. They were too close onto him, both of them. And they had the bad look of knowing their business all too well.

Heading the black for the woods, he twisted in the saddle and shot the forward trooper through the body. The youngster fell, dangling his left foot in the onside stirrup. The trained mount reared but brought up quickly, and stood. The distorted body of its rider did not move.

The black had Jesse almost into the timber now. Another dozen jumps would do it. But the dead sergeant's companion had too much horse under him. Twisting again, Jessie emptied his left-hand gun. He cursed as he missed his man but laughed wildly as he saw the horse, hit three times through the barrel, stumble and go down.

The second sergeant was no militiaman. He hit the ground on his feet and with his carbine unslung. He had two seconds before the black would have Jesse within the safety of the oak scrub. He used them: the first to drop to one knee, the second to squeeze off a cool, aimed shot.

The .54-caliber Spencer ball caught Jesse still twisted in the saddle from his downing of the sergeant's horse. It entered low in his left side, ranged up between the ribs, deflected against the right shoulder blade and burst out high under his right armpit. The rupturing pain of its exit told him it had torn his lung in passage.

Within the same second, and while he still clung to the racing black, two ragged volleys blended with the sergeant's single shot.

Even while the pain of his wound tore at him from within and the first of the scrub oaks slashed at him from without, Jesse's dimming mind automatically catalogued and separated the two volleys. The first came with the unmistakable bull's bellow of .54-caliber carbine fire:

the Union Spencers getting into action from the road. The second broke with the familiar staccato rap of .36-caliber Navy Colts: Cole and the boys, faithfully following him and firing from God knew where—or how.

His next memory was of his horse stumbling. He knew the black was mortally hit. Knew the feel of a bullet-drilled mount going out from under a man. Knew it from Centralia to Cane Hill. And from half a dozen places in between.

With the last flash of consciousness, he wrenched himself free of the saddle. He fell sideways and heavily away from the stricken animal. Waiting for the jolt and crash of the ground to rush up and smash him senseless he felt, instead, the life-saving shock of cold water. He knew from that, and from the distant feel of the moss and the sliding rocks under his numbing hands, that he had fallen into a stream. He struggled clear of the creek's shallows in time to see the black pitch and slide into the middle current and lie there, head under, flanks heaving, welcoming and awaiting the swift mercy of drowning.

The next instant the blue mud of the creekbank was reaching for Jesse himself. He came into it gratefully, belly first, head twisted grotesquely to the left. There was no movement and no sound, save where the slowing pump of his heart lifted the bright blood up into his throat from the torn lung. And pushed it, pulse-driven, through the clamped set of his teeth, out upon the waiting clay. Presently that sound, too, ceased. The hemorrhage welled and fell away, the clenched jaw slackened.

If the breath of life lay yet within it, no least sign stirred the last stillness of the body on the creekbank.

The faces above him moved in, then away. They loomed brightly, shifted, grew dim, disappeared altogether. They came again, fled again, now clean and brilliant, now shadowed and blotted out, like rainstorm stars among the broken clouds of a clearing night sky.

Shortly, one of the stars came too near. He saw its curled sideburns and wide gray eyes. And, moving in the whirling orbit of its familiar face, he saw the withdrawing satellite of the glazed clay jug. In the same moment he felt the bite of the forty-rod scalding its way from his throat to the pit of his belly. He came retching up on one elbow, vomiting the whiskey, cursing and crying aloud in the torture of the pain from his bandaged chest.

*"Oh, Jesus, I caint stand it, Bud! Help me, Bud, help me—"*

Cole seized him, forcing him back on the straw pallet, his eyes tightening at the use of the forgotten name.

He had not been *"Bud"* to anybody for more years than a man could remember. It was a little boy's name, going far back into childhood, back even beyond the hazy days of Uncle Eben and Old Sam Pettis. Back to the six- and seven-year-old days when he and Frank had sung in the Centerville Baptist Boy's Choir. And when Dingus had been a lisping three-year-old perched big-eyed upon the hard pine pews beside the fierce-proud Mrs. Zerelda James, while the Reverend Robert James lashed righteously forth from his pulpit on the furies of hell and the forgivenesses of heaven.

"Lay still. Goddamn you, Dingus! Lay still—"

Cole swallowed hard, fighting the words past the thickness growing around his Adam's apple.

"Ease back now, you hear? I got aholt of you, Ding. I aint going to leave go of you, old pardner. Hang on, damn you! You hear me now, Dingus!"

Jesse nodded, hand tightening on Cole's arm. He moved his head again, trying to say something. The words would not come but the blood would. The hollow bubble of it, building once more in his throat, caught at his breath and drowned it. The sound was not new to Cole, nor to any of the five rough men standing, white-faced, behind him. Each had heard, before now, the stertorous breathing of a lung-shot man. Each knew well the meaning of the choking rattle now filling Jesse's throat.

With the first thick gasp, Cole's big arm was behind Jesse, raising his slight form from the dirty pallet. He held him close until the rack of the coughing had spasmed and subsided, continued to hold him when it had.

Oll Shepherd looked at Billy Gregg. The latter

73

nodded to Jim Cummins.

"He's gone, Cole." Jim's hand touched the big man's shoulder gently. "Leave go of him and come along now, man."

Cole did not answer and George Shepherd added softly, "Do like he says, Cole. Jess's done for and we aint got no right to stay here at the Widder Bowman's no longer. She's put us up for nigh on a week now. It aint fair to put off on her no longer. The Feds will play it mighty rough on her if they jump us here."

Cole still did not look up. "Fetch the Widder's spring wagon," he said slowly. "Bust a bale of hay into it and borry some spare blankets off of her."

"Jesus Christ, Cole!" It was the bad-tempered Clell Miller stepping forward. "You aint going to try toting him back to Centerville! I say we put him under, right here, and clear out quick. We done already hung our hides on the wall fooling around this long, Goddamn it!"

"Clell's right," growled Billy Gregg. "Jess's dead. Bury him and have done with it."

"He aint dead," said Cole, talking to himself again. "He's sleeping. I can feel the breath in him here against my chest. Fetch the wagon."

The others exchanged quick looks. It was George Shepherd who said it for them, before they turned and went out of the Bowman cabin.

"He's sleeping all right, pardner. Only he aint ever going to wake up again."

# Death Of A Legend

Cole brought Jesse from the cabin, carrying him like a child in his arms. When he had put him in the wagon, he swung to the driver's box, unwrapped the reins, nodded to the already mounted and waiting guerrillas. "All right. When we hit the main road turn north for Lexington."

In the stillness which followed, the rusty file of Jesse's breath rasping at the torn lung carried harshly from the wagon bed. None of the mounted men said a word; all sat their horses staring at Cole, waiting for the rest of it.

"I'm taking him home to Centerville," said the latter. "But not like no damn hunted dog. I'm going in to Major Rogers again and try and get a military pass, along with a sergeant and a squad of men, to clear Dingus and the wagon through to Clay County. We caint put him on a horse and we got to have a proper pass and an escort to get the wagon acrost the Lafayette County line. These here paroles Rogers give us obviously aint paper enough for the job."

He slowed down, dropping his voice. "Dingus meant to come in and give himself up, open and honest. And he done it. Just like he promised his ma he would. I mean to see that part of it set straight. I'm taking him home to her, by God. I reckon there aint nothing else me nor anybody else can do for him now."

"I reckon there aint," said Jim Cummins softly. "Let's ride."

"You boys aint beholden to come along."

There was no bitterness in Cole's nod. "Likely, as I said, them paroles Rogers give us aint worth the paper they're writ on. Especially after us tying into them Federal troops and leading them off of Dingus like we done back yonder on Persimmon Creek."

"Likely," grunted Billy Gregg.

"Figures," vouchsafed George Shepherd.

"Wagon path's bad betwixt here and the main road," offered Clell Miller.

"Yeah," growled Oll Shepherd, eying Cole. "See you watch them potholes and don't jar him none on the way out. . . ."

Cole watched the potholes. It was a slow, nerve-strung journey, the wagon's five gaunt outriders holding their restive saddle mounts down to the inchworm crawl of the farm horses, their watchful eyes constantly alert for the chance Federal patrol that would spell disaster to their risky mission.

That jealous fate which always hovered over Jesse stayed with him now. The wagon reached the rutted heading of Lexington's Main Street without a blue tunic or brass cavalry button being sighted. It was 11:00 A.M., Thursday, April 21.

At 11:05 Union Provost Marshal Major J. B. Rogers looked up from his desk to see his orderly shoved rudely to one side of his guard post at the office door. Three seconds later the major was moving his chair back, staring up at the six-odd feet of ex-Confederate guerrilla which had done the shoving.

"Morning, Major, sir," said Cole. "Come along outside. We've brung you what's left of one of your paroles."

At six minutes after eleven, Major Rogers stood outside his office beside the Widow Bowman's spring wagon, while the gathering curious gaped and the hard-eyed escort horsemen glared stonily over their heads. And at seven minutes after eleven, he was back at his desk again, his pen scratching a frowning signature to the Area Order passing one spring wagon, contents and driver, along with one disgruntled Union sergeant and eight unhappy, escort troopers, from Lafayette into Clay County. It was 11:08 when he folded the document, looking up at the waiting guerrilla.

"Mr. Younger," he said quietly, "I would advise you not to linger on the way. This is a *military* pass for you and the wagon. The sergeant and his squad will see that it is honored as far as the county line. But I'm sure I don't have to remind you of the *civilian* temper your followers may encounter. If you heed my suggestion, you will disperse your men the moment you leave Lexington. This area is full of patrols not under my command. Therefore, I cannot, as you have discovered, guarantee your paroles even *in* Lafayette County, let alone outside it. I'm sure you understand that, sir."

Cole took the pass, answered just as quietly.

"Yes, sir, I understand it. I'll push to the river, lay up there in the willows till dark, cross over and drive on through tonight."

"An excellent idea," nodded the officer. He stood up, offering his hand. "Good luck, sir."

"Thank you," said Cole, meeting the grasp.

He turned for the door, checked his stride, came back to the desk. "One thing, Major—"

"Yes?"

"How about Jesse's own parole? Seeing how he is, and all. Caint you leastways guarantee *his* for him?"

Major Rogers stepped around the desk, brought up facing him, eyes narrowed thoughtfully.

"Seeing how he is, Mr. Younger," he said gently, "it won't be necessary. His parole has already been guaranteed by a higher command than mine."

The details of the following three months, were they known, would by themselves make the most incredible novel of all. Under the simple title of *The Ninety Days of Jesse James* they would tell more of grueling hardship, heroic sacrifice and unbelievable courage than all the guerrilla raids, bank robberies, train holdups and highway outrages combined.

They would tell of Cole Younger bringing his dying leader safely to Centerville only to find Dr. and Mrs. Samuel hastily departed from the anti-Southern climate of the post-bellum bor-

der for the relative security of Nebraska and the
Indian Territory. Of his returning to Lexington
and gaining from a reluctant Major Rogers extended permission to leave Missouri and attempt to bring his stricken comrade to his
distant parents. Of his subsequent regathering
of Jesse's remaining faithful, less by three now
that Gregg had suddenly disappeared and
George Shepherd and Clell Miller had fled to
the sanctuary of their kinfolk in Logan County,
Kentucky. And of their setting out, the other,
constant three, Cole, Oll Shepherd, Jim Cummins, through the drear rain of April 29, upon
the 500-mile wagon drive to Rulo, the tiny Nebraska hamlet to which it was rumored Jesse's
family had gone.

And then of that impossible hegira itself. Of
the thirty days of trial upon the way. Of the sixty
nights of travail at destination. And of the two
weeks of eventual return by riverboat down the
Missouri in early August, all attended solely by
three ex-guerrilla horsemen, an obscure frontier physician and an indomitable gray-haired
woman.

And each jolting mile, every endless, pain-
racked hour, was endured and survived by an
eighteen-year-old boy whose ghastly complex of
shattered rib and punctured lung would have
killed a normal man within twenty breaths of
its reception.

But beyond these brief facts only one other is

known. And the novel of *The Ninety Days* will never be written.

On the 14th of August, 1865, the western mail packet *Yellowstone Belle* reversed her stern paddles and backed into a routine landing beneath Kansas City's crown of red clay bluffs. The leadman in her bow heaved his line ashore. The *Belle* was warped in and made fast. As the cleated bridge of the gangplank was dropped, the grateful cry of "Plank's down!" arose among the deck passengers, signaling the end of the weary voyage.

None of the dockside hangers-on recognized either of the quiet, watchful men who so tenderly bore the stretcher down the *Belle's* plank. Jim Cummins? Cole Younger? That raunchy pair? Why, they weren't nowhere near big nor mean-looking enough. They would have known old Cole or old Jim in a minute, by damn!

Nor did they mark anything memorable about the black-bearded face of the scowling ruffian who followed the two with the stretcher. Oll Shepherd? That ragtag rack of seedy whiskers, big Ollie Shepherd? Well, I lay not! A man would know Oll as quick as he would Jim or Cole.

As for the gray-haired, nervous couple bringing up the rear of the procession, they were given even less than passing note. Doc Samuel? Zereldy James? Don't be a ninny, man. Anybody knew Doc and his missus were long-gone somewheres out in the Indian Territory. They would never be back, you could bet.

Nope, that boy was just some poor devil with a passel of close friends or blood-kin and a worried pa and ma—that was all. No use sparing him a second look either, as far as that went. From the pasty-faced look of him, those friends or kin of his would be carrying him in something a mite squarer than a stretcher before the month was out.

But the month was not yet out. Fate had a savior ready in the wings, waiting for Jesse James. She was slight and blonde and barely seventeen.

*Her name, too, was Zerelda!*


She stood beneath the catalpa tree by the front gate of her father's farmyard when they brought him from the *Yellowstone Belle*. She followed them as they moved him carefully through the parlor and into the waiting bedroom—her bedroom. When at last his eyes opened, the others were gone. She alone was still there, faint and unreal in the curtained shadows, standing, waiting.

He looked at her, wondering who she was. The fever, building again in him from the exhaustion of the long river trip, made his eyes uncertain, his mind unable to collate the scatter of his fitful thoughts, or to bring them to any meaningful conclusion.

She was small, he could see, and golden-haired. Just a girl, too, she was. Not more than sixteen, maybe seventeen. But already a woman grown for all of that. The clean starch of the gingham pinafore was prim enough, the stays of the corselet and the billow of the petticoats beneath it proper as ever need be. But there was that about the intenseness of the oval face and the long, slow look of the dark blue eyes which burned into a man despite his fever. And which brought his wandering thoughts together and his tired eyes to bearing full upon her.

He smiled, that queer little quirking smile of his reserved for those signal occasions which might strike the grim iron of his fancy, or touch the guarded vein of his hard humor.

"Jesse James, the Great Missouri Raider, at your service, ma'am," he said. "You'll excuse me if I don't get up. I've bin poorly of late. . . ."

She continued to stare at him, not answering, fascinated, as would have been any frontier girl, by the presence beneath her own roof of the fabulous Jesse James.

She had never seen him before, though the recountings of his heroic adventures in the lost cause of the Confederacy were a part and parcel not only of her general day and time but, in the particular case of the John Mimms's household, a matter of actual blood heritage. Her mother had been born a James, the younger sister of that same ordained, largely forgotten Baptist minister who had died so quietly in faraway California—the Reverend Robert James. As a full, first cousin, the glorious exploits of Aunt

# Death Of A Legend

Zerelda Samuel's second-born were as familiar to her in fancy as were the faces of her own family in fact.

The peculiar circumstance of her never having seen her notorious cousin, though she was but a year younger than he, is a remarkable testament to Jesse's passion for anonymity. Even among the trusted blood of his own kin he was a shadow moving behind solid forms of flesh and substance. Frank she had seen many times. Dr. and Mrs. Samuel, as many more. Cole she knew well. And even the Shepherd boys had passed her way on hurried occasion. But Jesse never.

It should be of more than passing note to mark this peculiarity, this passion, of Jesse's. To the day of his death, with one strange exception, he practiced it relentlessly. Other than a reluctant handful of ex-war comrades, fellow guerrillas and actual gang members, not fifteen persons in the state of his birth could, *or would*, take certain oath to the identity of America's most famous outlaw. Beyond these hesitant few, of those who actually knew his shadowy face and legendary form, there remained only the immediate family, and its blood-kin. And, indeed, even among these latter, only the two Zereldas, his lean, gray mother and the slender, golden-haired girl who stood now at his bedside, were to come forward within the final hour of that sullen inquest at St. Joe and state, with legal certainty, "Yes—this is Jesse James."

More than any other single factor this inherent wild-animal shyness, this inborn distrust of people and of places of habitation, would hold the key to the lock of Jesse's seemingly charmed life. It was to remain the simple secret of his success, the reason for his survival.

The girl's racing imagination, stirred by her fabled kinsman's history, slowed now as her wide eyes took in the sobering fact of his actual presence.

She had pictured a handsome, dashing soldier of the South. A tall, fire-eyed hero of the oppressed. An eagle-fierce enemy of the Union wrong. A glamorous, striking partisan of the Confederate right. A demigod of faultless face and form.

What she saw was a dying boy.

A boy no larger in the skeleton-stark wasting of his slender frame than a teen-age girl. A boy with his long dark hair faded a sandy auburn from the guerrilla years of wind, driving rain, and sun. A boy with a strange, ugly face. Wide and high of brow. Short and badly pugged of nose. Receding and narrow of chin. Thin and sparse of downy, red-brown beard. Freckled. Fish-belly white of skin. Weak and crusted of chronically granulated eyelid. A miserable, mud-homely, frightened boy. Sick unto death. *And having the gall to smile about it*.

"I'm Zerelda," she said at last, halting the march of the long seconds across the stillness between them. "Your Uncle John's girl."

He nodded, the wry smile chasing the pain lines from around his mouth corners. "Uncle John's got a powerful purty girl," he managed. "And his girl's got a powerful purty name."

"It's your mother's," she said simply. "I was named for her."

He nodded again. The smile was gone now. The pain in his chest grew, seared up into his throat. He coughed heavily, trying to press it back, biting his bloodless lips, turning his head into the muffle of the pillow's ticking. When the paroxysm had passed, he knew she had moved closer, sensed, rather than felt, the coolness of her slim hand holding his.

"Why don't you go now, girl?" Her name was in his mind but somehow he failed, awkwardly, to use it. "It's 'most dark. Your ma will be needing you in the kitchen, likely. I'm beholden to you."

He felt the loneliness of the room closing in, even as the words came.

Why had a man to be that way? The way he always was with people who wanted to help him. Eternally pushing them away from him. Wanting to back into a corner or crawl into a hole, and wanting always to be watching them and never wanting them to be watching him.

Looking at the girl now, seeing the quiet way she was smiling down at him, he wished he had not said it. Wished he could say, instead, what he really wanted to. What was crying out in his mind but would not come out of his mouth.

Wanting to tell her to hold his hand, to hold it and hold it, and never to let go of it.

"Go along," he said roughly. "There aint no point in your standing around. I'd rather be by myself, you hear?"

He felt her hand tighten, felt the slim weight of her ease to the bed, felt the roundness and the warmth of the soft hip where it pressed his shoulder, the cool pressure of her free hand where it lay, fresh and light as a first snowflake, against his burning cheek. It was suddenly very dark in the room, and the fragrance and softness of her lap drew his head swiftly in. He said nothing, letting the hungry press of his hand say it for him. The coolness of the night reached out for him. The darkness folded itself about him.

"I'll stay, Cousin Jesse," she said softly. "I'll wait along a spell with you."

Jesse did not hear her. He was safe at last and, for the first time within the memory of the hunted years, no longer alone. The labored rhythm of his breathing lost its harshness, fell easily away into sleep. When the moon came an hour later, tipping the room's darkness with its prying silver, Zerelda had not moved.

For nine years she was to wait for Jesse. Then, for seven more, to stand beside him. Standing and waiting, waiting and standing. Always in Jesse's shadow. A shadow of sixteen years of terror, violence and the sudden roar of six-gun unprecedented in the annals of American outlawry. And in the end, when the last gun had spoken, she stood beneath another tree in another farmyard, still watching, still waiting, while the rough pine box was lowered, the last clods fell, and the final words began:

*"Man that is born of woman—"*

This much remains to us of Jesse's love—he was as strange about it, as enigmatic, as contradictory and confusing as he was in any of his remembered traits.

Many damnations of Jesse James exist in cold fact. But upon one point of romantic record all accounts remain unanimous. Jesse looked once upon Zerelda Mimms, and never took his eyes away. Figuratively, she was the first woman he saw and, literally, she was the last.

The others of his wild band, notably the handsome, light-natured Cole, who never married and who left a string of fractured frontier pearls from Rulo, Nebraska, to El Paso, Texas, were normal patrons of their hard calling's accepted trilogy of moral trespass—bad whiskey, sharp cards, shady women.

Not so their unsmiling leader.

He would drink upon infrequent occasion. In even rarer moments, he would draw to the inside straight or to the bob-tailed flush. Even in his speech he was cleaner and more careful than the others. And with the grinning Cole, who shared the pious perversity of his religious fervor, he more than once sang in some small-town church choir with his Navy Colts belted in hidden sacrilege beneath the buttoned sanctity of his cavalry coat, the while, just beyond the town, his cursing followers held the horses and anxiously scanned the south road for dust-sign of the approaching posse.

This much must stand upon the ledger of latter-day judgment, against any spelling of murder or inscription of social rapine, to the singular credit of Jesse James: he abode with his chosen woman, in sickness as in health, *until death did them part*!

# HIGH
# NOON

# Chapter Five

*Liberty*

The fall of 1865 was an autumn of evil vintage
for ex-guerrillas in Old Missouri. State and local
offices were filled with Northern radicals—
"charcoals," as the disdainful Southerners
called them. The known followers of the late
Charley Quantrill and his chief lieutenants continued to be hunted down throughout the "guerrilla counties." Masked vigilantes rode the
back-country lanes incessantly. Lynch ropes
once more sailed over lonely oak limbs and
were stretched tight to the dead-swung weight
of the luckless champions of the thirteen-
starred battle flag. It was a time, in the words
of a contemporary historian, "when men again
tilled their fields with muskets by their sides
and slept in expectation of combat."

It was also a time during which a minor miracle of frontier medicine and faithful home nursing took place. But, in the way of minor miracles, a political one had preceded the medical.

In October of 1865, rabidly Southern Clay County had elected a Republican sheriff. His name was Joe Rickards, and he cared no more for "Todd's terrible revolver fighters" than he did for the town drunk. A solid, stumpy, unimaginative man, history strangely cut him out for a distinction no other man before or after him was to know—and cut him out, in the process, for the second and more remarkable of Clay County's autumn miracles.

Rickards tilted his chair against the boarded front of his Liberty lockup, scratched his middle-aged paunch, enjoyed the growing warmth of the late November sun. It was a fine Saturday morning. Across the square, and around it, the normal traffic of a border town on market day moved in orderly, busy progression. Beside him Tunk Johnson, his right-hand deputy and a local boy of some repute, adjusted the tilt of his own chair, cleared the boardwalk with a thin stream of Clay County Burley, made comment on the deplorable lack of excitement.

"It don't seem like old times no more," averred Tunk. "Things has been quieter than a free nigger in Memphis, since Jess got winged and his boys done took to the brush. How you reckon he is, anyways? Old Jess, I mean. I hear they're draining that hole in him twice a day. Boys tell me they got to hold him out over a dishpan to let the pus run out. They say his ma and that Mimms girl aint been out of sight of him since he was packed in off the *Yellerstone Belle*."

Rickards shot his own stream of Burley at a fly that had tarried too long on the far edge of the boardwalk. He held his counsel until the fly had decently drowned, then nodded.

"You can hear anything you want when it comes to that rooster. Personally, I'll believe he's dead when the box is shut and covered up. Meantime, I got a hunch he aint so bad off as they leave on."

Tunk started to answer, then glanced across the square. "Speaking of the James boys," he said, pointing, "aint that Sam Holmes coming yonder? Looks to be in a tolerable rush, don't he?"

Richards watched the horseman spin his bay around the near corner of the square, spur it toward them. Not of the caliber to fit into a reg ular guerrilla gun, Sam Holmes was a known hanger-on of the outlawed irregulars and, accordingly, a fair source of backwoods information. Rickards dropped his chair forward, nodding wordless answer to Tunk's questions.

Holmes slid the bay up, wasted no time in Saturday morning amenities. "Jess and the boys has been over to the Platte County Fair. They said to tell you they're coming into Liberty this

93

morning and that no Goddamned Republican is going to arrest or take them, neither!"

"Thanks," grunted Rickards. "Don't spur that bay none in getting him out of here. You throw any more mud on my front stoop, I'll jug you."

The partisan horseman glared at him a moment, threw back his head, laughed harshly. "Big talk!" he sneered. "Save it for Jess!"

With the warning, he wheeled the bay and departed. It may or may not have been significant that he held the lathered animal to a careful chop-step walk until he had him well clear of Sheriff Joe Rickards's "front stoop."

With the guerrilla courier out of earshot, Tunk turned to his superior. "You sure as hell had yourself a tall hunch," he said quickly. "They must have drained that hole in Jess powerful fast."

"Uh-huh." Not a wasteful man with words, Sheriff Joe Rickards.

"You reckon he's really up and around? That he actually means to come into Liberty like Sam says?"

"Uh-huh." Rickards persisted in his verbal economy.

"By damn, you'd best leave for a long trip right sudden, Joe!" his deputy advised nervously. "Them young'uns aint healthy to meddle with."

"Uh-huh."

"I can hold the jail down. They know me and won't give me no trouble, once it's spread around you've gone. How soon can you pull out?"

Rickards stood up. He scratched his belly again, looked up and down the square, nodding to himself. Shortly, he looked back at Tunk.

"I reckon I'll stay around," he said quietly, and turned and went into the office.

There were thirteen horsemen in the happy group. They entered the town at ten o'clock, Jesse, peacock-proud, though still pale as a quality-folk bedsheet, cantering a black gelding at their head.

The reunited bravos included brother Frank, newly returned from his unfortunate following of Quantrill into Kentucky, George Shepherd, who had sided him in that misguided adventure, Jim Poole, one of the "tattered twenty-five" who had accompanied Jesse to Texas and who had arrived back in the home state only days before, Clell Miller, fresh from the brush he had taken to after his parole by Rogers, and of course Cole and Oll Shepherd.

After a proper hand-galloped payment of respects twice around the square, during which a suitable number of store windows were shot out, they headed their mounts at a dead run down Main Street in the direction of Fred Meffert's Saloon. On the rip-roaring way, the last of the good townfolk were driven off the street by a further fusillade of wild revolver shots and

hair-raising guerrilla *"yip-yip-yahs!"* of returning triumph.

Despite the band's roistering good humor, the
denizens of Liberty remembered all too well the
real article. The least perceptive dullard among
them realized that just the wrong-turned word
or crossing of uncertain temper could ignite the
present invasion into as bona fide a raid as a
man would want to recall. They sought the
sanctuary of home and fireside without notable
argument, those of their number who had ridden recent Union vigilante tours along the back
roads being particularly prompt in vacating the
public thoroughfare.

When the carefree boys had haunch-slid their
horses up to Meffert's hitching rail, thrown
their reins and clumped across the boardwalk
into the saloon's musty interior, the sole inhab-
itant remaining on Liberty's main stem was a
short, squat stranger in a ragged overcoat and
pulled-down hat, lounging in front of Harlan's
feed store across the street. None of the gang
gave him a second look. It was an oversight not
like Jesse James, and one that was to cut his
loudly advertised "return" uncomfortably short.

Cole, arm around his pale comrade, billfold
already open on the polished mahogany of Meffert's bar, boomed out his big laugh and called
for forty-rod on the house.

"Boys!" The ham's heft of his fist crashed the
bar, bouncing the filling glasses. "I reckon there
isn't a one of us aint glad to see little old Dingus

out and around! I aint much of a one for speech making but I say the first drink goes to Dingus's ma and the Mimms girl. I allow they brought old Dingus around where there wasn't anybody else could have done it. Here's to Mrs. Samuel, boys, and to little Zerelda Mimms! I reckon there aint nobody left in Liberty is going to take a set at arguing that point. I say, throw 'em down!"

He was raising his glass, suiting action to toast, when somebody in Liberty "took a set."

As a matter of fact, not only somebody in Liberty, but somebody in Fred Meffert's Saloon.

" *And I say, throw 'em up!* "

The quietly spoken command came into the smalls of the celebrants' backs like the cold probe of a Navy Colt. But it was no six-gun, Sam Colt's or otherwise, that the overcoated stranger held hip-ready and hammer-cocked in their directions.

Jim Poole knocked his glass over in the involuntary jerk of his drinking hand. Oll Shepherd, always the first to wet the social lip, had his forty-rod halfway down the hatch. He gasped, strangled, spewed white lightning in four directions. Cole lowered his brimming tumbler to the bar without spilling a drop.

Not bothering to turn, the big guerrilla looked speculatively into the mirrored back of the bar, made due note of certain aspects of the reflection there. The stranger, hat back now and overcoat collar turned down, bore a striking resemblance to Sheriff Joe Rickards. Further, he handled the sawed-off 10-gauge as if he was not meaning to hit bobwhites with it.

"Boys," said Coleman Younger gravely, "we're outnumbered. One to thirteen. You may play your hands the way you see them, but personally I never bet against a pair of tens showing on the board."

He turned with the sober observation, bowing gracefully toward the twin muzzles of Rickards's shotgun.

"Now then, Sheriff, you may play your double tens. Me, I'm throwing in." He gestured with his raised hands toward his crossbelted Colts. "I got nothing but a pair of sixes!"

" '*Now then*' "— Rickards's mimicry of Cole's phrase was humorless—"you loudmouthed bastards. You said no Goddamned Republican could arrest you. I'll learn you a trick or two about that. *You're arrested*."

The terse words were no sooner out than Tunk Johnson, clearly as miserable as a streetwalker at Sunday services, slunk in through the saloon door and relieved the dumbstruck guerrillas of their guns. Within sixty seconds of his following them into the saloon, Sheriff Joe Rickards followed Jesse's bad men back out again.

It is still a favorite story in Liberty today: that march of the empty-holstered revolver fighters across the town square and directly into Judge Philander Lucas's waiting courthouse. At the time, the sheepish guerrillas took it for the most part in good course. Cole, as usual, set the temper for the occasion by doffing his hat and bowing handsomely to the ladies among the gathering groups of curious, and returning the grins and banter of their jibing menfolk. By the time the courthouse steps had been traversed, any remaining element of seriousness to the affair had evaporated in the November sunshine and under the obvious good nature of the famous captives. Liberty let out its collective breath and had itself a good laugh.

With one memorable exception.

A certain member of the outmaneuvered Clay County bravos failed, notably, to find anything funny in the situation.

Jesse was a man who could take a joke or leave it very much alone. In the present case, while as aware as any of his fellows of the ironic humor of Joe Rickards's single-handed capture of thirteen *cum laude* guerrillas, he did not, like them, write the experience off as good clean fun.

While he outwardly played his part with as much aplomb as Cole or Oll or any of them, the inner darknesses of his mind were furiously at work. The subsequent fact that Judge Lucas, for want of any serious standing charge against them, reluctantly ordered their release after a sharp warning to "leave Liberty out of their future plans" brought no light to those inner darknesses.

Analytical as always, and learning where the others laughed, Jesse saw far beyond the rough banter of his comrades, as the chastised guerrillas galloped their horses defiantly out of Liberty an hour later. What could happen once could happen again. What was luckily a joke could unluckily be a tragedy. It was what came of running in a bunch, and of showing yourself off in a crowd.

Riding beside him, Cole threw a side glance at his brooding leader. He took note of the fact that the infallible barometer of the blue eyes was at storm-warning blink. Losing his grin, he asked quickly, "What's eating you, Ding? There aint no harm to come of it, is there? We was lucky, the way I see it."

Jesse had a penchant for the old saws, the pithy sayings. No doubt it was a habit well drilled into him by his mother, an omnivorous reader of the standard classics. When he was worried, Cole had noticed, he was wont to express that worry via the handiest aphorism. He returned Cole's look now, merely nodding. "Fool's names and fool's faces—"

Cole laughed at him, clapping his big hand to the hunched shoulders. "Aw hell, Ding! You got to get over that sweat of yours about being spied on in public. Forget it, man! There aint no harm to come of it, I tell you."

"You don't tell me nothing." The reply was as quickly made as the blink which came with it. "Once bit, twice shy. Goddamn their dirty souls to hell. They'll never take my gun away again!"

Cole knew his man too well not to let it lay right where Jesse had dropped it. Dingus was mad clean through. He never horsed you when he was blinking like that, and as far back as a man could remember, clear back and beyond boyhood, even, Cole had never heard him make an empty brag. You had to reckon he wasn't making one now.

*Fool me once, shame on you. Fool me twice, shame on me.*

They never arrested Jesse again.


No man has left a record of what Jesse did from the date of his arrest by Joe Rickards until six o'clock in the morning of February 13, the following year. The missing weeks are another *Ninety Days*, one more of the baffling blind spots in his carefully covered trail.

But the morning in question was something else again.

Captain Minter's house stood on the south side of the Kansas City Road, where it wound down to the river from the west. Below the house, a scant six hundred yards, the road ended abruptly at the Blue Mills Ferry. Beyond the ferry station, on the north bank of the Missouri, it began again, though now in a different direction, toward a different terminus, and bearing from that point a significant change in name—the Liberty Road.

At 5:45, Rush Stepp, an itinerant farmhand,

pulled his cloddy team and boxbed wagon up to the loading dock east of the house. Captain Minter was a man of ambition as well as intellect. In addition to supervising the Blue Mills Ferry, he maintained a profitable feed mill on the residence's premises. He came out of the house now, crossed to the dock, nodded to Stepp.

"Morning, Rush. How's Mr. Hobart and the folks? You've come for another load of meal, I suppose."

"Yes, sir, Cap'n. Twenty sacks this time, I reckon. Mr. Hobart's fine. Missus is ailing agin, though, and the middle boy's down with the measles."

The small talk went along as Rush loaded the sacks and Captain Minter wrote up the account. At five minutes of six, the last sack was in. Rush climbed up on the box, unwrapped the reins. As he did, Captain Minter looked over his head, frowned quickly, nodded in the direction of the Kansas City Road.

"Hold up, Rush. Look yonder there—"

Rush looked, turned uneasily back to Minter. "I dunno, Cap'n. Mr. Hobart's in a tolerable fret to get this meal. I reckon I'd best ease right along."

"You'd best stay right where you are, till we see what they want. There's something familiar about that big man in the lead."

Rush started to answer, thought better of it, made himself as small as he could on the wagonbox, sat furtively watching the approaching horsemen.

There were thirteen of them, all finely mounted, all wearing long cavalry coats of Union blue. Three rode in the lead, ten hung a little back. Only the three turned off the main road and came for the loading dock.

"Morning, Captain."

The man who spoke, a big, pleasant-faced man, addressed Minter with the easy familiarity of an old friend. There was, significantly, no answering recognition in the Captain's reply.

"Yes, sir. What can I do for you?"

"Well now, sir, we've had a long ride and our horses are in need of a good feed. We figured to buy us a sack of your fine meal."

Captain Minter was a merchant of discretion. He did not bother to inquire into the dubious merits of feeding fine-ground meal to hungry horses. He employed the pause in looking at his questioner, and at his two companions.

The first of these was no more than a boy of nineteen or so. He was small, appeared nervous, had a marked peculiarity of blinking his eyes. The other rider was older and taller, though just as slender in build. The first rider was over six feet, and big from his bootsoles up. All were well dressed and clean-shaven.

"You want the Kansas Winter," said Minter, still watching them, "or the Missouri Spring Hard?"

"Wheat's wheat," grinned the big man. "But

seeing's we're Clay County boys, give us the Missouri."

*A Missouri wheatsack*! A passing horseman said, "make it Missouri," and the whole course of a folklore was altered. But Captain Minter was a soldier of personal fortune, not a chronicler of frontier legend. Business was business, a sack of wheatmeal was a sack of wheatmeal. Some minutes after six o'clock Captain Minter was the richer by ninety cents and the first of the fabulous Missouri wheatsacks was abroad the Blue Mills Ferry in the attentive company of the blue-coated horsemen.

Watching the ferry grow small toward the Liberty shore, the Captain, as was his habit in moments of preoccupation, tapped his prominent front teeth with the second finger of his right hand.

"Rush," he said to the staring farmhand, more thinking aloud than actually addressing him. "You know who that big rascal was?"

"Beats me, Cap'n," shrugged Rush. "I think I seen him somewheres, but I lay I caint place him."

"*I lay I can*," said Captain Minter quietly. "That was Cole Younger bought that sack of meal."

Greenup Bird and his son, William, cashier and bookkeeper respectively of the Clay County Savings & Loan Association, arrived at the front doors of that institution's fine brick building on

104

the northwest corner of the Liberty square promptly at 7:45 A.M. At five minutes before eight those doors were thrown open to whatever legitimate business might be thus early abroad.

Also at five minutes before eight, two ambitious students, early-bound for their classes at William Jewel College upon the hill beyond the square, came out of their front doors and stood a moment sampling the brisk cold of the February morning.

Presently, Jimmy Sandusky, a second-form lad of fifteen, spied his pal George Wynmore. Waves were exchanged, the two boys starting for their regular meeting-place on the corner opposite the bank. George, a nineteen-year-old and popular enough around town to have earned the nickname "Jolly," reached the square first and stood waiting for Jimmy to come up.

Those were a fateful five minutes. During their brief course some even-earlier risers were about their particular calling.

They came into Liberty from four directions, in groups of three and four. Young George paid the first group scant heed. Its three horsemen were well dressed, clearly upright in bearing, headed by a most pleasant, imposingly large gentleman on a fine bay gelding. Their innocence was further established by the smiling nod of the big man as they cantered past George, and by the cheerful, "Morning, son.

Fine day, aint it?" with which the big man greeted him.

Shortly, however, the first group was joined by a second, then a third and fourth. George counted thirteen horsemen in as many seconds, and began to wonder. Even a lad as "jolly" as he was adept enough at frontier arithmetic to see that something unusual was adding up in front of the Clay County Savings & Loan Association.

He glanced excitedly up the street, waving to Jimmy Sandusky to hurry it along. This was some doings. A boy naturally wanted to discuss it with his pal. At the moment Jimmy was only minutes away. But George Wynmore's wave was the last communication he would ever have with his friend—or with anybody else.

Three of the horsemen detached themselves from the gesturing, quick-talking group. They rode only a short way, then separated and took up independent stations several hundred feet from the bank. The remaining ten rode directly to the bank. Before its doors, they split up. Three rode away along the street to the north, three along the street to the west. Neither of these groups took up a station, but continued to wheel their mounts back and forth along the storefronts facing the square, clearly on the *qui vive* for the first move of interference from patron or proprietor of the opening business establishments.

The original three horsemen now dismounted, threw their reins over the bank's hitching rail, moved toward the waiting doors. There, the third man stopped, posting himself in a lookout position commanding approach to the bank entrance from either direction. The other two, one of them the big man who had spoken so pleasantly to George, hurried into the building.

Inside, the two strangers paused, returning the questioning looks of Mr. Greenup Bird and his worthy scion.

"Good morning, gentlemen." Mr. Greenup Bird later remembered that the pair's official greeter was a fine-looking, six-foot man of scholarly address. "Are you open for business, good sirs?"

"Why, yes," stammered the elder Bird. "Yes, of course. Name your pleasure, gentlemen."

The senior cashier was understandably new to the type of business he was inviting. He grew old to it very rapidly.

His immediate education consisted of a grinning nod from the larger of the strangers, to the smaller.

"You take the old man. He's more your size."

Jesse returned Cole's nod sans the grin, moved across the floor to the cashier's counter. Where the big Navy Colt came from, Mr. Greenup Bird never could remember. He remembered very distinctly, however, that it wound up probing the region of his right temple.

"All right," said Jesse unheatedly. "Open the

vault, and don't drag your feet about it or I'll blow your head off."

Cashier Bird was an astute banker, had a quick head for clear figures. He wasted no time adding the .36-caliber hole in the end of the Colt to the six capped chambers of the cylinder which lay behind it. He opened the vault.

Meanwhile, Cole had implanted his Navy Colt in the younger Bird's shrinking belly, and now backed him toward the vault, following his father and Jesse. Inside the vault, the shelves were admirably cleaned. Both captive Birds watched helplessly as the smaller man swept bonds, greenbacks and minted coins alike into the capacious maw of the Missouri wheatsack which the bigger outlaw had produced from beneath his long coat.

With the sack full, the two bands stopped outside the vault. The larger doffed his hat to the elder Bird, who had followed them out of the vault.

"A pleasant good morning, sir. Thank you for your courtesy."

With that, he and the bulging wheatsack were on their way to the door. But his smaller companion, pausing, eyed the indignant cashier narrowly. In his subsequent deposition, Bird avowed that the following instruction came with a crooked grin and a notably nervous eye-blink.

"All birds should be caged," philosophized the small gunman. "Get back inside the vault,

Mr. Bird, and step to it!"

Mr. Bird stepped to it, wondering, even in his haste, at the casual use of his name. Joining his son in the vault, he heard the slam of its door, saw the accompanying departure of the slender bandit from behind its heavy grillwork. He saw something else, as well.

The spring lock on the vault door had failed to catch in the hurried slamming.

Cole was still tying the wheatsack to his saddlehorn, and Frank was still waiting for Jesse outside the bank entrance, when Mr. Greenup Bird's outraged cries for aid and succor began echoing from the bank's raised front window.

Circumstances along the main stem of Liberty altered forthwith.

Alarmed citizens began to run about, repeating cashier Bird's outcry. And for the first time, as they were to do on so many a subsequent, similar occasion, the chilling rebel yells of the ex-Centralia raiders began to terrify the morning air.

Shortly, Cole had the sack adjusted to his unhurried liking. By the same time Frank and Jesse had found stirrup and were mounted. Also by the same time, the atmosphere on the northwest corner of Liberty's square was beginning to whistle a bit.

Several quick-thinking individuals among the astonished citizenry had found firearms.

But Jesse had not failed to apply his usual care in such professional matters. His men were well drilled in the parts each had been assigned in the master plan.

The three outflung pickets took off in as many directions, yelling and firing their revolvers to draw attention off the main pack. The two groups of patrolling guerrillas raced their horses back and forth along the storefronts, pouring a hail of high-aimed lead into them which had Liberty's shopkeepers sweeping up glass for a week. Under the crash and confusion of this galloping destruction, Jesse, Frank and Cole headed their mounts around the square in the identical direction whence they had come not five minutes before. Behind them, their rear guard firing a last volley into the stores, drew racing together, and swung their horses to follow those of Jesse and his companions.

George Wynmore, sole firsthand eyewitness to the original approach of the three outlaw leaders, was still standing on his cross-street corner. As the trio of fleeing bandits thundered back toward him, he lost sudden interest in the whole proceedings.

Turning, he began to run.

One of the three horsemen leveled his Colt, shot him twice through the back as he ran. He fell immediately, rolled over, came halfway to his knees, still clutching the leather-thonged pack of his schoolbooks. The second wave of guerrilla horsemen, running up on the ironshod heels of the first, finished the job.

The boy pitched on forward into the dirt of

the square—excused from school forever.

Clay County tradition insists the coroner's inquest over the mutilated body of "Jolly" Wynmore disclosed five .36-caliber revolver bullets: two entering from the back, three from the front and right side. No document of any such finding remains. If it did, its pathological detail could interest only the insatiably morbid. What is certain, and what is to the larger point, was that Liberty's most popular, harmless young citizen lay murdered in cold blood—and the Clay County Savings & Loan Association stood divested of sixty thousand dollars in government bonds, greenback currency and mint-gold coin of the realm.

It was the first daylight bank robbery on the North American continent. As a matter of further fact, for any evidence to the contrary turned up in the ensuing eighty years, it was the first on any continent. In either event, there exists no reasonable doubt in whose devious mind the assault was conceived, nor by whose slender hand executed. Mr. Hurlburt Peabody, years-gone seer of the Pleasant Grove School District, had penned the name into his attendance book with prophetic accuracy.

It was still spelled Jesse Woodson James.

The virgin triumph was now being loudly shared by the hard-riding guerrillas as they swung their mounts out of Liberty, driving them down the east road toward the Ray County crossing of the Missouri. Of the thirteen unscathed horsemen, only the three in the lead held their silence and hoarded their various thoughts.

Jesse's face revealed nothing. He sat his black easily, eyes blinking, thin lips straight, his slim body moving rhythmically to the hammer of the gallop. Frank's attitude was similar, compounded only by the repeated, worried glances he flung back through the settling dust of the escape route.

But Cole's handsome features were set in a cement of rare ugliness. When, presently, he kneed his bay up to side his leader's lathered black, his words were as hard as the look which backed them.

*"Goddamn you, Dingus. Why'd you do it?"*

He had never cursed him in earnest before. But the chill of the soft-voiced question was plain as the hoarfrost along the road's muddy edges, and no man could miss it. It bit into Jesse like a lash, cutting at his thin temper.

"You son of a bitch! Don't you cuss me, you hear! Don't you *ever*. I won't take that from you, nor any man alive!"

Cole watched him, knowing as well as any man what went on in that dark mind of his. Dingus was *different*. Cole had always known he was. You could love him better than your own brother, follow him not only to hell and back, but twice around the devil on the way. But when you were done with your ride, or even before you swung up to start it, you knew one thing. Somewhere in Dingus, God had left something out. Something most men, no matter how mean or wicked, had in them. And something which they had to face up to, like it or not, short of cold-blooded murder.

Dingus didn't have that *something* in him.

When the pressure built up in him it just ran around in that crazy brain of his until it came to that empty place. Then it just jumped. When it jumped, Dingus pulled the trigger. It made no mortal difference to him *who* was standing in front of the gun.

Cole looked at him again now, and knew that if his next words hit that empty place in his head, he would kill him as quick as he had that poor damn boy back yonder.

"Dingus," he said softly. *"You'll take it."*

Jesse favored his left-hand gun. And Cole was riding on his left.

The small hand flashed downward. But not so swiftly as the big one did, outward. Cole's long fingers came around Jesse's reaching wrist like the released jaws of a baitpan trap. "You'll take it," he repeated, voice unraised, "and you'll take it straight."

Jesse made no attempt to free the pinioned wrist. The two rode on, the little drama so swift, so close between the flanked horses, that Frank, riding ten yards to the rear, saw nothing.

"You ever again pull a trick like downing that boy," Cole concluded, "you and me are through.

You know what I'm talking about, Dingus. We've been here before."

Watching Jesse's eyes, he saw the blink steady down, knew from that that the killing minute had passed, the empty place been jumped. He brought his hand slowly away then, nodding softly.

"You understand me, boy?"

Jesse looked at him, the bad-wild light Cole knew so well gone from his blue eyes. He did not look at him long, and he dropped his head with his reply. His words were still hedged with defensive anger, but Cole had a fine ear for the high, thin voice of his boyhood idol. Within the limits of his wild way, Dingus was ashamed. He was ashamed and he knew that Cole *knew* he was.

"Sure, you damn fool." He looked up now, but still away from Cole. "I know that 'noble heart' of yours. It'll get you killed or caught one day, too, you hear? Let's jest forget it. The boy saw me, spit-close. I didn't cotton to the way he kept looking at me when we rode in. It don't pay to take chances. I reckoned he might have knowed me from somewheres. That's all. . . ."

His big companion didn't answer, save with a slow nod. It was a nod only of understanding, not of agreement.

Cole Younger never forgot Jolly Wynmore. He buried him quietly in his mind, alongside Old Hickory. He knew as he did that it was the last such ceremony he would perform for Jesse.

There was no room left in his one-time unquestioning loyalty for a third of the senseless headstones. He had meant what he said. There would be no third interment. For Cole, the graveyard was full.

# Chapter Six

*Corydon*

In the light of our later day's law and order it is hard to understand the shameful failure of witnesses to come forward following the rape of the Clay County Savings & Loan Association. In the light of certain techniques of Jesse's band with regard to incidental witnesses, already apparent in the senseless murder of Jolly Wynmore, this remissness becomes not alone understandable but, to the degree that men are entitled at all costs to protect their own hides, highly reasonable.

The gang began operations on the old reliable theory that dead men are seldom loquacious. It proved a theory which, through practice of ready Colt and restless trigger finger, was to protect them from identification for a dozen years.

The fact of the Liberty affair was that Jesse, by his use of Greenup Bird's name in ordering the cashier caged, demonstrated that he knew the man. It would seem to follow that Bird knew him. They were local boys, as well known in Liberty as they were in Lees Summit. But both Greenup Bird and his discreet son, William, refused to testify on the question of whether the James boys and Coleman Younger had composed the trio which entered his bank.

The prior fact of the Liberty affair was that Captain Minter had positively identified Cole as the man who bought the sack of meal on the morning of the robbery, the identical sack later found abandoned at the Ray County crossing of the Missouri. Knowing Cole as he did, the proprietor of the Blue Mills Ferry could not have failed to recognize his two companions at the feed mill negotiations: the blinking-eyed, nervous boy and his taller, thin-faced comrade-in-waiting, or more explicitly, his older brother-in-actual-blood.

But educating Rush Stepp as to the notorious identities of that morning's meal customers and repeating the same testimony under oath at Liberty proved two vastly different proposals. When he was queried, Captain Minter's memory took a sudden vacation. For the official record he had never even heard of Jesse and Frank

James, much less sold them and Cole Younger a sack of Missouri wheatmeal at Blue Mills Ferry the morning of the robbery.

The exact situation was no different than would be a similar situation today. Police protection meant little or nothing to witnesses who had far more fear of the given word of *certain* outlaws, than respect for the bounden promises of *uncertain* law officers. That given outlaw word was very simple: "Shut up or get shot."

It is a singular fact that in the eight major "bank failures" which followed the Liberty fiscal collapse of February 13, in each of which the James boys were named, off the record, by scores of witnesses, not one Missouri citizen's name appears under oath on the surviving courthouse records of inquiry, in connection with the identification of Younger, Thomas Coleman, or James, Jesse Woodson or James, Alexander Franklin.

This "Missouri immunity" is hardly an idle observation. It must be borne in mind if one is to accept the incredible record of the next six years. The facts of the record alone are peculiar enough. Let us consider some few of them.

In late October, 1866, Jesse and six men, as usual described by witnesses as riding "fine Kentucky thoroughbreds," held up the banking house of Alexander Mitchell & Company in Lexington, Missouri, making off without any killings, and with the slim haul of two thousand dollars.

In early March, 1867, five men, again described as "led by Jesse and riding matchless thoroughbreds," entered the private banking firm of Judge William McLain in Savannah, Missouri. This time there was no haul whatever. Judge McLain bravely fired on the bandits as they entered his office, surprising them and driving them off, becoming in the process a local hero, and the only man ever to shoot it out with Jesse James and live to boast of it.

On May 23, 1867, it was the Hughes & Mason Bank in Richmond, Missouri, largest county bank in the state. But by this time Jesse had apparently learned some lessons in his new profession. The innocences of Lexington and Savannah were not compounded. Four thousand dollars in gold went into the wheatsack, and the mayor of the town and a teen-age bystander were killed in the getaway.

The last case serves as a notable example of the workings of that "Missouri immunity" which made it, and all the other cases, possible.

Eight warrants were eventually issued for the Richmond killings. Jesse and Frank James were named in private by a dozen witnesses, but of the warrants actually drawn not one held the charmed names: James, Jesse Woodson; James, Alexander Franklin.

Three of the eight minor bandits identified were subsequently cornered and killed, one by gunfire, two by Judge Lynch. Jim Cummins was arrested and released. Cole Younger, like Frank and Jesse, was given a "scared-white and mile-wide" berth in the entire matter.

This was the peculiar occasion of the notorious "alibi cards," those amazing documents written by Frank and Jesse and distributed throughout Clay County by their friends. The cards announced with bland innocence that the two peace-loving James boys were at home tending their "dear and ailing" mother at the time of the Richmond murders. We are left to believe, for lack of any evidence to the contrary, that these cards were accepted at face value by the so-called law enforcement officers of Old Missouri.

The only result of the whole affair was that Richmond was crossed off the preferred banking list of the investment firm of "Woodson & Franklin," and Jesse's men were the more affluent by a shabby $2.69 apiece.

The interim, then.

Jim Cummins was to declare, following his "coming in" many years later, "Conditions at that time in Clay were getting too warm. I took a trip to California."

The force which gave primary impetus to Jim's urge to leave was an unrelenting, incorruptible, private organization of professional manhunters. It was as well known then as it is now—the Pinkerton National Detective Agency.

Founded in 1850 by Allan Pinkerton, the Pinkerton Agency has aptly been described as the "civilian Federal Bureau of Investigation of the

1880's." Pinkerton had been the head of the Northern Secret Service during the War between the States. He was a man of known tenacity and absolute integrity. His services and those of his grim organization, under the competent field leadership of his son, William Pinkerton, were now called down upon the head of Jesse James by the panicky members of the Missouri Bankers Association.

The entrance of the Pinkertons was made in 1867, directly after the Richmond robbery. The event marked the ending of an era for Jesse. In a description of the day, "they took to his trail and never left off of it till poor Jesse lay dead in St. Joseph." The pressure the Pinkertons put upon "poor Jesse" was for no single moment relaxed in the fifteen long years to come. Gone was the careless freedom of the old reliance in the clan. Gone was the former ease of vanishing into the family sanctuaries of Clay and Jackson counties. Suddenly, any friend of yore might be a Pinkerton of present. Overnight, every stranger was assumed to be a professional detective, every passing man on horseback a hired killer of the hired law.

The saga of the Pinkerton Agency in its trailing of Jesse James must, however, remain for another story , another storyteller. The Pinkertons *followed after* Jesse. If we are to ride with him, we cannot at the same time gallop with them. The simple truth is, relentless pressure or no, brilliant effort or otherwise, they never caught up to him. He remained, in the end, too wise and too wary for them. And he rode too fast.

Mr. Nimrod Long was well pleased with the day and date—March 20, 1868. The confounded war was three years over, reconstruction was shaping up nicely in southwestern Kentucky. Particularly so in the guerrilla-torn county of Logan and the up and coming city of Russelville. The books of the financial house of Long & Norton were in their best balance since Appomattox.

Mr. Long allowed himself the luxury of his second cigar since opening hour.

The panetela had built but half an inch of ash when he glanced up to see six strangers ride up in front of the bank. Two of the newcomers at once dismounted and started for the building's entrance.

The first of these was a strikingly handsome man of well over six feet, his companion a smaller fellow of rather mean appearance. Both were well dressed and—at once apparent to the eye of a Kentuckian—both superbly mounted on blood horses.

Seconds later, the larger of the newcomers was introducing himself in a soft drawl which bespoke at once the presence of a fellow Southerner and a gentleman of some culture.

"Good morning, Mr. Long, sir. My name is

Colburn, Henderson Colburn, sir. From Louisville way."

"A good morning indeed, Mr. Colburn," smiled Nimrod Long. "May we assist you in any way, sir?"

"As a matter of fact, you may, sir," answered the other, producing a hundred-dollar bill. "I am a cattle buyer and have just delivered a small herd in Nashville. I should like this bill changed so that I may pay off one of my hands, uh, Mr. Woodson, here."

Mr. Long looked at Mr. Woodson, sniffed with well-bred disdain.

Mr. Woodson was an uncommonly ugly fellow, short, pale, high-foreheaded. His eyes were red-rimmed and granulated, as though from some chronic infection—an infection which no doubt accounted for the continual squinting blink with which he surveyed the interior planning of Long & Norton's house of business. Completing his distasteful mien, a two-weeks' growth of sandy-brown whiskers overlaid his narrow jaw. It was clear Mr. Woodson was beginning the losing struggle of raising a beard to compensate for the handicaps of nature.

Nimrod Long could not be blamed for his failure to understand that he was looking at the origins of that "dark-sandy" beard which was destined to become the hallmark of the king of all highwaymen. Nor for his inability to comprehend that the nervous eyes were memorizing every professional detail of vault, teller's cage, cash counter and money drawer within their watery range. Mr. Long was a teller of the bank genus, not of the fortune variety, and as the former he was astute enough.

"Mr. Colburn, sir," he observed, suspiciously examining the proffered greenback, "I'm sorry to say that this bill is counterfeit."

Nimrod Long's suspicions came a shade late in the afternoon. Nevertheless, Mr. Colburn's courtesy held faultlessly. "Well now, sir," the big cattleman agreed, "I reckon that bill *is* counterfeit, just like you say. But I do believe I have something here which isn't." He was still smiling apologetically when he reached inside his coat and produced the real article.

*"Open that vault, Mr. Long."*

Banker Long appraised the authenticity of the Single Action Army Colt, decided forthwith that it was genuine. As were, he concluded, its two counterparts now occupying the nervous hands of Mr. Woodson.

But Nimrod Long was six feet tall. Brave as a badgered bear. Wiry as a Logan County wildcat.

He got a bony knee into Jesse's groin, sprang away from him, leaped for the alleyway behind the bank. Doubled over with the blinding pain of his injury, Jesse staggered after him. He was in perfect time to get in the way of Cole's aim, and the banker was safely away down the alley, broadcasting the facts of financial life in Russelville at the top of his lungs.

"They're holding up the bank! Hurry up,

everybody. They're holding up the bank!"

Inside the building, the indestructible Cole grinned at Jesse. "Well now, Ding, I reckon we dassn't let Mr. Long down. He's advertising a holdup and I allow we're beholden to furnish him one."

"Get the vault!" snarled Jesse, not amused. "I'll take the cash drawer!"

The vault—pure luck of the profession—was open. Under the practiced sweep of Cole's hand, better than five thousand dollars in greenbacks and bagged coins went into the wheatsack. Outside the vault, similar luck was Jesse's. The cash drawer added nine thousand dollars in currency to the sack's treasure.

The combined loot was so heavy it required the efforts of both Cole and Jesse to drag it across the bank floor and out to the horses and the waiting confederates. More precious minutes were lost making the wheatsack fast to Cole's saddlehorn. By the time the mount-up was made, they were in trouble.

"Ride north! Ride north!" screamed Jesse, spurring his black away from the bank with the order.

Obediently, his followers formed up behind him, making the charge out of town in cavalry fashion. The luck of the damned held. They broke through the hail of squirrel rifle and shotgun fire put up by the aroused citizens and won through to the north road.

But Jesse's furious back glance, checking the

miracle of the escape and its attendant wonder—none of his henchmen had taken a dangerous wound—saw something else.

Something which boded a bad ending to a bad beginning.

Back toward the town, the dust of their exit-gallop still hung over northern Main Street. Coming through that dust, no more than a short mile away, were the first horsemen of a huge posse. Ten, twenty, thirty horses, Jesse counted. Still they came. Fifty of them, anyway. And not five minutes behind!

They would need all the luck they had ever had, now. He had tailored that Russelville job pretty careful. But he had cut the britches a little too close for comfort!

Jesse was right.

In the weeks succeeding the Logan County robbery, the Pinkerton's top operative, the famous A. B. "Yankee" Bligh, took up the trail.

The gang fled into Allen County east of Logan, there split up on the unplanned basis of every man for himself—and Allan and William Pinkerton's pet devil to take the hindmost.

Bligh got on the trail of Big George Shepherd, ran him down to Nelson County, Missouri, cornered him in a clansman's farmhouse, wounded him in a running gunfight, captured him alive and put him away for three years in the Missouri State Prison.

Exit, Big George Shepherd. He never returned to the outlaw wars, but fate had him marked for a strange, brief future in Jesse's wild life.

Next on Yankee Bligh's list was brother Oll.

The Pinkerton detective ran Oll down in a second farmhouse, only a few miles from the Samuel place at Centerville. Refusing surrender, Oll made an early-dawn dash for the surrounding woods and freedom. Bligh's posse cut him down. They buried him, sans shroud or benefit of clergy, where he fell.

Yankee Bligh expunged the second name on his seven-man list, headed back for Kentucky where his fellow Pinkertons had located Jesse himself.

But the grapevine of the guerrilla telegraph was still working. News of Oll Shepherd's death reached Jesse before Bligh did.

There was a brief council of war with brother Frank. This damned Yankee Bligh was a bad actor. When he started after a man with company orders of "dead or alive," he clearly favored the first option. It was time for a trip. California called. It was hurriedly conceded that Jim Cummins had had an excellent idea the year before. And even more hurriedly concluded that no better time than the present could be selected for joining Jim in an extended vacation on the coast.

The outlaw brothers implemented their decision with characteristically opposing methods.

Frank went quietly and directly, by Overland Stage and horseback, out the Oregon Trail. Jesse traveled in style, riding the cars to New York, seeing the big city sights on his Norton & Long expense account, taking first-class passage via steamship for Panama, and then going to San Francisco.

Tradition has the brothers hiding the year away as outpatients in a sanitarium operated by an uncle on the James side, in Paso Robles. And spending the long months tenderly searching for the lost grave of their "beloved clergyman father," who, according to local accounts, had been buried somewhere near Marysville.

Knowing Jesse, if not Frank, one may be excused for imagining that the former managed to steal a few not so touching moments from this tender exploration to clean his Colt and polish the marksmanship which had been so miserable at Russelville. And to curse William and Allan Pinkerton, along with Yankee Bligh, while at the same time sparing himself a soulful hour now and again to consider future ways and means of illegal reentry into the banking business of Old Missouri.

Whither went the courteous "Mr. Colburn," following Russelville, remains among the Clay County imponderables. He was not in Missouri with the Shepherds. He was not in California with Frank and Jesse. The legend has him living high and loving wide, the whole time, down around Dallas and Fort Worth in Texas.

The description fits young Thomas Coleman like a kidskin glove. He was known to favor the longhorn state, and to look with more than passing approval on the looser-limbed of her fairhaired fillies. *Requiescat in pace* the fable of his Lone Star amours.

Cole, like Frank and Jesse, had earned a considerable rest. Like them, too—and history is at least sure on this point—he took one.

It was two full years, lacking but three months, before the wheatsack was seen again in Old Missouri.


Zerelda Mimms sat by the front window of her father's farmhouse, staring into the December twilight.

It was the third day of the month, and her birthday. By the calendar she was twenty-one. And by any other witness, a woman full and beautifully grown. But her thoughts were not of birthdays, nor of beauty, nor of womanhood attained.

The catalpa tree, yonder by the picket fence, was bare now. Its limbs stood skeleton-stark against the winter dusk. Yet Zerelda was seeing it in its summer bloom, rich and fragrant and freshly green, as it had been that August day when they brought Cousin Jesse from the *Yellowstone Belle*.

Five times, since, the catalpa had shed its waxy foliage. Still she waited, as she had from that first shedding, for Jesse to come back to her.

Through the lonely years, she had seen him but a few times. Each of the hurried meetings had been the same—short, fleeting, midnight affairs, with bandit lookouts posted along both approaches of the North Kansas City Road, and with the hulking, faithful Cole Younger holding Jesse's saddle horse in the rutted wagon tracks beyond the catalpa tree.

Jesse had never so much as held her hand, let alone taken her in his arms or asked for her promise.

A man who is riding with blood not his own still drying on his saddle fenders does not think in terms of ordering orange blossoms or naming the day. Zerelda knew he loved her. She accepted the long separations as the price of their unspoken vows, and she accepted them without question.

A blood member of the James clan, she was of course aware of his crimes. At the same time, and because she was a member of that clan, she accepted the family view of Jesse's career, which was to say the view of Zerelda Samuel. That view, since his ambush and near death outside Lexington, had been that Jesse, far from being a criminal, was a hounded and hunted Southern hero. From the day of her misguided advice that he turn himself openly over to the Federal authorities, the harsh-faced matriarch of the clan had become a full champion of her outlaw son's insistence that his war was still with the Union, and that his bank-raid killings were conducted solely on the old Biblical principle of an eye for an eye and a life for a life.

Forgotten, or not admitted, were such little inconsistencies as the assault on Norton & Long in Southern-state Kentucky. The time had grown too late for legal niceties. The legend insisted that the persecuted James boys stole only from the cursed Northerners, and Zerelda Samuel had become the blind, bitter heart of the legend.

The lonely girl's thoughts had turned quite naturally from Jesse to his vengeful mother. Only that morning Mrs. Samuel had brought her the happiest present of the day—news, at long last, of her missing love. The letter had been posted from Marysville, California, three weeks earlier. It was addressed to Jesse's mother, and meant for her, all save that wonderful, nineword postscript: "Ma, please let Zee know I am coming home!"

Still, that had been hours ago. The quick uplift of the long-awaited news had worn away under the oppressive grayness of the day-long cold. Looking now down the darkness of the wagon road, Zerelda fought back the growing emptiness of her thoughts, left the window, went into the kitchen to light the lamp and begin preparing her father's supper.

As she did, she heard the ring of the horse's hoofs on the frozen dirt of the front drive. Ignoring them, she smiled wearily. One thing about men you could always depend on, John Mimms no less than any other: they never failed to show up at suppertime.

She still thought nothing of it when she heard the horse go through the barnyard and into the barn. Her father was a horseman, like any Missourian. He would naturally want to blanket and feed his mount before looking to himself.

When she heard the quick lightness of the booted tread on the snowcrust of the rear stoop, she knew it was not John Mimms, but when the hesitant knock came a moment later she answered it, automatically, only wondering, disinterestedly, which close neighbor or kissing kinsman it might be.

"Evening, ma'am." The stranger's slight bow was made yet more unbending by the heavy stiffness of his sheepskin winter coat. "I was just passing by and seen your lamp go up. It's some cold, ma'am, and I've come a powerful long ways. Clean from California, as a matter of fact, and I sure could use a bite to—"

The first, numbing shock of it passed. The continuing easy drawl of the familiar, thin voice was broken sharply off by Zerelda's glad cry. *"Jesse! Cousin Jesse!"*

"Shhh!" Jesse put an exaggerated finger to his lips, stepped grinningly past her, heeled the curtained door quickly shut. "Quiet down, girl. You want to scare up every blamed Pinkerton in Clay County?"

"Oh, Jesse, Jesse!" The tears came then and the clumsy humor of his entrance was washed embarrassingly away in their fall.

"Hush, Zee, honey. Don't cry like that. Now, please, you hear me, girl?"

He stood there, his hands outstretched awkward and stiff, not knowing what to do with them, or with *her*.

She looked up, seeing his mute gesture, stepped hesitantly toward him, the tears still thick and glistening on her dark lashes. The awkwardness and stiffness were suddenly gone, then. He took her in his arms, holding her close and hard, neither of them saying anything, or needing to.

To Jesse, having her next to him, feeling the tremble and cling of her slim body against his, breathing in the wonderful fragrance of her soft skin and thrilling to the wispy touch of her blonde hair against his frost-burned lips, the moment itself was everything. He had never had a woman in his arms before. The rare, warm flood of blessed relief set loose in him by the eager press of Zerelda's young body swept over him, burying the tortured past as swiftly as it did the bleak future.

For Zerelda Mimms, the moment itself was but a small, precious sample of happier times to come. Jesse was home. And he was safe at last. Nearly two years had passed since Russelville. The Pinkertons had not since been seen in Clay County. She and Jesse would go away, make a new start somewhere else, raise their little ones far from Clay County and the dark shadow of their father's name.

With the hopeful thought, she clung tighter still to Jesse. For the first time, shy and backward about it as a schoolboy, he tilted her chin uncertainly upward, kissed her full on the mouth.

Their lips were still together when the iron tattoo of the galloping hoofbeats broke Zerelda away from him in sudden fear.

The moment, too, was gone for Jesse.

"Rest easy, now," he grinned quickly. "It's only Cole." But she saw the twist that set in around the thin mouth when he said it, and the cat-crouch that came into his step as he turned for the door.

He didn't reach it. It swung open without a knock. Black hat brushing the top sill, bear's hulk filling the whole frame, Cole Younger only nodded quickly and did not come in.

"Sorry, Zee, old girl," he grinned. "Hope I didn't bust up anything that might lead to wedding bells." Then, grin flicking out like a trimmed lamp: "Grab your hat, Dingus. We got company up the road."

"Is it *them*?" gritted Jesse.

"I think so. God knows how they get wind of things so quick."

"The Pinkertons—!" Zerelda's frightened gasp went unanswered. She got neither look nor nod from either man.

"Well," blinked Jesse, suddenly high-voiced, "if they're so damn set on smelling something, we'll raise them a stink they won't get out of their nostrils for six months. Let's go, Cole."

They were through the door and away into the night before Zerelda could cry out after them. Seconds later, the driving hammer of the two horses, coming from the barn, swept past the still-open door, cleared the front picket fence on the deadgallop fly and was lost in the swirling snows of the North Kansas City Road.

The only answer to Zerelda's single, broken cry of "Jesse—!" was the whoop and howl of the December wind throwing her own voice back upon her.

The seventh day of December, 1869, was as miserable as a wet, blowing snow could make it. The clay roads of Daviess County were standing rut-deep in frozen slush. Along the central thoroughfare of the river town of Gallatin, the hoofchurn of the mud was banked from storefront to storefront.

Inside the Daviess County Savings Bank, John W. Sheets, one-time captain of Union cavalry, current cashier and teller-of-all-trades, shivered and poked up the woodstove.

As he did, two heavily overcoated strangers entered, one of them presenting a hundred-dollar bank note and requesting change. Ex-Captain Sheets began to count out the bills. Shortly, he was aware that the two strangers

135

had produced four Colt revolvers and a Missouri wheatsack.

"Hand over the keys to the inside vault," said the larger of the men, pleasantly. "We'd admire as little fuss as possible, if you don't mind."

Sheets looked at them. He said nothing and did not move.

The big man cursed softly, moved on around the counter to help himself. He cleaned the cash drawer, came back around the counter. "Let's get out of here, Ding," he said quietly to his companion. "I don't cotton to the smell of this one."

"Wait a minute," rasped Jesse. He stared at Sheets. "Isn't he the bluebelly that downed Bill Anderson at Missouri City?"

"How the hell should I know?" asked Cole nervously. "I was in Baton Rouge."

"Get on outside with the sack," ordered Jesse.

Cole stood still, not liking the tone of his voice. Outside the bank, the sudden roar of a fanned Colt put its barking period to his hesitation. "That's Frank's .44," he scowled. "Let's get the hell out of here." His advice was compounded by Frank's shout from without.

"Hurry it up in there, boys! They'll be onto us!"

"I'm gone!" shrugged Cole, the old grin flickering. "Frank aint the one to grab hisself if he aint been kicked!" With the observation, he ran for the door.

Jesse watched him go, moved into the

counter, leaned across it, both pistols leveled on Sheets.

"You ever with the Union cavalry?" he hissed.

"Yes, I was—" began the cashier.

"Name of S. P. Cox, lieutenant with Jenni-son's Fifteenth?"

"No. John Sheets, captain, Fourth Iowa—"

"You're a damned liar!"

The left-hand Colt moved up and across the counter. The blast of the black powder filled the tiny room. The burst of its smoke and the stab of its orange flame obscured Sheets's face. The ball passed through his right eye, blew out the back of his skull, smashed the window behind him. Jesse, waiting to watch him fall, turned and ran for the door.

Outside, brother Frank had not exaggerated. A score of citizens had found guns, were working up the street toward the bank. Both Jesse's and Cole's horses were acting up, especially Jesse's black. Between trying to hang onto them, control his own mount and still thumb a delaying fire into the aroused townfolk, Frank had both his gun hands full.

Cole came out first. He vaulted into his saddle, the nearly empty sack impeding him not in the least. Jesse was no more than thirty seconds behind him. But as he legged up on his rearing black, Frank lost the reins. He saw Jesse clutch for the saddlehorn as he spun his own mount after Cole's. The latter, looking back as Frank galloped up, slid his horse to a mud-showering halt.

"God Amighty, Buck, look yonder!" In his excitement he unconsciously used the old boyhood name.

Fifty feet from the bank, Jesse's black had thrown him, hanging his left foot in the onside stirrup. He was dragging him now in a lunging, crazy run. As Frank and Cole watched, Jesse fought his foot free of the stirrup, fell under the horse, was struck by one of the driving rear hooves, struggled halfway up, collapsed back into the mud.

"We'll pick him up between us!" shouted Cole. "Then I'll handle those eager bastards for you!"

"All right!" yelled Frank. "I'll take him on the offside!"

Cole to the left, Frank to the right, they drove their horses down upon the huddled body, firing over the heads of the advancing townsmen. Cole stood in his stirrups, his bull's voice bellowing over the gunfire. "Get up, Dingus! Get up!"

The half-conscious Jesse responded, staggering to his feet as the two horsemen thundered up. They took him, one on each side, at a dead gallop, swinging his slack body up between their careening mounts.

"Leave me have him!" roared Cole, dropping his reins to seize Jesse with both great hands. Frank released his grip and Cole raised Jesse bodily, to jam him astride Frank's horse behind the saddle.

Without waiting to see the continuing success of the transfer, the big bandit heeled his bay gelding into the closing crowd. Three times, from streetside to streetside, he drove the excited animal through its ranks, breaking them, scattering them, riding them down, his hoarse curses mingled with enraged guerrilla yells. He forgot the bank, the wheatsack across his saddle, the double-mounted Frank, the fact that his Colts were snapping on empty chambers. He only knew that somewhere in the red haze which swam before him were the screaming faces of the miserable cowards who had been swarming in on foot to tramp down his fallen idol where he lay, helpless as a drowning swamp rat in the main-street slush.

His madness faded as the last of Jesse's would-be tormentors fled before the crazy lungings and wheelings of the gelding, and the street lay suddenly deserted before his clearing eyes. Reason returned with the physical shock of a cold rain. He wheeled the bay with a final yell, sent him bombarding up the street after Frank's laboring mount.

Behind him, the men came quickly into the street again. Horses were brought up, carbines booted, grim riders swung to saddle. Within ten minutes of Jesse's shot within the bank, the posse was on its way.

Again, Jesse's incredible luck held.

A mile southwest of Gallatin the fleeing outlaws encountered a farmer, Daniel Smoot, on
his way into town aboard a fine saddlehorse.
Cole shoved a gun under his nose with the crisp
suggestion that he dismount and take to the
brush with minimum delay. Farmer Smoot
thought it an excellent idea.

Fully remounted, the bandits rode on. During
the delay the Gallatin posse drew within long
range, lobbed a few shots after them, but with
the fresh horse the fugitives soon drew clear
again.

Six miles later, outside the village of Kidder,
they rode up on the Reverend Abner Helm, a
Methodist circuit rider. With a Colt muzzle in
his back, the good man showed them a back
road around the settlement. Once clear of the
dwellings, Jesse took his pistol out of the minister's kidneys and spoke his first words since
running out of the bank at Gallatin.

"Reverend, I want to tell you something. I am
Jim Anderson, Bloody Bill Anderson's brother.
I just killed S. P. Cox who works in the bank
yonder in Gallatin. He killed my brother in the
war and I've got him at last."

They rode on, pushing the horses, Jesse silent, Frank echoing him. Cole, too, held his
peace. But in his mind was trouble.

He knew that Bloody Bill Anderson had been
killed by a Lieutenant Cox. And that Bloody Bill
had a brother named Jim. He also knew, or
thought he did, that Jesse had no more ever laid

eyes on the Union officer than *he* had. Or on Bill Anderson's brother, Jim, for that matter. At any rate, he had never heard him mention either one of them, save in the past minutes.

He eased his bay alongside Jesse's black.

"Dingus—"

"Yeah?"

"You kill that boy back yonder?"

"You heard me say so," answered Jesse, not looking at him.

"Why for, for Christ's sake?"

"He was looking at me."

"Then he wasn't Cox, at all!"

"Goddamnit, I said he was!"

"But you *knowed* he wasn't."

Jesse looked at him then. And twisted the thin rarity of his grin at him. "Maybe so, maybe not. Leastways, he'll learn to pass over vault keys next time he's asked, polite."

They rode on in silence, stirrup to stirrup.

"Ding."

Jesse whirled on him. "Now shut up, Cole! Don't keep crowding me. I said it was Cox. I said I knowed him and I said he knowed me, you hear?"

Cole nodded, thoughts dividing between loyal heart and worried mind.

"Then why the yarn about Jim Anderson to that preacher back to Kidder?" he asked presently.

"That's for me to know and you to find out!" snapped Jesse. Then, as quickly, the scowl was

141

gone. "There's one thing you *can* know, though," he grinned. "And that is that you'll sure as hell *find out* before long!"

Cole found out, all right. And in the finding had cause to wonder anew at the wolf-sharp workings of his friend's mind.

Back in Clay County, Jesse wasted no time putting that mind to work.

The alibi grapevine of the clan was jangled into motion. Within hours of their return, it was being spread that three days before the Gallatin Bank robbery Bill Anderson's brother, Jim, had visited the Samuel farmhouse. He had pleaded with the hardworking Jesse to join him in a dastardly raid on the Daviess County Savings Bank. Indignantly, Jesse had refused. But he had, at Anderson's urging, and after extracting a sacred promise from him to forego the heinous crime, loaned him his favorite black saddle gelding—the very animal, *by strange coincidence*, which had been found galloping loose in the streets of Gallatin after the murder of poor Mr. Sheets.

As usual, the loyal constituency of Clay County bought the yarn, wholeskein. And just in time.

A week after the robbery, the sheriff of Daviess County rode up to the office of the sheriff of Clay County, leading a fine black saddle-horse. The animal had been painstakingly traced to a Clay County lad, one Jesse W. James of Centerville. Action was demanded and, for once, was forthcoming. A posse was made up immediately. Meaningful departure was taken for the Samuel farmhouse. Frank and Jesse were forewarned, of course. They were not at home. There were no arrests.

Behind the Daviess County sheriff, a scant three days, came the Pinkertons, having worked out the trail in their own plodding way from Gallatin to Centerville.

Their reception by the Clay County sheriff is best put in the words of William Pinkerton in a subsequent address to a Chicago convention of peace officers from fourteen states.

"When I asked the assistance of the officer in arresting a part of the James gang, he said that he would deputize me and aid me secretly, but owing to the relatives and sympathizers of these men residing in the county, he dared not lend a hand openly.

"He said that I did not have to live there after the arrest had been made but that *he* did."

The Law of the Clan stood unsullied.

Jim Anderson was a dirty murderer, Jesse James, a persecuted hero.

Cole Younger was left with his worried mind and divided heart. And with 312 dollars as his bloodstained share of the Gallatin Alibi.

The trail breaks. The tracks fade. And the summer sun shines brightly on the public square of Corydon, Iowa, June 3, 1871.

143

The square is full of farmers in their Sunday best; the lager beer is flowing by the barrel. Atop the bunting-draped platform the Honorable H. Clay Dean, a Missouri politico of Southern stripe, is addressing the Iowans on the evils of Black Republicanism. A high old time is being had by all and, up the street in the deserted town, history is being stowed into a wheatsack.

The clerk in the Corydon County Treasurer's Office looked up to greet the three men and the six large-caliber revolvers.

"No noise now, sonny," requested one of his visitors pleasantly. He was a tall man, the clerk remembered, and had a smile that lit up his whole face with kindly good humor. "We're tax collectors, too, you see, and would like to relieve your office of the burden of counting all those county receipts in the safe yonder."

"Sorry, gentlemen—"

The clerk backed away, white-faced, his desperate gesture going to the safe.

"But it's locked. Honest to God—"

The ex-officio tax collectors exchanged casual glances. The small hairs at the nape of the clerk's neck took on individual life, lifted chillingly.

"Why don't you try the Obocock Brothers Bank down the street, gentlemen?" he asked pleadingly. "It just opened this very morning!"

*Just opened—*

The big man turned his grin on his two companions. "You hear that, boys? What do you say, Ding?"

"I say, I reckon we'll be its first customers," announced the smaller of the two, blinking his blue eyes rapidly.

The Obocock Brothers Bank occupies a unique niche in America's hall of banking fame—it closed two hours after it opened.

Its contribution to the wheatsack was forty-five thousand dollars in cash. The teller was impressed with the expertness displayed by the three bandits in cleaning the vault's shelves. Five minutes after they entered, the largest of the outlaws turned to the smallest. "She's clean, Ding," he said. "Let's go." Knowing a good job when he had pulled one, the smaller man nodded, directed the binding and gagging of the lone teller. Then he nodded again, holstered his guns, led the exit.

At the door, and grinningly, they stood aside for the new bank's first legitimate customer. The Reverend Moseman Jones was the ordained shepherd of Corydon's Negro Baptist flock. He was, as well, a good and simple man. And a pathetically trusting one. In the frayed flour sack in his right hand, he held the lean rewards of a long and frugal life. There was, hence, an understandable pride in the quiet dignity with which he peered at the bandits over his steel-rimmed spectacles, and inquired, "I beg your pardon, gentlemen. Can you tell me where I may deposit my savings?"

The smaller of his listeners nodded sympathetically. In the same motion he produced two .44 caliber Colts and jammed them into the terrified minister's stomach. His tall companion stepped forward, bowed graciously, opened the bulging wheat sack. "Right in here, Uncle," he directed politely.

The Reverend Jones was plainly new to banks. And to bank robbers. He was not new to cap-and-ball revolvers. Nor, to soft, Southern drawls.

His savings went into the sack.

Outside the bank, the three disrespecters of the colored cloth joined the four horsemen who were waiting there, holding their mounts. The sack was tied, the retreat begun. Not a shot had been fired, no voice raised in protest. It was pleasant work and well paid—something better than a thousand dollars a minute for each of the seven riders.

Down in the square, the Honorable H. Clay Dean was booming to his climax. Neither he nor his spellbound audience noticed the jogging approach of the seven horsemen. Nor the pause they took upon the outskirts of the crowd. One of the riders, the smallish man with the heavy beard of sandy hue and spade cut, who had directed the bank withdrawal, looked at his big-shouldered principal assistant. Between blinks of his blue eyes, he managed a broad wink. Standing in his stirrups, he waved to Dean across the heads of the crowd.

"A point, sir. If you please—"

Dean, the crowd securely in the palm of his skilled hand, its members helpless under the anesthesia of his golden voice, felt he could afford the luxury of charity and largess. His return bow was a mirror of courtly mien and manner.

"We yield to the gentleman on horseback!" He returned the interrupting wave regally. "Your question, my young friend?"

"Well, sir," the bearded rider called soberly. "Some fellows were just down to the bank and tied up the cashier. All the drawers are cleaned out and I reckon somebody had best get down there in a hurry."

H. Clay Dean gasped.

The crowded Corydonians stood dumb-struck.

The silence was too much for the bearded horseman. He broke down completely. He choked, snorted, threw back his head, slapped his dusty thigh. His high-pitched laugh was echoed by the bass guffaw of his big companion and by the delighted yells of their five fellow riders. The outlaw laughter was still breaking across Corydon's stunned square when the seven horsemen spun their mounts away down the street to vanish in a cloud of June dust. Yelping back from within the dust cloud came the screaming beast-bawl of the border guerrillas' *"yip-yip-yah!"* of final farewell.

147

It was the belated key to the lock of Corydon's community silence.

"My God!" gasped a farmer on the edge of the crowd. "It's the James gang! They just robbed the bank!"

So it was, and so they had.

And in the dust of their passing, they left us one more fleeting glimpse of that rarest of Jesse's strange contradictions—his sometimes wonderful sense of deadpan humor.

# Chapter Seven

*Adair*

Not too long ago there were oldsters still alive in Clay County who remembered that summer of 1873. By June it had turned uncommonly hot, and in July the greening corn stood sear and shuck-dry along the parched furrows. It was a spell of heat without parallel in the memory of fifty years.

Through its wilting stifle, early in the evening of July 7, rode Cole Younger. His destination was the Samuel barn, his summons an urgent message from Jesse. There was more than the suffocating humidity of the July night pressing in on Cole as he kneed his mount along the Centerville Road.

Off through the darkness of the woodlands, the fireflies wound in endless, fairyland flight over the bottomlands of the Little Blue. Down in the slough, the peep-frogs sang in contented answer to the eager chirrup of the roadside crickets. A bullbat twittered softly overhead, his wheeling wings banking noiselessly in pursuit of the succulent June-bug. Beyond the hunting nighthawk, the summer stars hung fat and bright, lighting a man's way, trying to let him see the peace and beauty in the night about him.

But Cole was only in the night, not of it. His mind was full of Jesse James.

*Since Corydon, Dingus had murdered again.*

It had been more than a year now, but Cole's thoughts took him back to that April day in Adair County, Kentucky, as starkly as though it had been but hours before. . . . There was the Deposit Bank in the little town of Columbia. Outside it, Clell Miller and his own brother, Jim Younger, raced their horses back and forth across the public square, firing, guerrilla yelling, terrorizing the townfolk. Inside were he and Jesse, backed by Frank and Bill Chadwell, a new recruit. There was the unarmed cashier boldly defying Jesse.

"Give me the keys to the safe!" he could again hear Dingus saying. And the cashier, incredibly, replying, "I'll be damned if I do that!" There was the quick, maddened blink of Dingus's eyes, the furious demand, "Damn it! Hand over those keys!" Then, the cashier's still more amazing, "You go to hell!"

Jesse had his gun in the youngster's belly. Cole could still hear the muffled burst of the three shots, smell again the stink of the powderburn on the cashier's shirtfront, see again the stare of those tortured eyes, dead and set before their brave owner fell into the counter and spun to the floor.

Cole remembered, too, the price of that cashier's life—less than four hundred dollars from the counter till, to be split among seven men.

Two weeks later it had been the Savings Association in Ste. Genevieve, on the banks of the Mississippi.

Four thousand dollars had jingled into the wheatsack then, and the getaway had been easy. But Jesse had let Cole's "baby brother," Bob Younger, ride along on that raid against Cole's vehement objection. The tomfool kid had got his taste of quick money. Any man as long in the business as his big brother, Cole, knew what that meant. And cursed Jesse for it.

Then in September it had been the Kansas City Fair, where Jesse and Frank and Clell Miller had carried off the tin cashbox containing nearly ten thousand dollars. Cole had stayed out of that one, and made Jim and Bob stay out of it, too. He hadn't even believed Jesse would do it. That was homefolk money, kinsman's cash, not Yankee bank loot or bluebelly savings bonds. It made a man hold up and wonder what had become of the old rebel spirit. Whence had gone the fun and free conscience of cleaning out Union treasuries? And where, *really*, had disappeared Dingus's all-the-time brag about robbing only the rich sons of bitches who could afford it, never taking from the *good folks*, which was to say the poor ones like Cole and Frank and Jesse themselves?

Yes, a man had thought much on the matter since Corydon and since Columbia.

Cole was still thinking on it as the lamp in the Samuel window loomed ahead.

"Cole, this here is Ed Miller."

Jesse grunted the introduction of the stranger as Cole squinted to adjust his eyes to the glow of the lamplight in the barn.

"Any kin to Clell?" asked Cole, eying the newcomer unsociably.

"Brother," the man in question answered for himself.

Cole had never liked Clell Miller. He knew at once that Brother Ed was not going to fare any better in his books.

The head of the Younger clan was a humble, easygoing man. There was not in his big body a small or a mean or a superior bone. But there had always existed between his family and Jesse's a bond of background and border breeding across which few of the gang's lesser members were privileged to trespass.

Both the James and Younger families were of better than border average. Both bloodlines were of High South, First Family heritage.

While in the matter of formal education neither Cole nor Frank nor Jesse had progressed beyond the Pleasant Grove grammar school, the parents of both clans were well educated, widely read, and of marked religious bent. The Bible was as familiar to the front parlors of both as were the more standard of the old literary classics. Frank, for instance, was a bona fide student of Shakespeare. Either Cole or Jesse could quote chapter and verse from the Old Testament. All three were omnivorous readers and, despite the obvious frontier crudities of their speech, were regarded by most who had occasion to come in social contact with them, either happily or unhappily, as "definitely well-bred gentlemen, with polite, scholarly bearings, who possessed rather broad grasps of current affairs, as well as showing themselves remarkably fluent and easy of address."

By marked contrast, their followers, with the sole exception of the quiet-spoken Jim Cummins, were rough, unlettered men. Of these Clell Miller was typical. A ruffian in the classic sense, he had neither formal nor family leavening in any education other than that of first-degree murder and armed, felonious assault. His kind were to Jesse and Cole as lesser bustards to an eagle or peregrine falcon. Birds of little imagination and no appealing plumage, they followed after their fierce leaders, picking querulously at whatever remains the latter might deign to leave them. In a two-word triteness, common criminals.

Looking now at Ed Miller, Cole rated him not
alone a fowl of low feather but, from his pale
beak and furtive, practiced shift of eye, an ex-,
and not long ex-, jailbird.

Jesse's terse conclusion cemented the guess,
drove it home with customary bluntness.

"Ed's just out from State's Prison. Clell's sent
him to me. Ed's got an idee you'll cotton to. Got
it from John Reno, while they was in jail together."

"Such as?" Cole asked slowly.

He knew about John Reno. He and his three
brothers had run a gang pretty much like Jesse's, only up in north Missouri, Illinois and In-
diana. But not with Dingus's luck. The
Pinkertons had caught up to them. And John
had spent his last three summers in the Missouri State Prison. Still, any man in Cole's profession had to listen when John Reno's name
was called out in the meeting.

"Such as easier pickings than banks," nodded
Jesse succinctly.

"Go on," said Cole, still not liking it.

"*Express cars!*" blinked Jesse. "Government
and big company payroll gold, on through
trains!"

"Yeah, I know," grunted Cole caustically. "It's
a powerful grand idea. Look at where it's wound
John Reno up."

"That aint the point, you big ninny!" Jesse
flashed his twisted grin deliberately. "Reno was

just getting the kinks worked out of it when he was took. Ed, here, claims Reno give him all the details on how it *ought* to be done. Says Reno reckons bank busting caint shine with trains."

He paused, eying Cole, and saw he was losing ground.

Jesse knew the big bandit's mind better than he knew his own. He knew that Cole was tired of the killing and the murder that went with forcing banks in broad daylight. He knew, too, that the tall outlaw was splitting away from him, was more and more getting out of hand— was, in addition, influencing his brothers, Jim and John and young Bob, in the same direction. And Jesse knew, finally, what he would never admit to any man, not even to Cole. *He had to have that big devil with him*!

In the late war years, he had known what it was *not* to have the grinning giant at his right hand. He remembered that night in the cave above the Little Blue, when Cole had come back to him. And remembered, too, what seeing him and hearing him had meant then.

Even so long ago, he had known he could not go along without Cole, had known he had to have him beside him in the dark, had to have his hand there to reach out for when he needed it.

Now, in his whole shadowed world, a world which had lately shriveled and shrunk in upon him with frightening speed, there still remained only that one big hand. If he lost that hand, if it were somehow plucked away from him—

He reached impulsively for the big shoulder. The words came easily, instinctively, low with feeling and quick and tense. If the burden of their sentimental rush was a naked deception, Jesse did not know it himself. He did not hear the lie, even as he told it—if it was a lie.

"Bud!" The old name stirred Cole uneasily. "I'm just as fed up with all this as you. I'd like to go with you like you're always saying. Down into Texas and take up that piece of land to settle on. The hell of it is, we caint do it. Not without we've got one hell of a lot of money, we caint. They aint going to leave us be. Them lousy Pinkertons have fixed that. They've got us wanted 'dead or alive' in eight states already. We aint no more chance to live decent and normal in Texas than we have right here in Missourah. Not without we make that one big haul, we aint. You know that, well as me."

"It's so, Ding. Goddamn it, it's so—" His mind, always slower than Jesse's, never so complex, fell unwillingly into the pattern of his bearded chief's enchantment. "But what in God's name is a man to do? We caint just go on killing and robbing and riding off into the Goddamned woods all our lives. I'm sick to my belly of that."

"No sicker than me!" protested Jesse soberly. "But honest to God, Cole, I say Ed has brought us our way out!" His slim hand came again to Cole's shoulder, his blue eyes as innocently wide as a child's. "You know I aint never horsed you. There aint nothing would ever make me."

"Aw, I know that, Ding. God Almighty—" He was embarrassed now, and awkward, the way Dingus always made a man feel when he went to halfway backing out on him. "It aint you— you know that. It's just I caint see what you're getting at—"

"Money!" snapped Jesse. "Big money!" His eyes blinked furiously. "Cole, some of them trains carries up to a hundred thousand dollars in gold cash!"

"The hell!"

"The hell, yes!" He gave him no time. "You know what that means to us? It means you and me can get enough in three, four jobs—maybe, by God, even in *one* job—to get clear of Clay County and stay clear of it!"

"Ding—" It was Cole's turn to put his hand on his friend's shoulder. "You mean that, old hoss? You really mean that if we get that hundred thousand dollars, you're through and done and shut of robbing? And will go along to Texas with me?"

"I mean it, Cole! So help me!"

"Dingus, I'd give a mortal lot to believe it—"

"You can! Damn it, you can!" said Jesse eagerly. "And I'll promise you something else!" He played his hole card carefully, knowing what it meant to Cole, saying it as if it meant the same thing to him. *"There'll be no more killing."*

Cole shook his head slowly. "Some of it caint be helped, Ding. You know that, well as me."

"Not the way these train jobs work. They aint the same. You aint dealing with street crowds and getaway gunfights and posses riding up on your tail ten minutes after you're out of the vault."

"I caint see that," said Cole doubtfully. "You got a Colt in a man's guts, it aint no different he's in a express car or a teller's cage. He kicks up, the trigger gets pulled. Naw, Ding, I reckon—"

"Listen a minute and I can *make* you see it, you big blockhead!" He grinned it off, pulling a dog-eared army map out of his coat with the grin. "Just crowd up here and look at this map, and how I've got her figured. *That's all!*"

"I'm looking," nodded Cole, stepping forward, not meaning to *really* look, not meaning to even *listen*.

Jesse flipped the map open, spread it expertly to the yellow fall of the lamplight.

"Honest to God, this is something like!" The feel of the map, the look of it, the rush of another plan building like wildfire in his mind, flared up in his pale eyes. "I never seen a prettier layout. You see this here roadbed? She's the Chicago, Rock Island and Pacific. Now, north here is Council Bluffs. Yonder's Adair, that flyspeck just east of the bluffs. Now me and the boys will hole up outside Council Bluffs. Meanwhile, I figure you and Frank will ride a wide swing north up into Nebraska, here. . . ."

He swept along, the old, infecting magic of

his excitement working into Cole like bad whiskey, picking him up and carrying him along,
painting the easy picture of the hundred thousand dollars, drawing the long-dreamed-of conclusion of the speedy retirement and final safety
it would bring to them—and holding out the
bait of that "little place" in Texas that Cole had
always planned for him and Dingus "after the
war."

Within ten seconds of his coming forward to
lean over the map and to listen to Jesse's high-
voiced, swiftly pointed detailing of the new
campaign, Cole was lost.

And in the following five minutes the particulars of the first major train robbery in world
history were set forth in the Samuel barn.

The subsequent implementation of those particulars made page one of every principal newspaper in North America, as well as those in
Europe and around the globe. But the hidden
heart of the whole thing—the truth or the lie
behind Jesse's promise to Cole Younger—did
not appear upon the printed page.

It could not then, nor will it ever.

At Adair, Iowa, fate delivered the hundred
thousand dollars twelve hours too late!

After supper, Jesse, restless as always, left the
camp, walked up through the undergrowth,
climbed the low river bluff to the edge of the
county road. He stood a long time looking
northward up the road.

Finally he turned, disappeared again in the trees.

At the fire, he squatted across from Jim Younger, saying nothing. The others, Clell and Ed Miller and Comanche Tony, a halfbreed Frank had met in Texas, were already asleep in their horseblankets. Presently, Jesse blinked the smoke out of his eyes, glanced over at Jim.

"What you reckon is holding them up?"

"Nothing," grunted Jim. He was a big man, like Cole, but lacking his brother's happy-go-lucky temperament. "It takes time—that's all. Cole and Frank aint the ones to hurry a job past doing it proper."

"Well, I reckon I don't like this here camp. Too open and we been here too long. 'Most a week now. We'll be spotted before long, if they don't step to it."

"What's to spot? We're fifteen miles out of Council Bluffs. We got the Missourah to one side of us and plenty cottonwood and willow to the other. There aint been six people up that road since we lit here."

"We'll move tomorrow," was all Jesse said.

The stillness held for five minutes. Shortly, Jim nodded. "Likely you're right. It aint only twenty-five, thirty mile across the river to Omaha. Seems they should have got that train schedule smelled out and been back before now. Tomorrow's the twenty-first, aint it?"

"From sunup to sundown," grunted Jesse.

"Well, maybe they'll show yet tonight. I hate

to move out on them. It might mess up everything."

"We caint risk it no longer. I'm losing my feel for this job. I don't like that, at all. Not ever."

Jim's brother, Cole, could have told him something about Jesse's "feel" for a job. Lacking that knowledge, Jim merely shrugged. "I got a hunch they'll show."

In the present case, his hunch was better than Jesse's feel.

The sound of the shod horses being held on a high lope came, muffled, down to them from the roadway above. Quickly, the lope fell away, was replaced by the rattle of sliding dirt and gravel along the face of the bluff.

"We'd best douse the fire, don't you reckon?" asked Jim nervously. "I'll go roust the boys out."

"Set down," said Jesse, not moving from the fire. "Leave the boys be. It's them. That bay of Cole's racks late with his off forefoot. I could pick him, blindfold, out of a cavalry charge."

Seconds later, the riders eased their lathered mounts into the reach of the firelight, legged down off them, letting the reins trail. Cole's broad grin brought the meeting to relieved order.

"Dingus, you're a prophet! You didn't miss it a damn red cent!"

"Leave off the tail-wagging," growled Jesse, on his feet now, with no grin forthcoming. "What'd you find out? Frank, how's she lay?"

"She lays good," said his sober-faced brother. "But tolerable close."

He paused thoughtfully with the statement, the others waiting, narrow-eyed.

Time had changed Frank James, as it had Jesse.

With maturity, he had lost the stumpy squatness of his boyhood, had thinned up into a tall, bony man. Unlike Jesse and most of the others, he was smooth-shaven, wearing only a brown droop of sunburned mustache. He was, by contrast to his more famous brother, narrower and leaner of face, with a better mouth and firmer chin line. Frank's was the perfect outlaw face: plain as dirt, common as clay, undistinguished as a livery stable saddle.

He could have, and time without number he did, pass in any crowd without notice. If Cole had become the gang's "public relations counsel," Frank developed into its "undercover contact."

He carried out the bulk of the dangerous and touchy preparatory work for many of the bands biggest jobs. He did it quietly and without reward, either in his own time or subsequently. If Cole was Jesse's strong right arm, Frank was his subtle left. Still he paid then, as now, history's high price for the lack of personal color. Where, to the gang, Jesse was always "that Goddamned, wild-eyed Dingus!" and Cole "the handsome, dashing Cole!" Frank was simply "good old Frank," and never anything more.

It is a guessing game, running down the reasons for a man's unpopularity eighty years after, but in his memoirs quiet Jim Cummins has left a logical hint. "He was," says the thoughtful Jim, "eternally spouting that cussed Shakespeare at us till a man just naturally got so fed up on it he didn't have room for any more of it in his belly." The pay rates of men's opinions do not appear to alter a great deal. Frank, almost certainly, put up the going price for erudition among the unenlightened.

In the present instance, however, he was not dealing with the likes of Jim Cummins.

"Well, damn it!" snarleed Jesse. "Get on with it! How close *does* she lay?"

"Tomorrow night, 8 P.M."

"That 8 P.M. in Adair?"

"That's right," said Frank quietly.

"You certain sure?"

"We paid off the express company clerk in the Omaha yards. It's a shipment from the Black Hills diggings, and it's like Cole said."

"What you mean, it's like *Cole* said?" Jesse was blinking now.

"You didn't miss it a red cent," answered Frank quickly.

"How much?" rasped Jesse, moving into him.

It was Cole who boomed out the answer, his laugh loud enough to be heard in Adair, had the wind been right. "A hunnert thousand U.S. dollars, to the Goddamned nickel, Dingus!"

\*  \*  \*

Jesse picked his spot just east of the bluffs, selecting a sharp curve a mile south of the C.R.I.&P. waypoint of Adair. By 7:15 P.M. there was still too much of the late July daylight lingering on, but he could wait no longer. The spades, saddle-packed all the way from Clay County, were put to work loosening a stretch of half a dozen ties beneath a rail collar on the curve. Meanwhile, Frank and Cole, under Jesse's personal eye, unbolted the joining collar. In half an hour, all was ready.

What was left, was for Frank and Cole. It was ticklish work, not to be entrusted to hands less old and steady in the trade.

The long ropes were quickly passed beneath the loosened rails, half-hitched around the ties, repassed beneath the roadbed steel and made fast to the horns of Cole's and Frank's saddles.

The two horsemen swung up and eased their mounts into the slack, testing it. Satisfied, they nodded through the growing twilight to Jesse. He nodded back, turned his own mount toward the timber and the restless shadows of his waiting men.

Pulling the black in, he sat him uneasily.

The minutes wore on. He counted them away against the audible ticking of the battered silver watch in his breast pocket. Five. Ten. Fifteen. Still no sign of the 8 P.M. from Omaha. Suddenly, he held his breath, cursed softly. The damn watch had stopped ticking. He pulled it out.

"Strike me a light, here!" he rasped to Clell Miller. His henchman scratched the match, held it out. Jesse leaned from his saddle, toward its cupped light.

"What's the trouble?" said Clell.

"7:58!" grated Jesse. "The son of a bitch has quit on me!"

He hurled the watch from him, voice and hand alike, trembling with the instant violence of his temper. It struck a tree in the darkness, shattering with a thin *ping* of flying springs. Thirty feet away, down at the tracks, Cole heard the curse and the tiny crash of the watch.

"What's the trouble, Ding?" His low call repeated Clell's query.

"I dropped my watch," answered Jesse levelly, the blind flash of the tantrum as swiftly fled as it had flared.

"Well, don't cry no more," advised Cole tenderly. "Daddy'll get you a new one."

"Don't give me none of your sass," called Jesse quickly. "What time *you* got?"

The question was overlaid by a hoarse, lonesome wail from beyond the bluff-cut. Again, it came. Plaintive, sad, long-echoing. The lostsoul cry of a steam locomotive's haunting whistle, keening through the night.

"8 P.M.!"

Cole laughed across the darkness. Then he boomed out above the growing hum and clack of the rails, "Pull up your blinders, boys! We might have to shoot somebody we know!"

165

He and Frank, masks already in place, eased their horses forward again, into the full pull of the ropes. Up the tracks now, along the clay walls of the cut, the shimmering dance of the engine's headlamp was flashing and jumping. In the shadow of the timber, Jesse and the others adjusted their masks; the same cheap calico bandannas destined to become the exclusive trade mark of the train-robbing firm of J. W. James & Co.

The engine was through the cut then, and they could see the bloody glow of its firebox staining the night. They watched the swing and jerk of the following cars pound rockingly along the narrow-gauge roadbed toward the curve. Heard the cast-steel drivers of the locomotive bite into the bending rails, and heard the harsh warning scream of the whistle as the engineer picked up the two horsemen alongside the track in the jolting of his headlamp.

"Pull 'em!" yelled Jesse. "For God's sake, pull 'em!"

Cole ignored him, he and Frank holding their fear-crazed horses until the last possible second.

The locomotive and tender were so close onto them now that they could see the engineer clearly limned by the leaping flare of the firebox, leaning from the cab and frantically waving them away.

Like good boys, they obeyed.

The two horses jumped under the drive of

their masked riders' spurs. The ropes sang tight, stretched, came away, springing the loosened rails outward.

It was a big train, close to twelve cars.

The locomotive, tender, five day coaches and two sleepers left the tracks, lunging wildly along the embankment. The tender-coupling broke free of the lead coach, hurtling the locomotive on down into the river bottom. From the tangled mass of its bursting boiler and broken steamlines, the fireman staggered free, voice screaming in the agony of the oil-soaked overalls burning on his back. The engineer, trapped in the hissing wreckage, was already dead, instantly scalded by the live steam.

Miraculously, the coaches stayed upright.

The wheels of the overturned locomotive were still spinning crazily in mid-air when the first of the dazed passengers tried to fight their way clear of the shambles of wooden seats and shattered glass within the cars. Their efforts were met at the broken vestibule doors by five, courteous gentleman in calico masks.

At the same time, Cole and Jesse had run their mounts alongside the express car, still on the rails and undamaged. Leaping from their saddles through its open doors, they put the express company messenger under pistol point.

"Open that damn safe!" rasped Jesse. The company man responded with suspicious alacrity. Cole produced the wheatsack, swept the gold into it. It was plain from the thin stream of it and from its empty jingle in the bottom of the hundred-pound sack that there was far from a hundred thousand dollars, or even any good part of that amount.

"All right!" snarled Jesse angrily. "Where's the rest of it?" With the demand, he drove his Colt into the messenger's belly.

"That's all there is of it!" cried the terrified clerk. "Honest to God. That's the whole shipment. There aint no other safe—you can see that, boys!"

They could, and all too well.

"I ought to kill him!" whimpered Jesse, eying the cowering clerk wildly.

The man said nothing. He did not move. He was a literate man, a man who could read. In the red-rimmed blink of the staring eyes above the knotted bandanna, he read death.

"*Get out!*" said Cole to Jesse. He said it flat and harsh, and he took him by the shoulder, shoving him roughly toward the vestibule door at the car's end. "*Keep moving. I'm right behind you.*"

Twisting his head, he hissed under his breath to the clerk: "Don't you move, and don't you say nothing!"

He was back to watching Jesse, then, waiting for him to wheel about and come for him. But he never did. He only kept moving, head down, mumbling incoherently. At the door he hesitated a moment, but still did not turn. When he had gone through it into the connecting coach

168

ahead, Cole moved after him. At the door he, too, paused, nodding softly to the white-faced messenger.

"You won't never come no closer to it, my friend." He added thoughtfully, "You got any kids?"

"Three," stammered the clerk. "A little boy and two girls—"

Cole nodded for the final time, voice going softer still.

"When they grow up," he murmured, "they can tell their kids their grandpap knowed Cole Younger."

In the coaches ahead, the rest of John Reno's new technique, as imported by Ed Miller and interpreted by Jesse James, worked more smoothly.

The bandits fell quickly into the organized spirit of relieving the bewildered passengers of their wallets, rings, watches, petty change and personal trinkets. The whole of the scrambled loot went swiftly into the wheatsack. Cole, in charge of the sack, was the Southern gentleman incarnate, bowing to the younger ladies, insisting that the older keep their seats and, here and there where he detected a Dixie dialect, their valuables as well. The rest of the gang, caught up by his good humor, enjoyed the entire performance.

Jesse would have no part of it.

He stood at the vestibule entrance of each car,

in turn, scowling and blinking and ordering his followers peremptorily on to the next car. Repeatedly, he snapped at Cole to "cut out the monkeyshines and get on with it!"

Within twenty-five minutes of the crash, the gang was on its way.

They rode twelve straight hours, Jesse pushing the flight unmercifully. When daylight and staggering horseflesh demanded an end to it, they halted and split up the loot. It came to less than seven thousand dollars.

Jesse was coldly furious.

Openly and bitterly he assailed Cole and Frank, charging them with the entire fault of the failure. Frank said nothing. Cole, typically, had a go at taking it in stride.

"Ding," he announced, straightfaced. "I been holding out on you."

"Don't put off on me," warned Jesse, sensing his towering lieutenant's mood. "I aint in no humor to put up with none of your damn nonsense."

"No, sir," drawled Cole, owl-sober about it. "But when old Cole promises something, he delivers it. Here—"

He fished the fat gold watch out of his vest, handed it toward Jesse. "Now, don't drop this one. It's a genuwine, twenty-one-jewel Swiss super. I borried it off of a jewelry drummer from Peoria. Nice young feller in Car Four. He—"

Jesse did not move to accept the watch. "You can take that *genuwine*, twenty-one-jewel Swiss

170

super of yours and shove it!" he interrupted angrily. "Your promises aint worth a Goddamn cent. If they was, we'd have a hundred thousand dollars to divvy-up, rather than that sack of junk we come off with."

"Jess," broke in Frank, quietly, "it aint Cole's fault, nor mine either. That express clerk in Omaha said that money would be on the eight-o'clock train. He held us up five days to be certain on the train and the time."

"Aw, the hell! You two chuckleheads make me sick. You're the ones need a new super. If you'd learn to tell time, maybe we'd get somewheres. You got the wrong train, Goddamn it—that's all!"

That night, the gang rode on. And for the ten following nights.

Their harassed way led south into the Indian Territory and looped back up to the west, through eastern Kansas, covering a distance of six hundred miles. The Pinkertons, put on the trail by the C.R.I.&P. and the Adams Express Company within hours of the robbery, pushed them every relentless foot of the way. It was only when they succeeded in losing the detectives in the Missouri River bottoms by crossing and recrossing the Big Muddy three times in twenty-four hours that they were finally able to slip safely into Clay County.

Much has been claimed and disclaimed as to who *really* robbed the C.R.I.&P. at Adair, Iowa, July 21, 1873. The interests of objectivity have fortunately been served by two surviving documents. The first of these, the claimer, exists in the official files of Pinkerton's National Detective Agency. It reads, in pertinent part:

. . . furthermore, our operatives learned that the day subsequent to the robbery, the gang stopped at an outlying farm in Ringgold County, Iowa, just north of the Missouri border. They were given supper and spent the evening on the porch of the farmhouse in lengthy discussion with their host. The conversation varied from Shakespeare through current politics to modern farming methods and practical theology. According to the farmer there were seven men in the party, their leader being a man about five foot seven inches, with light blue eyes, heavy sandy beard, goodly shoulder-width, turned up nose and prominent forehead. He appeared to be fairly well educated. . . .

"This," adds Allan Pinkerton in a masterly understatement, "is a fairly good description of Jesse James."

The second document, the disclaimer, is in the form of an affidavit from one Marshall P. Wright of Jackson County, Missouri, an acknowledged "old friend of the boys."

. . . In 1873 I was living in Clinton, Missouri, and was there on July 21 when the train was robbed in Iowa, west of Des Moines. The Younger brothers, including Coleman and James, were charged with the robbery. I knew all the boys well and had known them for years. On the day after said robbery, early in the morning, I met the boys at Monegaw Springs, St. Clair County, Missouri. I had a copy of the paper giving an account of the robbery. Cole and Jim Younger were there and I read the article aloud to them, remarking on their ability to be in so many places at once. The place where the robbery was committed, Adair, Iowa, is more than 200 miles from St. Clair County, Missouri, which distance—if guilty—they must have traveled in 24 hours. It was stated by people living there whom I know that the Youngers had not been away. There were no cross lines of railroad making it possible for them to cover that distance.

I have every reason to believe and do believe that the charges of that robbery to the Youngers was the work of their enemies who were seeking to drive them out of Missouri. . . .

Verity? Perjury? Truth, half-truth, no truth at all? Who can say after eighty years?

One thing remains certain, a thing in the

realm of fact, not needing to be sworn to either by hated Pinkerton or kin-loyal clansman. Cole's and Frank's espionage in Omaha had been faithful—but not quite flawless.

On July 22, just twelve hours after the wrecking and robbery of the Adair train, a second C.R.I.&P. train passed over the identical, repaired section of track outside Adair. Frank and Cole, it would appear, had made a slight miscalculation in train schedules. It was the 8 A.M. they wanted, not the 8 P.M.

Aboard that second train were seventy-five thousand dollars in government mint-gold!

# Chapter Eight

*Kearney*

The year 1874 was full of fate for Jesse James. It saw death in his own camp and in that of his enemy. It saw, conversely, love as well, both he and Frank marrying within its span. Its twelve months marked the belated turning of the local law against them, the governor of Missouri for the first time coming officially forward to put down their outlawry.

Jesse was at work early in the year, laying the cornerstone for the latter, overdue result.

The lonely flag station of Gad's Hill, a hundred miles south of St. Louis in Old Missouri's big piney section of southwestern hills, stood in customary winter evening quiet. A few minutes after 5:00 P.M., January 31, the village blacksmith, the town physician and three of their fellow natives foregathered at the stationmaster's shack, as was their custom, to await the passing of the Iron Mountain Railroad's Little Rock Express.

Promptly at 5:30, ten minutes before train time, five strangers rode up out of the gloom to surround the station. They were big, rough-looking men. Their workaday attire—boot-long blue overcoats, flat black hats, cheap calico masks—at once commanded the attention and respect of the Gad's Hillians.

Clell Miller, acting on Jesse's unhurried order, ambled down the track and jammed the station agent's red flag between the ties just beyond the depot. As soon as the flag was planted, and as though it had been a signal, five more masked men rode out of the woods and joined the original group. The newcomers, under Jim Cummins and Bob Younger, took over the guard detail at the depot, freeing Jesse and his chosen elite for the really important work.

On schedule, sharply at 5:40, the Little Rock Express chuffed to a noisily steaming halt. Frank took the locomotive, inviting the engineer and fireman to join him in a short stroll toward the depot while Jesse, accompanied by the faithful Cole, entered the sleepers. At the same time, the second crew of bandits, headed by Jim Younger, invaded the day coaches.

Business in the sleepers was brisk. One after another the passengers were aroused from their seats and cordially invited, via Jesse's prodding

pistol, to contribute to the Missouri wheatsack
being dragged down the narrow aisle by his affable assistant. One passenger alone, a lumber
company executive, consigned five thousand
dollars in payroll cash to Mr. Younger's burlap
collection plate.

Frank, coming through the car moments
later, saw they were doing admirably, started to
move on and join the second crew in the day
coaches. Jesse looked up at him, grinning in his
rare, quick way.

"To hell with those Jim Crows, Frank. Leave
them to the boys. Give us a hand with these plug
hats, here."

Jesse was on one of his occasional high
swings. True to the pattern, he put his memorable touch to the next moment.

He had his Colt in the flowered weskit of one
of the plugged hats when that upset ticket-
holder made the mistake of offering up a pocket
watch of worthless German silver. Jesse passed
the instrument to Cole, not noting its inferior-
ity. The latter frowned in professional disgust,
tapped his leader on the shoulder. Jesse looked
around, grinned with his nod of understanding,
took the watch back. Tossing it to its owner, he
laughed. "You're out of our class, mister. Get
the hell up front with the cheapskates where
you belong!"

With the laugh, he planted his trim boot in
the startled passenger's rear, kicked him stum-

bling toward the sleeper's exit and the day coaches ahead.

The Jim Crows and plugged hats all cleaned alike, the gang entered the baggage car. There was no express safe, the registered mail yielding two thousand dollars. The Gad's Hill job was done.

There remained only the postscript, as irresistible a piece of evidence as remains to us of Jesse's character, and a collector's item of Americana.

Frank and Cole now ordered the engineer back into the cab, Cole advising him to "give her a toot and get the hell on down the line." As the train began to move, Jesse galloped up to the engine. Running his black alongside the cab he pulled a folded paper from his pocket, tossed it through the open window to the engineer. "Give this to the newspapers," he yelled above the gaining churn of the drivers. "We aim to do things up in style whenever we can!"

Scrawlingly handwritten on the back of a Postal Department reward notice for information leading to the arrest of Jesse and/or Frank James, the document was Jesse's personal press release on the Gad's Hill robbery—complete with capitalized headline.

### THE MOST DARING
### TRAIN ROBBERY ON RECORD!

The southbound train of the Iron Mountain Railroad was stopped here this eve-

ning by five heavily armed men and robbed
of——dollars. The robbers arrived at the
station a few minutes before the arrival of
the train and arrested the agent and put
him under guard and then threw the train
on the switch. The robbers were all large
men all being slightly under six feet. After
robbing the train they started in a southerly
direction. They were all mounted on handsome horses.

P.S. There is a hell of an excitement in this
part of the country.

\* \* \*

Their names were Louis J. Lull and James
Wright. They had been assigned to the Gad's
Hill robbery by their employers, Pinkerton's
National Detective Agency. Carefully they
traced the gang's flight. The trail led into the
Younger clan's hideout area of Monegaw
Springs, and to a certain farmhouse outside
nearby Roscoe, Missouri. Posing as cattle buyers, the detectives stopped at the farmhouse late
in the afternoon of March 16. The owner of the
property appeared ill at ease. He had no stock
for sale. The Pinkerton operatives rode on, their
preliminary mission of scouting the suspected
premises accomplished.

Minutes after they left, two men came out of
the farmhouse. Going hurriedly to the barn they
mounted up and departed in turn—in the same
direction as the detectives.

Lull and Wright were scarcely out of sight of

the farmhouse when they were joined by a third operative, a local peace officer named E. B. Daniels, who had acted as lookout while they scouted the farm. "We may be in trouble. Two men left the house just after you did," was all Daniels had time to say, before Wright's voice cut warningly in on him.

"No maybe about it, boys. Watch yourselves. Here they come."

The lawmen halted their horses, spacing them carefully like the old hands they certainly were at the game. In the little time it took the approaching horsemen to ride up, they saw they had their hands full. Both were big, hard-looking men, both heavily armed, the first rider with a cocked shotgun and two belt revolvers, the second, with a pair of beltguns and a booted carbine.

"Wait up a bit," said the taller of the two horsemen, checking his restless horse. "We want to talk to you."

Detective Wright was a brave man, and not in a mood for talk with armed desperadoes. He drew his revolver, fired over their heads, yelled to his two companions to "get out fast!" put spurs to his horse and ran for it. Luck rode with him on the try. The second horseman threw two revolver shots after him, succeeded only in knocking his hat off. The next instant Wright was around a bend in the road and safely away.

His companions never moved. For the best of reasons. They were directly under the cover of the first horseman's double-barreled shotgun.

"Now," said the latter calmly, "We'll have our little talk. Take off your pistols and drop them in the road."

The detectives unhooked their gunbelts, let them fall. The second horseman dismounted, picked them up. "These here are damn fine pistols," he grinned up at them. "You boys must make us a present of them."

The first horseman was not grinning. "Where did you come from?" he barked at Daniels.

"Osceola." The local detective kept it short.

"What are you doing in this part of the country?"

"Just rambling around."

"Yeah? We hear you been rambling around quite a bit. You was seen over at Monegaw Springs two days ago."

"We were at the Springs, yes. We were certainly not inquiring for you gentlemen, however. What is it you want?"

"Pinkertons!" growled the younger of the two horsemen, losing his good humor. "No God-damn detectives are ever going to catch me grinning through a grating."

"You've got us wrong," broke in Lull, hastily. "We're not detectives. We can show you who we are and where we're going."

The older of the horsemen, the one with the shotgun, laughed harshly. "No need, my friend. We know who you are and right about here we'll show you where you're going."

# Will Henry

There was no mistaking his meaning, nor the way he suddenly shifted the shotgun onto Lull. Detective Lull read both signs clearly, knew the little talk had come to its abrupt end. Swiftly, he reached for a hidden Smith & Wesson pocket pistol, one of the blunt-nosed No. 2 Models carried by plainclothesmen of the day. He cocked and fired it on the draw, point-blank, into the man with the shotgun.

His horse bolted as he fired, and he heard the second horseman's Colts begin to bark behind him. He felt the two slugs rip into him. The first was a harmless flesh wound in the upper arm, but the second took him low in the left side, knocking him off his running horse and into the roadside ditch. He felt the smashing impact of the fall, and remembered no more.

The grim action, above reported, was contained in the deposition of detective Louis J. Lull, made as he lay dying twenty-four hours later in the Roscoe Hotel.

He didn't live to know what effect his single shot in the battle had taken. It was a harsh one.

While his own wounds were occupying Lull, the second horseman, in addition to downing the brave Pinkerton operative, had killed Constable Daniels. But the Pinkerton detective's single, opening shot with his No. 2 Smith & Wesson had not been wasted. The first of the accosting horsemen, shot through the base of the throat by the heavy ball, lay hemorrhaging his life away in the dirt of the Roscoe road even

182

# Death Of A Legend

as Lull was receiving his own fatal wounds.

The postscript is short. Lull's "two hard-looking men on horseback," were Jim and John Younger.

Jim buried his brother that same night in the lonely twilight of the farmhouse orchard. What he carved upon the rough pine headmarker, which tradition has him fashioning "half wild with grief," will never be known.

It could simply have been *R.I.P., the first of Jesse's men*.

History has it carved that way.

On Monday, March 23, the domed hall of the Missouri state legislature was crammed to capacity. The rumor persisted that Governor Silas Woodson, distant kin to the outlaws or not, was determined to cry a halt to Cousin Jesse's depredations. All political ears were acutely tuned to what the chief executive would say about "the boys."

What he did say, in a surprisingly angry oration, was this:

"There exists in this state a certain band of outlaws who, in disregard of all social and legal obligations to God and to country, have been murdering and robbing with impunity and defying the peace officers in this locality.

"These desperadoes one day enter and rob a bank and cold-bloodedly murder a

183

cashier. The next day they visit an agricultural fair in the most populous part of the state and in the midst of thousands of men, women and children rob the safe and make good their escape.

"Anon they enter another town, rob a bank and shoot down in cold blood its officers. Then they deploy murderously and feloniously into our sister states. Soon they return to Missiouri and rob a railroad train.

"The law is inadequate. The authorities are powerless to deal with these outlaws. Life and property are unsafe.

"The time has come to put an end to these conditions of affairs that have become uncontrollable."

Climaxing his denunciation, Governor Woodson demanded an appropriation of ten thousand dollars to form a special cadre of secret police to track down and destroy the Clay County brigands "to the man."

What ensued only serves as another demonstration of the gangs dark and—to this day—unexplained influence in the high political places of their native state. The appropriation was passed by an overwhelming majority of the legislature, then promptly ruled "out of order" by the president *pro tem* of that august body. Woodson's attack on the gang was bitterly assailed by the Democratic press of the state and the entire sordid matter died miserably aborning.

Detective Lull was still alive when the third of the Pinkerton "eyes," dispatched in rageful haste from the Chicago home office, arrived in Clay County. He was James W. Whicher, described in the terse company files simply as "twenty-six years old, an excellent operative."

Enlisting the aid of "certain local interests friendly to his employers," he determined to pose as an out-of-work farmhand and thus to move directly upon the Samuel farmhouse. The locals, aghast at such lunacy, did their best to dissuade him. They failed.

Early Sunday morning he set out on foot for Kearney, as the old hometown of Centerville was now being called. Arrived at Kearney, he began at once working toward the Samuel farm, stopping along the route to inquire for work at the neighboring places. When and where Jesse's vicious counter-espionage picked him up is not known. It is known that one James Latche, a jackal to Jesse's pack of lions, left Kearney shortly after Whicher did—and arrived at the Samuel farm considerably *before* him. The mills of the Clay County demigods were agrind.

Whicher approached the Samuel farm at sundown. It was his last known movement on the 30th.

At 1:00 A.M. the following, morning, the ferrymaster of the Owens Ferry, operating across the Missouri between Clay and Jackson counties, was dragged from his shack by three horsemen. All wore woolen mufflers pulled high about their faces.

Their leader, "a smallish, nervous man with a dark beard," identified his group in a "high, excitable voice."

"We're Deputy Sheriff Jim Baxter's posse," he growled. "We caught a horse thief and we aim to take him to Jeff City where we'll get his mate."

The ferryman at once explained that, his assistant being on the far side of the stream, he could not handle the crossing alone. They would have to wait until morning.

The nervous man grabbed him by his nightclothes, "displaying a terrible temper."

"If you don't want your Goddamned boat cut loose, along with your damn throat," he snarled, "get started and see you step to it!"

As the ferry left the Clay County shore, its frightened pilot looked in vain for the familiar face of Deputy Sheriff Jim Baxter among his mounted passengers. There were only the three face-hidden horsemen and the unfortunate "horse thief," bound and gagged aboard the fourth, led, mount. On the far side, the posse paid its proper fare, rode quickly away.

At 10:00 A.M. the same morning, the body of a man "with a rope around his neck, nine shot wounds in his chest and head, and his face and

186

arms partly eaten away by wild hogs," was found facedown in a pool of blood on the Independence Road. A week later a sharp-eyed reporter from the *Kansas City Times* identified the remains by a small, tattooed "J. W. J." on the right wrist. It was Jim Whicher.

But, again, the shadowy postscript.

On the Tuesday night following the murder, five of the James gang, headed by Jesse (Cole and Frank not mentioned), rode into Kearney.

Heavily armed and in a hurry, they paid a series of abrupt social calls. Each stop was at the home of a citizen rumored to have discussed the death of the Pinkerton operative in the same breath with the hallowed name of James. On each darkened stoop the message was repetitively short, easy to understand.

*"Keep quiet if you don't want your Goddamned head blown off."*

The latter part of the same week the *Missouri World* carried this eloquent footnote from its unnamed Clay County correspondent.

So great is the terror that the James and Youngers have instilled in Clay County that their names are never mentioned save in back rooms and then only in a whisper. Clay County has a population of 15,000. . . .

The citizens kept quiet, all 15,000 of them.

The long time of waiting was past. The nine years of standing by were done. The date was April 24, 1874.

# Will Henry

In the Kansas City home of her married sister, Zerelda Mimms watched out the front window. Behind her in the prim neatness of the frontier parlor, a nervous clansman-of-the-cloth coughed uneasily, thumbed his bookmarked Old Testament repeatedly. About him, equally ill at ease, flitted a dozen "friends of the family," all watching the girl at the window, all waiting, with her, for the delayed approach of "Cousin Jesse."

At last, he came. And with him, right and left, came Cole and Frank.

The three horsemen rode the center of the street.

In their lead, Jesse danced his sleekly groomed black. His red-brown beard was barbered to a precise spade. The knee-high cavalry boots shone with polish. His new black cutaway fell gracefully and spotlessly from his wide shoulders. A new hat, black and broad-brimmed in his unfailing custom, sat the carefully combed thickness of his long, dark hair. To the curious, already gathering outside the house, he smiled and called easy greetings, bowing soberly to the gentlemen, doffing the wide hat sweepingly to the ladies.

The onlookers stared, most of them having their first sight of the notorious outlaw. They nudged one another in amazement. This man, Jesse James? This pleasant, slim, smiling fellow on the tall black thoroughbred? Why, they had seen him many times before on these very streets, and never even imagined who he was!

Others among their number, not so new to their man, made note of certain things beyond the fresh trim of the beard, the shine of the boots, the flash of the smile. Making the note, they exchanged guarded nods.

The fall of the cutaway was slightly disturbed below the waist, as would be only natural to the cross-belted sag of the two heavy revolvers beneath it. The small hands, gloved as always to cover the missing tip of the middle finger of the left hand (shot away, tradition says, by Judge McLain in the long-ago Savannah robbery), were carried properly enough across the saddlehorn. But also carried across that saddlehorn, unbooted and naked in the April sun, was a late model '73 Winchester Carbine. The blue eyes, free for once of their dangerous blink, darted, none the less, from streetside to streetside, missing no single face among the curiosity seekers, overlooking no solitary physical fact obtaining along the avenue of his advance. And behind him, his brother and Coleman Younger, while apparently as gracious and unconcerned as their famous leader, still kept their horses wide and clear of his, their carbines, in turn, unslung and ready.

Even on his wedding day, Jesse James was taking no chances.

Away down in the southwest corner of the state, in the limestone and pine ridge heartland of historic Barry County, midway between the present sleepy mountain towns of Cassville and Seligman, lies the little known, eighth wonder of Old Missouri's Ozark world—Roaring River.

It is today a state park, and still one of the least spoiled treasures of natural wilderness left upon the continent. What it was on that early May morning, these eighty years gone, when the young couple in the newly painted spring-bed wagon halted their team of fine bays to gaze down upon it from a high abutment of the Seligman road, can only be imagined.

Mile on reaching mile, the dark evergreen cover of native pine stretched unbroken. Here and there, a limestone escarpment or rearing, sandy bluff rose up above a bell-clear, graveled creekbed. Winding off through the forest, an occasional, snaking loop of the Seligman road showed briefly to lure the traveler on. Below the lookout point from which the young couple gazed, the turquoise course of Roaring River rushed brawlingly along its abbreviated journey to the White. To the east, barely visible beyond the silent pines, the subterranean rock fortress of its cave-born origin shouldered juttingly against the spring sky.

It was a wild and lonely and lovely place, well fitted by remoteness and rugged inaccessibility alike to serve its present, fleeting purpose in the marked lives of the young people in the spring-bed wagon.

"I allow it's a mite lonesome," said the man

softly. "And likewise a mite far from town."

"Oh, it's beautiful!" cried the girl. "So wild and strange quiet, and all—"

"Well," nodded the man, putting his arm lightly about her shoulders, "I reckon it don't shine with Niagara Falls, honey. But we'll make it do, I'll lay."

"Do!" laughed the girl excitedly. "Why, Jesse, it'll be the best honeymoon either one of us ever had. You just wait!"

"Coming to that, Zee, girl," Jesse said, grinning broadly, "I've done waited just about all I'm a mind to. Let's get on down to the river."

As he put the bays down the steep grade, Zerelda clung to his whip-arm in properly put-on alarm, snuggling close into him on the swaying seat. He did not object noticeably. The soft feel of her hands and the warm press of her young body were not exactly the things a man would complain about. Not when he was only a short ten days married, and meaning to make a life-long career out of staying that way.

"Zee, honey," he said happily, "you'll love it down yonder. You aint never seen anything to beat the way the river comes right out of the solid rock. We can go back in the cave a good ways and you'll see things dripped and twisted out of pure stone like you never thought could be."

"Jesse, tell me now," she teased. "How are we going to get along? To eat and sleep and suchlike, I mean. You haven't said a word about that and a wife rightly wants to know about those things. We can't keep going on kisses and cold box-lunches forever."

"Never you mind, girl," was all he would say. "You will see soon enough."

Half an hour later, she was seeing. And gasping with delighted disbelief.

The little cabin was hidden in a grove-thick cluster of pines on the edge of the five-acre meadow fronting the river's exit from the cave. You couldn't see it until you drove right up onto it but, once you saw it, it was like something out of a storybook. It was old, its peeled logs weatherworn to a soft silver gray. And tiny, so one-room small it looked like a make-believe dollhouse tucked away in a fairytale woodland. But old and weathered and deep-hidden as it was, you could see at a glance that it had been more than somewhat spruced up of mighty recent date. And not by any band of elves. It would have taken a pretty muscular company of sprites to cut and stack all that new stovewood along the north wall. And to scythe and rake back all that wild hay from around the front yard. Not to mention hand-splitting those six-foot planks that made the new stoop for the door. Or filling the two big rain-barrels with fresh river water and lugging them up the footpath from the cave.

"Jesse! How ever in the world did you do it?"

Zerelda could not get over the surprise of the place, nor the warmth and wonder of its isolated, mountain-guarded meadow.

"Didn't," grinned the proud bridegroom. "Old Cole and some of the boys come down last week and rigged it up for us. It's an old hideout we aint used since the war. I mentioned it to Cole and right off nothing would do but that he had to come down and set it right for you. He thinks you're about the greatest, Zee."

Busy, as he talked, with getting their trunk out of the wagonbed, he did not notice her quick silence at the mention of "Cole and the boys." Nor did he see the uneasy shadow that came into her eyes as she glanced across the meadow toward the fringing pines.

But in the moment of that shadow's passing, Zerelda had seen beyond the pines. Beyond them, and to the limestone ridge they based. Far enough along that ridge to pick out the motionless guerrilla horseman silhouetted against the skyline at its crest. And to recognize, even at the half mile distance, the towering bulk of the rider. It was Cole Younger. She did not need to turn her glance to the other ridges surrounding the little meadow. Those other grim-still watchmen would be there upon them, she knew. And, knowing it, her heart sank chillingly within her. Even as she forced a gay answer to Jesse's cheerful call from within the cabin, and hurried down from the wagon to join him, the honeymoon was over for Zerelda Mimms.

\*    \*    \*

Where the laws of Missouri had failed, the tenacity of the Pinkertons did not. Three of their operatives had been slain in one month. In the words of Allan Pinkerton in a directive to his nationwide organization the situation was declared: *"War to the knife, and the knife to the hilt!"*

The summer and fall of 1874 were devoted to the patient planning of that war. September passed, and October. November wore away. The gang had vanished again. Still the Pinkertons waited, knowing their enemy, long trained in the ways of his guerrilla mind.

On December 12, the waiting was ended.

At Muncie, Kansas, eight miles west of Kansas City, a band of eleven calico-masked outlaws boarded the 4:45 express. The passengers and the two bonded express messengers were relieved of sixty thousand dollars in cash and jewelry. There was no shooting. The getaway was familiarly succinct: the bandit leader rode easily up alongside the cab of the locomotive, waved his pistol and airily instructed the engineer: "Get going and give our love to Kansas City."

There were no identifications.

The Pinkertons crouched, spreading their net, saying nothing. Two weeks later they closed it on their first bird.

Early in the evening of the 28th, the marshal of Kansas City arrested one Bud McDaniels on the routine charge of shooting up the town. On

Mr. McDaniels's dead-drunk person was found one thousand dollars in fresh cash. The Pinkertons took over.

We may assume that Bud was persuaded to part with more than his money. Here and there, through the smokescreen put up by their champions then as now, we are able to imagine that the Pinkertons were no strangers to the rubber hose, or its 1874 equivalent.

Mr. Daniels talked.

He had been at Muncie, Kansas. No, he didn't remember all the others.

Did he remember any of them?

Oh, sure: Clell Miller, Clell's brother Ed, Jim Cummins, Charlie Pitts, a couple of others.

Maybe the James boys?

Well, naturally, Frank and Jess!

That all? How about the Youngers? Bob? Jim, maybe?

Well, yeah Jim anyways.

Nobody else? Say, Cole, for instance?

Oh, Cole. Sure. Anybody ever see Jess without that big bastard?


The Pinkertons were ready. On January 5, 1875, their operatives covering the Samuel farmhouse sent a coded message to their headquarters in Kansas City: Frank and Jesse had been seen entering their mother's home. Their reply was a three-word telegram: ATTACK CASTLE JAMES. Zero hour was set at 10:00 P.M.

The ungainly posse, fortified by local peace

officers and just plain citizens who had had enough of the gang's terrorizing, left Kansas City via a special train supplied by the Hannibal & St. Joe Railroad. The coaches were darkened, the members of the posse slipping aboard at five-minute intervals. Once across the Hannibal Bridge into Clay County, the train was pulled onto the spur at Kearney. On foot, its passengers spread through the snowy timber toward the Samuel place.

The Pinkertons took charge.

The house was dark. No warning was given.

Through the west window, a flaming metal object was tossed. By its glare, the posse saw the room's occupants: Dr. and Mrs. Samuel and the two small Samuel children. Suddenly, there was a flashing explosion. The Pinkerton men rushed forward.

In the house they found Dr. Samuel unconscious, bleeding from multiple wounds. By the blackened fireplace stood Zerelda Samuel, her right arm a shapeless pulp. On the floor lay eight-year-old Archie Samuel, Jesse's half brother and prime family favorite, a gaping hole torn in his side.

The boy died the next morning, even as Dr. Samuel was amputating his wife's mutilated arm.

National repudiation followed for the Pinkertons. A wave of public indignation denounced the "bomb-throwing" incident as an "inexcusably horrible crime." Forgotten in the clamor were the surpassingly more criminal outrages of Centralia, Lawrence, Liberty, Adair and Owens Ferry.

But even so, and even now in the removed objectivity of the passing years, one wonders about the Pinkertons.

What was it they threw into the Samuel living room?

One answer is supplied by William Lewis, a personal friend of Frank James, writing in the *Morning Telegraph* fifty years later:

There was no bomb. Frank James himself, supported by Sheriff Timberlake, stated there had never been a bomb exploded in his mother's house. The James boys were believed to have been in the house, but they were not. They had been there, but the instinct of the partridge had sensed the hunter from afar and they had fled. The house was surrounded by detectives who were decidedly anxious to get any members of the train robbing gang, for several of their number had been assassinated and one or two killed in open fights with the outfit.

Mrs. Samuel, mother of the James boys, who was extremely gifted in an executive and practical way, was in the house with two children of her husband, Dr. Samuel, when the detectives and the posse surrounded the house. Mrs. Samuel extinguished what few lights there were, and what conversation was held with the besiegers was carried on in the darkness. The law officers and members of the Pinkerton staff who surrounded the house had prepared for an emergency in the Samuel house. They carried with them what was known as a flare. It was a lamp with a hemispherical bottom of cast iron. The top was of brass and two tubes about six inches long carried the wicks.

This flare, then, the detectives lighted and tossed through a window. Immediately the interior of the living room was illuminated and the occupants were palpable targets. Dr. Samuel, who found himself measurably aided in his daily coming and going with a cane, beat at the light with his cane and then pushed it into an open fireplace full of dying embers where it exploded.

The attack on the house had been made about two and a half hours before midnight when the family was preparing for bed. The so-called "bomb explosion" was the explosion of the flare lamp.

The other side is represented by an earlier *Courier Journal* interview with George Hite, the James family grocer, fellow clansman, Jesse's lifelong friend and defender.

Jesse James went to Chicago to kill Allan Pinkerton and stayed there for four months but he never had a chance to do it like he wanted to. That was after Pinkertons made a raid on his mother's house, blew her arm off and killed his stepbrother. He said he could have killed the younger one [William? Robert?] but didn't care to. "I want him to know who did it," he said. "It wouldn't do me no good if I couldn't tell him about it before he died. I had a dozen chances to kill him when he didn't know it. I wanted to give him a fair chance but the opportunity never came."

Jesse left Chicago without doing it but I heard him often say: "I know God will someday deliver Allan Pinkerton into my hands."

One black? The other white? Both half gray, perhaps? The choice is the reader's, but one thing is certain. There can be no question as to Jesse's personal conviction, nor history's immediate reaction.

*It was a bomb.*

On the heels of "the bomb" now burst Missouri's peculiar Outlaw Amnesty Bill. This measure, introduced by the Honorable Jefferson Jones of Calloway County, incredibly called for outright forgiving of the James gang. It nominated Frank, Jesse, Cole, Jim and Bob Younger (by name) for local sainthood, and

contained such well-nigh unbelievable passages
in their behalf as: "WHEREAS, believing these
men too brave to be mean, too generous to be
revengeful, and too gallant and honorable to be-
tray a friend or break a promise . . ." and:
"WHEREAS, under the outlawry pronounced
against them they are, of a necessity made desperate, driven as they are from the fields of honest industry . . ." and: ". . . that the governor of
the state be requested to issue said proclamation notifying them that full and complete amnesty and pardon will be granted them for all
acts charged to or committed by them. . . ."

Of course, this bill was disguised by specific
references to the activities of the outlaws during
the war, detouring their later adventures. It
fooled no one. It was intended as the opening
wedge toward a full pardon. The Democratic
press tacitly endorsed it; the powerful *Kansas
City Times* openly and brazenly lobbied for it.
The Republican papers ridiculed it for the trav-
esty it was. Voting in the legislature was along
divided party lines, a solid Democratic majority
bloc sustaining it, a mixed minority coalition of
Republicans and Democrats denying it.

For the last-minute honor of "poor old Missouri," the bill's enemies succeeded in having it
declared out of order, and shelved. But what
served the honor of the state severed the final
thin cord of hope for Jesse and his men. The
defeat of the amnesty bill was a bell of doom.

And they knew for whom it tolled. *It tolled for them*.

Like a starving wild beast who has come hungrily in to sniff at the staked-out calf or the bleating goat, only to be shot at, Jesse leaped snarlingly away.

And, in leaping, struck blindly out.

The two horsemen waited beside their saddled mounts, watching the Kearney road. Presently, a third horseman rode up through the growing moonlight to join them. There was a muttered exchange of greetings, after which the newcomer paused and asked suspiciously, "Where's your trained ape at?"

"Cole's gone to Texas, along with the others," grunted one of the other men. He then added bitterly: "Anyway, he wouldn't be of no account for what we got in mind. Maybe not for anything, nowadays. He aint the same no more."

"He's the same," rasped the third horseman. "I allus said he didn't have no real guts."

"Yeah," the second of the men who had been waiting for him said softly. "Only you never said it in front of him."

"I wouldn't dirty my hands on the big dumb bastard," gritted the other. He paused, scowling, then nodded to the first man. "What you got in mind?"

"*Dan Askew*!" His answer came sharply muttered.

Askew was an elderly farmer, a near neighbor of the Samuels. He was a Kearney church elder, a gentle, popular, much respected man, and a longtime good friend of Dr. Samuel's. Some months back, completely innocent of the man's real identity, he had hired on an itinerant farm hand named Jack Ladd. Subsequent events had revealed Ladd to have been the principal Pinkerton agent in the undercover work preceding the Samuel raid. He was, in fact, the operative who sent to Kansas City on January 5 the coded announcement of Jesse's and Frank's arrival at their mother's home.

"It's about time," was all the third man said. "Let's ride."

It was 7:45 P.M., April 12.

At eight o'clock (the time was only an estimate, being but the guess of the coroner's jury at the inquest), Askew came out to stand on his front porch. Shortly, he crossed to the springhouse for a drink of water. He drew a fresh bucket, started to lift it to his lips. The greeting came quietly from behind him.

"Hello, Dan."

Farmer Askew stiffened, his face going gray in the moonlight. *He knew that voice!*

All three shots were unhurried. All were in the back.

Askew dropped the bucket, twisted both hands to his kidneys, slumped across the well-casement, slid away from it to the ground. His wife and grown daughter, running out of the house, heard the high laugh down by the springhouse. A moment later, three horsemen rode by the porch, "not ten feet away in the moonlight."

Their leader touched his hat.

"Evening, ma'am. Sure is a purty night."

The women did not answer. The horsemen left by the front gate, the one who had spoken to Askew's wife dismounting beyond the gate to swing it carefully shut.

The Henry Sears farm was midway between the Samuel and Askew places. At 8:30, Farmer Sears answered a polite knock on his front door to discover a young man standing below the stoop. The lamplight from the open door revealed him clearly. Behind him, the moonlight did equal service for his two mounted companions. None of the men wore masks; none of them was more than twenty feet from the startled farmer.

"Sorry to disturb you, Mr. Sears, but we just killed Dan Askew." The man at the porch steps made the announcement in a voice that Sears had heard before. "Now, if any of his friends want to know who did it, I reckon you'd best tell them it was the detectives."

Ordinarily, the advice would have been more than sufficient. But the times were on a tide of change. Henry Sears remembered names and faces as well as he did voices. And the names and the faces he remembered were these:

*Jesse James. Frank James. McClellan Miller.*

The identification of Askew's murderers marked the beginning of the end of Jesse James.

He was yet to ride for six wild years, to kill and plunder and kill again, but never, from that day, with the same magic immunity. The brute murder of one gentle old man did what a score of front-page crimes of major violence could not. Into every partisan mind along the hitherto impregnable border, the question struck its sudden chill: If such as Daniel Askew could die in the dark, what was the life of *any* man worth?

In farmyard, corner store, parlor, church pew and public square across Missouri, men met and nodded, grim-faced. Even in deepest Clay and Jackson counties the voices were stilled, the hearts dark, the eyes unraised.

Jesse James had lost his people.

# Chapter Nine

*Lamine River*

May is a beautiful month in any state, Texas no less than Old Missouri. Collins County, north-west of Dallas, was young-green with the coming curl of the buffalo grass. Overhead, the blue sky swept unbroken from El Paso to the Gulf. Watching the slow drift of the high clouds, the young rider on the steps of the JD-Bar bunk-house shifted his glance from them, narrowed it along the distant bend of the Collins City Road.

Shortly, he arose, nodded in through the open door. "Company, Cole."

Cole Younger put down the awl, laid aside the waxed thread. Saddle-mending could wait. The soft months in Texas had not undone the lean memory of ten Missouri years. He eased out of the bunkhouse, hitching at the worn Colts.

"Looks to be alone," he drawled to the squinting Bob. "Where's Jim?"

"Up to the main house with the old man." The "old man" was J. D. Coleman, blood-cousin and sometime hideout operator for his clan's half of the James-Younger Wheatsack Combine. "Want I should fetch him?"

"Wait up a minute." Cole shook his head.

He was back out of the bunkhouse in a moment, uncasing the Union-issue field glasses. He swung them up, steadied them. "No," he said softly, face expressionless. "Leave me handle this bird my own self."

He went quickly around the bunkhouse.

Standing behind it, bits slipped, girths loosened, were three satin-coated, Missouri-bred horses. They had stood thus the whole of each waking day throughout the four months which had passed since their owners had ridden south from a certain train-detainment at Muncie, Kansas. Cole moved to his tall bay, popped the single-bar bit back over his tongue, shouldered up on the cinch. He rode swiftly over the rise behind the bunkhouse, slid the bay into the heavy greasewood of the narrow arroyo beyond.

Ten minutes later, he had followed the arroyo to its intersection with the Collins City Road.

Here a clump of chinaberry trees shrouded his ambush, and here he waited, carbine unslung, gray eyes narrowed. Presently he heard it—the dust-clumping approach of a single-footing horse. He drew back in the grove, letting the horseman pass him. Noiselessly, he slipped his mount into the roadway behind the stranger. His sudden order boomed in mock-anger.

"Throw up your hands, you Goddamn Clay County son of a bitch!"

The horseman wheeled his mount, blue eyes wide.

"Cole! You mangy old outlaw! How you been—?"

They were off their horses then, Cole pulling him into a bear hug that put up a rib-crack loud enough to be heard at the ranch.

"Dingus! Dingus! Jesus Christ, boy! How *you* been?"

"Leave go of me, you overgrowed buffalo, maybe I'll tell you."

"Ding, I just caint get over it!"

He stood back, looking at Jesse as though unwilling to believe God had been so good to him. "It's actually you, boy. Spit-ugly as ever and twice as puny. How in God's name did you find me, boy?"

"Oh, you aint so hard to find." Jesse flashed the old grin. "I just went into the first cathouse I come to in Dallas and showed the madam one of your Pinkerton pictures. Sixteen chippies jumped me afore I could turn around. They wasn't too much help though, at that. All wanted the same thing I was after—your address."

"Aw, it aint so, Ding." He grinned self-consciously, then sobered. "How *did* you do it, Dingus?"

Glad as he was to see the watery-eyed little devil, a man did not like too well the idea that he had been found out so easily.

"*Bowers*," said Jesse bluntly.

"The County Attorney!"

"Of Dallas," blinked Jesse, not grinning any more. "You kind of operate in style down here, don't you, Coleman, lad? Bosom pals with the Dallas County Attorney, sidekick of the sheriff. You know what I heard? From that damn sheriff, himself?"

"Naw, what?" Cole shifted uncomfortably under the growing blink of the pale eyes.

"That you had helped him bring in a bad man or two. That's a hot one, mister!"

"Well, I done it," defended Cole stoutly.

"Tell you something else I heard," sneered Jesse, ignoring him. "Got this from Bowers."

"Yeah?"

"Yeah. He told me you and them two ninny brothers of yours was singing in the Baptist choir and helping take the cussed Dallas scholastic census."

"Well, Goddamn it, I done that too!"

"I can just see it," said Jesse. He was grinning again now.

" 'Good morning, ma'am. I'm Thomas Coleman Younger, ma'am. Helping the sheriff take the census, ma'am. What kind of work is your husband in, ma'am? How many dear little'uns you and him got, ma'am?' " He paused, eying him suspiciously. "Say, Cole, what in hell's ailing you? You daft or something? What you got on this here Bowers?"

Cole looked at him. Finally, he nodded.

*"We was war comrades,"* he said softly.

In the four quiet words the big outlaw had named the main ingredient of the gang's long success. In a good part of the border, and in all of the Southern states, local peace offices were held by ex-Confederate soldiers. To the average Southerner the big three villains of postwar reconstruction were the banks, express companies and railroads. While the Clay County gang confined their operations to these "enemies of the people," they were covertly held to be doing a public service. To arrest an ex-war comrade for such patriotic endeavors would be unpardonable.

As was soon to be apparent, the magic of this old immunity was already fading in home-state Missouri. But in the solid South the charm still held. The James-Younger boys were still Reconstruction Robin Hoods. Particularly in "unreconstructed" Texas.

Cole went on now, putting his hand on Jesse's shoulder, talking low-voiced.

"Ding, we got it made down here. We can sleep nights, even if we still aim to keep a horse saddled, daytimes. Afore long that'll wear off too. We got it planned that in another six months we can move on over west into the Pecos country and buy us that ranch in our own damn names."

Jesse watched him closely.

"You got it planned how you're going to pay for that ranch?" he asked quietly.

He knew they could have but little money. The sixty thousand dollars from the Muncie holdup had been split too many ways. It would have taken too much of their parts of it to pay their way into Texas. He knew, also, all there was to know about the mysterious "Black Gonzales." Gonzales was a Mexican of mixed Negro blood, operating from the cattle-drive town of Doan's Store at the Red River Crossing in the Indian Nation. He was, in the modern parlance, the James-Younger gang's "fence." He would buy all the illegal gold the boys could bring him—*at a straight forty percent discount*! Jesse knew from bitter, repeated experience how much a man had left of his split after he had ridden three hundred miles to let Gonzales hack his cut off it.

Cole knew all this as well as Jesse, and the knowledge of it was working in him now.

"We aim to work as trail hands," he said uncertainly. "There's still herds going north, spring and summer. We can save enough in three, four years to get our place. I swear, Ding, all of us riding together, we can. Throw in with us, boy. Frank's agreed to. He's even sending for his missus next month."

"Where's Frank at?" Jesse was short with it.

"Over to the Scyene, working for Old Man Shirley."

John Shirley, owner of the Scyene Ranch, was famous in his own right—he was the father of Belle Starr. Jesse knew Belle. So did Cole, intimately. Rumor had long associated the roving-eyed right-hand man of Jesse James with Shirley's notorious daughter, and not by way of robbing banks. He now awkwardly defended that association, knowing what Jesse thought not only of Belle, but of all belles like her.

"Now don't get any funny ideas about Belle," the big rider frowned. "Frank's not fooling with her. Fact is, we aint none of us horsed around with her since Reed was killed."

Jesse remembered that John Reed, so-called "husband" of Belle Starr, had been downed in a gunfight the previous summer. He had always suspected Cole in the matter but the official credit had gone to a Collins City deputy. Now he merely nodded.

"I wasn't meaning that. Not about Frank. He's like me, I reckon."

It was Cole's turn to nod. Dingus reckoned right. Leastways, about himself. If he had a moral bone in his body, this was it—his remarkable continence with women. There had been, and were, but two of them in his hard life. Both were named Zerelda.

"Well, you needn't mean it about me, neither," he grinned. "I've swore off. She's too fast for this country boy, Ding. Besides," the grin broadened with the wink, "I aint the hawg to put his feet in the trough. There's plenty for everybody, leastways of Belle there is."

He sobered, letting the grin fade.

"What you say now, Dingus? Will you throw in with us on the ranch? You always said you and me would do it—"

"Let's get on up to the place," grunted his companion. "I aint forgot the ranch. I got something in mind that will make us more toward it, in five minutes, than eating trail dust will in fifty years."

Cole groaned inwardly.

"You aint got it in mind for me," he said miserably. He moved quickly for his horse. "I went for that yarn, once. Place called Adair, in case your mind is slipping. 'Once bit, twice shy,' you always said yourself."

"This aint Adair." Jesse swung up on his black, blinking hard at the unhappy Cole. "You and Frank won't be messing up no train schedules this time. Little Old Dingus will do his own dirty shirts on this one. There won't be no slip-ups, you can lay."

"Count me out," said the big horseman defiantly.

"Sure. Faint heart never won fair ranch, no-how."

Jesse shrugged the crude parody carelessly, adding nothing to it.

He let the silence ride along with them, watching Cole out of the corner of his eye. Presently, he saw the slow wheels of his friend's mind begin to turn. He could not have seen them better had there been a storefront window in the big lummox's forehead, he thought. They had not walked the horses halfway up the arroyo when those wheels clanked to their expected halt.

Cole checked the bay, turned to him.

"Where at?" he asked helplessly.

"St. Louis."

"The Mopac?"

He meant the Missouri Pacific. Jesse chucked his head in wordless agreement.

They rode a little farther, Cole scowling furiously. Jesse continued to watch him, his blue eyes wide with tender innocence. The telltale blink, controlled as always in moments of calculated deceit, was barely noticeable.

Shortly, Cole checked the bay again.

"How much?"

"Upwards of a hundred thousand dollars," murmured Jesse casually.

"You don't change your tune a damn cent, do you?" growled Cole irritably. "You're going to get that hundred thousand yet, aint you?"

"*We're* going to get it," amended Jesse quietly.

Cole kicked the bay on up the arroyo, glaring at his blue-eyed incubus. His faltering vow came with all the assurance of a man dangling over a thousand-foot precipice with one hand holding onto a prickly pear bush and the other grabbing his shrinking parts. "I aint a'going to do it! I aint—I aint—I aint." He spaced the words with desperate emphasis.

"You understand me once for all now, Dingus? I aint!"

"Sure. I aint deaf. It's a mortal shame though. . . . You should of seen that map—"

He dropped the bait deliberately, rode on, not looking back to watch it fall in front of Cole.

The big rider, in turn, tried not to watch it. He looked away, bit his lip, scowled his wavering best. He set his jaw, shook his huge head like a bear with a sheep in its teeth. It was no good.

Cursing aloud, he pulled over alongside Jesse's black. *"You got that map with you?"* he grinned.

On May 12, three days after Jesse's arrival at the JD-Bar in Collins County, five men held up the San Antonio stage, twenty-four miles north of Austin, Texas. They were, we are told, "big rough-looking men, riding fine blooded horses. They wore face masks of bandanna calico."

Bob and Jim Younger held the headstalls of the lead team. Jesse covered the driver, courteously suggesting that he "watch his cussed hands mighty careful and please to throw down the box." There was no profanity. Of the eleven passengers in the coach, three were women.

It is a curious commentary on the warped ideals, at least of the James-Younger members of the gang, that no witness to any of their many holdups ever reported a solitary instance, on the parts of Frank, Jesse, Cole, or the latter's brothers, of rough language in front of ladies.

But chivalry never interfered in the practical or professional sense.

Cole and Frank opened the door of the coach and bowed the victims out, one by one. The loot amounted to a little over three thousand dollars in cash. It was a short, sweet job, notable mainly for leaving a rare insight into the sober character of the least-known member of the band, and for showing, thereby, that the random James sense of humor was not the sole property of brother Jesse.

The last passenger out of the coach was the Right Reverend Bishop Gregg, of the Protestant Episcopal Church of Texas, Austin Diocese.

It was Frank's turn to do the honors. The long Colt barrel slid impiously into the belly-folds of the Bishop's frock. The good clergyman complained aloud over giving up his fine silver watch, citing his cloth as palpable immunity.

Frank, holding out his left hand for the watch, nodded compassionately.

"Parson," he observed, "the Good Book says when traveling take neither purse nor script. We therefore propose to put you back into the good graces of the Lord. Shell out."

The Bishop shelled out.

Bob and Jim now freed the lead team, Jesse advising the driver to "lay on the leather and give our regards to Dallas."

While the dust of the stage rolled Dallasward, that of the fleeing bandits piled high into the May sky, straight toward the Collins County hideout. Even as it did, Cole was anxiously calling its telltale question on Jesse.

"What you trying to do, Dingus? Lead the damn Pinkertons square down atop of us? They got an office in Dallas, you know."

"Yeah," nodded the latter. "I also know there aint no point in stirring up a dust down here unless *they* know who stirred it."

"What the hell you talking about?"

"Providing we lay them a trail right to the JD-Bar, they'll know it was our gang done the job—that's all. It's what I had in mind the whole time."

"For God's sake, why?" demanded Cole, shaking his head angrily.

"It's near a thousand miles from Dallas to St. Louie and the Mopac yards," said Jesse softly.

In theory, Jesse's ruse of raising a delaying dust a thousand miles south of where he meant to strike in earnest was sound bandit business. The only trouble was that he was matching minds with a mighty sharp firm of competitors. The Pinkertons had been in the business a bit longer than he had—plenty long enough to smell a bogus set of tracks once they had run them to the JD-Bar and had a little exploratory talk with Old Man Coleman. Before the day was out, the Dallas telegraph wires were humming northward.

In direct consequence, the projected robbery of the Mopac was shortly subject to some rescheduling.

On May 27 the gang, having separated to ride up from Texas in two groups—Jesse and Cole in the first and Frank James, with Bob and Jim Younger in the second, rendezvoused at the old Roaring River hideout.

Unknown to them, the trails of both groups had been picked up within the past forty-eight hours, that of Jesse and Cole at Siloam Springs, Arkansas, that of Frank and his companions at the little Cherokee town of Spavinaw, in Oklahoma Territory. Again the wires hummed. Pinkerton operatives from three states began closing in on Barry County before the last of the outlaws to ride in had had decent time to dismount and cool out his lathered mount.

But a telegraph wire will hum both ways. At Siloam Springs, once more showing that long-minded caution of his, Jesse had sent a message to his wife, then living near Clinton, Missouri, eighty miles south of Kansas City, with "trusted friends."

That "trusted" should not be misinterpreted. Zerelda was going under her maiden name; her hosts, non-native Missouri kin of her father,

John Mimms, didn't even know their great-niece was married, let alone to whom. It was, at the same time, a deception of limited possibilities. Had not Jesse's fateful wire disrupted it, it would soon enough have fallen apart under its own growing weight. Zerelda was four months pregnant and already having trouble retaining a figure to match the slender virginity of her claim to single blessedness.

Jesse's communiqué was typically to the point: "WILL BE AT HONEYMOON HOUSE. SEND HIBB DOWN IF ANYTHING WE SHOULD KNOW." It was signed: "LOVE, TOM," after his favorite alias, Thomas Howard.

The twenty-two-year-old girl, so soon to be the mother of Jesse's only son, was at once greatly excited. Only the day previous, young Hibb Woodson had ridden all the way down from Clay County with the alarming report that four strangers suspected of being plainclothes Pinkertons, had visited the office of the sheriff in Liberty. They had left town the same day, accompanied by three local deputies. The report had been set in motion along the clan grapevine by a James adherent who held a Clay County deputy's commission: "They know Jesse to be in northern Arkansas, approaching the Missouri line." All effort, Hibb had warned Zerelda, must be made to contact "the boys" in time. Had she had any late news from Cousin Jesse?

At the moment of Hibb's asking, Zerelda had not the least idea where her bandit husband might be. Now she had that dangerous knowledge. But Hibb was already gone back into the Clay County hinterlands, and there was no time to go after him.

It is a matter of folklore record that for seven days, commencing with her disappearance some time before the morning of May 26, Zerelda Mimms was missing from the Clinton home of her unsuspecting kinfolk. She returned there the morning of June 1. Her story was short and simple. She had "impulsively" gone to care for an ailing cousin "down near Seligman."

Where she had actually gone, and what she had really done, form as strange and stirring a part of the legend as any of Jesse's own rash deeds.

Cole sat on the crude planking of the little cabin's front stoop, smoking his cob pipe and watching the late moon creep over the limestone crest of Lookout Ridge. His thoughts were his own and he wasn't advertising them. Beside him, Jesse drew deeply on a cornshuck cigarette, flipped it spinningly away, glanced up to the ridge above, checking the tall silhouette of Bob Younger where it bulked black against the rising moon.

"About time we went up on the ridge and relieved the boys," he muttered uneasily to Cole.

"Yeah, I reckon. I'll go roust out Frank."

It was the 28th of May. They had been at the cabin twenty-four hours. Each had had but lit-

tle better than four or five hours sleep. They had
split the day into equal watches, only one man
sleeping in the cabin at a time while; of the remaining four, two stood watch outside the little
building and two on the ridge above it. It was
more than the normal precaution. All of them
cursed the restless premonition of their leader,
which demanded it. But even as they cursed,
they obeyed. They were only men, but Dingus
was different. He had the instincts of a brush
wolf—instincts which had more than once
through the hunted years saved them from
walking into a set trap, or from lingering on the
cocked baitpan of one until their own unwary
weight sprung it off.

"Wait up a bit, now." Jesse moved his head in
the negative, shaking off Cole's suggestion. "I've
got a feeling."

Cole didn't argue. He never did when it came
to those "feelings" of Dingus's. He eased back
on the stoop, knocked his pipe out. "Such as
what?" he asked quietly.

"Somebody's coming, I can tell. My damn
nerves are roached up worse than the hairs on
a scared dog's back. Set tight a minute."

"Yeah," breathed Cole, breaking his quick
glance away from the ridge above. "Likely,
you're right. Bob's dropped down off the lookout."

Jesse checked the ridge, saw only the moon
guarding its sharp crest. "All right," he said
quickly. "*Now* get Frank up. I'll fetch the horses

around. We'll know something by then."

It was an exactly accurate forecast.

Three minutes later, Bob Younger slid his mount to a stiff-legged stop outside the darkened cabin. He piled off him, crouching and squinting through the night-gloom. "That you, Jess?" His sharp challenge came as he moved toward the man bringing the saddled horses around the cabin.

"It's me. What's up?"

"We got company," drawled young Bob, voice easing softly. "Jim's bringing her in."

"*Her*!" The single word cracked into the stillness.

" 'Her,' " repeated Bob. Then, gently: "It's your wife, Jess."

"Not Zee, for God's sake, Bob?"

"As ever was, pardner," grunted his companion. "We heard this horse hammering down the Seligman road, slid down the ridge and jumped it in that stand of jack oak at the bend. It was her."

"What's she say?" Jesse's voice was back in its old thin rattle, snapping the question, wanting only the facts, ignoring the startling identity of their bearer.

"Didn't wait to hear no more than that she wanted to be took to you, quick. I cut and rode on down. Like I said, Jim's bringing her in right now. Ease down, Jess. We'll find out soon enough."

Soon enough was sixty seconds later.

Zerelda clung to Jesse for a sobbing, brief instant, and that was all. She stood back, then, and broke the eleventh-hour warning, dry-eyed.

Unable to reach a principal member of the clan in time, fearful of trusting any less than a blood kinsman, Zerelda James had hired a racing thoroughbred from the Clinton Livery, ridden the 159 miles to Roaring River in two nights and three days. She had ridden alone, guided along the unmapped back roads only by the year-old memory of her honeymoon trip by wagon the previous spring.

Jesse's young wife was a settlement girl, farmbred and born but city-schooled. She was not, in any real sense, a "frontier" or "pioneer" woman. She was not an expert rider, had never before ridden other than a properly ladylike sidesaddle. No details of her remarkable ride remain. Only its prime facts come down in the legend.

She did leave Clinton the night of the 25th, or early morning of the 26th day of May, 1876. She arrived at the Roaring River hideout shortly after ten o'clock the night of the 28th. Jesse and Frank James and the three Younger brothers had received and acted upon her desperate warning within minutes of that hour.

Past this point is anticlimax.

A mixed posse of Pinkerton detectives and Arkansas and Missouri peace officers closed in on the Barry County cabin in the gray daylight of the 29th.

They closed in on nothing. The coffee on the Buck's Range was cold. The trampled horse droppings in front of the little cabin had long since lost their warmth. The iron-shod, fifteen-foot strides of the fleeing outlaws' mounts marked the trail only as far as the rocky, wagon-tracked maze of the Seligman road.

Jesse James was gone.

There simply was not a better-liked, more popular couple in the farming community of Big Creek, some miles outside Nashville, Tennessee, than the Tom Howards. They were lively young folks and that new baby of theirs that had arrived last October was just about the brightest-eyed little boy you would ever want to see. His father called him Tim, his mother called him Eddie. From that, the Big Creek residents assumed the lovable tad's full name was Thomas Edward Howard. After his dark-bearded, beautifully mannered, culturally spoken daddy, no doubt.

Well, after his daddy, in any event. The kindly Tennessee farmfolk got that close, it must be admitted.

The baby's real name was Jesse Edward James.

The happy year was ended.

Sitting across from Jesse at the close of that last supper in the white-painted Tennessee farmhouse which had brought her her first and

only twelve months of home life with her restless mate, Zerelda knew that. Only the hour before, he had told her he was going, and where.

She had not remonstrated with him then. She
did not mean to now.

She had known when she married him that
he was a professional outlaw, with a price on
his head which could only be paid in one of
three ways: by his sudden death in the gunfire
course of some job; by his surrendering to the
Clay County authorities and accepting, thus, a
lifetime imprisonment in the Missouri State
Prison; by his continuing to rob and kill and to
lead the resultant existence of eternal flight and
constant vigilance which she had known since
the first hour of her Roaring River honeymoon.

When Zerelda Mimms had said "I do" those
twenty-four long months gone, she had done so
with full understanding of the words. To his
clear credit, Jesse had come to her in the week
before the wedding and made a clean, unvar-
nished admission of the ugly nature of his calling. He had not cloaked it in the old, outworn
robes of Confederate loyalty and lost-cause vengeance. But Zerelda had not waited nine years
to cry out, "Oh, Jesse, why did you not tell me
before?" She had only nodded at his confession,
and said nothing. Only held him the more
closely. And wept the more heartbrokenly when
he had gone.

Now, that same time had come again. The
time of quiet nodding when he said, "I'm going."

The time of brave smiling in the brief hour before he left. And the time of bitter tears after he had gone.

She glanced up, looking across the yellow coal-oil lamplight at the lean face of America's most fabled outlaw. He sat staring out the kitchen window, his coffee growing cold in front of him, unmindful of her, or of her watching him, his thoughts far away and riding, swift-mounted, on the racing back of a fleet black gelding.

Time had been kind to that famous outlaw face, and to the form that went with it.

Studying him now, Zerelda was seeing that face and figure as it was that long-ago August afternoon at that other farm-house "beyond the catalpa tree." And, as she did, her heart turned over, slow and deeply hurtful within her.

Gone was the dark fall of the lank, collar-length locks. Faded away was the crinkly pattern of the big boyhood freckles. Lost forever was the slight, short-statured, girlish slimness of the adolescent Dingus. Here was no longer the "pale-faced, sweet smiling boy" of her heart's first memory.

Jesse was barely twenty-eight that summer night outside Nashville. But the wild and wicked years had marked him hard and deep.

He had grown tall—an inch, perhaps two, shy of a full six feet. His body had widened and filled out with the thick muscle and sinew of ten years on horseback, and with the forced guerrilla marching-rations of constant danger and cold, fireless camps.

The freckles had been tanned over by the frostbite and windburn of years unending in the open. The long hair, sun-faded and bleached to a colorless bay-brown, was short-cropped and neatly brushed. The pug nose of boyhood had grown high-bridged and strongly arched, hawk-bent now in the same fierce curve as his mother's. The receding chin of his teens lay hidden under the harsh jut of the spade beard. Even the memorable thinness of his upper lip was covered by the dark mustache he had grown for his masquerade as Thomas D. Howard, respected Nashville squire.

Only the eyes remained unchanged.

They were still as raw blue as a rainwashed prairie sky. Still as red-rimmed and ugly as those of a barn-prowling ferret caught in the angry glare of a farmer's lantern. And they still blinked with the old, nervous uncertainty as he turned them now from the window to his waiting wife.

"I'd best be going along, Zee," was all he said. "It's full dark outside."

She was ready with the nod, knowing this was the time for it. "You'll want to say good-bye to little Eddie," she said. "I'll fetch him."

"No." Jesse's answer was quick. "Don't wake the boy. You wait on the stoop. I'll see him."

It was like him, she thought. Always wanting to be alone. Always afraid someone would see him being soft, or overhear him in a moment of unguarded sentiment. It was his way, she knew. To say what he had to say, or do what he had to do, with only himself and the one he meant it for to hear him say it or see him do it.

She nodded again, as gentle and slow as he had been short and quick. "All right, Jesse. I'll be outside."

He went into the darkened room, leaving the kitchen door inches wide, that the following lamplight might find his son's face for the one brief moment of farewell.

He stood over the sleeping infant for a full minute, not speaking, not moving. What thoughts were passing through his lonely mind can only be guessed at. But in their passing, for the one, hushed moment, they brought a look of strange peace and softness to the dark, savage face of Jesse James.

In the end, he only bent swiftly, kissed the satin cheek, gently tucked the light coverlet in place, turned and tiptoed away. At the door he paused, whispered "Good bye, boy!" across the baby-fragrant darkness, and was gone before the echoes of the whisper faded behind him.

All was quiet along the Mopac's right-of-way at Rocky Cut on the Lamine River, thirteen miles beyond the section stop of Sedalia, Missouri.

Just past the rickety trestle which bore the tracks across the Lamine, the green, all-clear lamp outside the watchman's shack winked cheerily through the July night. By its thin light the watchman chewed at his gag, cursed the luck which had stationed him at a lonely way-point in the Jesse James country. Forty yards farther up the track, in the throat of the cut, eight good men and true dropped the last of the piled crossties athwart the rails, laughed, spat into the trackside shadows, wondered what was holding up old Number Nine.

Jesse checked his watch in the day-bright glare of the summer moon. The Missouri Pacific's Train Nine was running twenty-seven minutes late. It was no matter. When Jesse bribed a railroad employee, he stayed bribed. On time or otherwise, Number Nine would be there. To Frank's worried query, he made this growlingly clear. Jesse was not in one of his higher moods.

"I told you she was due to lay over at Sedalia to pick up our express car. There's two companies shipping tonight, Adams and United. It figures to take them some time to hook up and get their invoices cleared. Our car will be up front, hooked back of the baggage car."

"What if she aint?" Cole had shadowed up to them from the darkness of the cut.

"If she aint," grated Jesse ominously, "there's due to be a new-made widow hanging around them St. Louie yards before the week's out."

The threat was no sooner stated than discounted.

Jesse threw up his hand, stopping the conversation. "You hear anything?" he asked after a moment.

"Nope," said Cole.

"Frank?"

"Me neither."

Jesse stepped up on the graveled roadbed. He pulled the omnipresent glove off his right hand, pressed his slim fingers to the cold iron of the near rail.

"I did," he nodded, stepping quickly back. "The steel's humming. She aint no more than two mile down the line. Clell!" he barked into the darkness.

"Yeah, Jess?" Clell Miller stepped into the moonlight.

"You and Ed stay in the cut and take the engineer. Frank—" His brother moved forward. "You and Chadwell get on the far side of the tracks. Jim—" The call went to Cole's second brother. "You stay on this side with Charlie." The reference was to Charlie Pitts, with Chadwell a relative newcomer. Jim Younger nodded, followed Pitts toward their horses.

"Bob, you come along with Cole and me. It's high time you learned a little something about railroading." Bob Younger grinned, moved eagerly for his horse. He was a handsome six-footer like Cole and, like his better-known brother, an easygoing man, slow to anger, quick to smile. Unlike Cole, and like Jim, he was not gregarious, fought inherently shy of excess conversation and those inclined to make it.

"Now, listen!" snapped Jesse, the rising pitch of excitement in his voice covered by the hoarse cry of the locomotive bellowing beyond the trestle. "When she pulls up, you boys race the hell out of your horses up and down both sides. I don't want nobody from the coaches or sleepers getting off that train nor sticking their damn noses out of it, you hear?"

He paused, barking it at them. "That goes double for any of the crew. I was seen too much around them St. Louie yards, you understand? Any brakeman or conductor goes to swing down on the tracks, you punch his Goddamn ticket for him!"

With the words, everybody was running for the horses. Number Nine's swaying headlamp had broken clear of the trestle bend, would in another minute be bouncing across the straightaway onto the pile of blockading crossties.

"Son of a bitch," muttered Cole, swinging up and seeing Frank mounting in the gloom beyond. "I wished I'd of stayed in Texas. Somehow I never get old to this stuff like that damn Dingus. I'm sweating like a windbroke horse."

"Some sweat, some spit, some cuss, some laugh." Frank's nod was tight. "Everybody does something just ahead of a job."

"You ever see Dingus sweat?" asked Cole quickly.

"No," said Frank, and swung his horse away.

*     *     *

Pete Conklin grabbed the arms of his chair, bracing himself as Number Nine bit into the trestle curve. It was a fairly short train and Pete knew the whipcrack that would come when the baggage car jerked out of the curve. He eased off his hold a moment later, spat out the open door. She was around the bend and running smooth onto the trestle straightaway. Pete yawned.

If only Johnny Bushnell would get the hell back in the express car where he belonged, they could get on with their chess game. Bushnell was the express guard. Bored with midsummer life on the Mopac, he had wandered up front into the coaches to pass the time of night with the conductor. There was no stop scheduled short of K. C., Johnny Bushnell knew. Moreover, Pete Conklin was a pretty dull chess player.

But boredom was very near an end for the Messrs. Conklin and Bushnell.

Suddenly, Number Nine locked her drivers, threw on the steam and sand. Her whistle hooted bawlingly and Pete Conklin started picking himself out of the pile of express packages where his tilted-back chair had thrown him. He was still on his knees when the three masked men swung their horses up to the open loading door, piled off of them, swarmed into the car.

Two of them were big and tall, and a man could see the crinkles of their wide grins beyond the muffle of their calico bandannas. The third man was about Pete's own size, which was to say only medium tall and not too hefty, and a man could look all night and not see any grin-lines past his bandanna.

"Hand over the key to the safe, young feller," he rasped.

"Honest to God I aint got it!" protested Pete. "I aint the messenger. I'm on baggage this run."

"All right, mister, where's the messenger?"

"Back in the train, gabbing with the conductor."

The slender man looked at him a moment. "All right," he nodded again, "let's mosey back and find him." He compounded the suggestion by shoving his right-hand Colt between the baggageman's kidneys, after spinning him roughly around with an openhanded blow of his free left hand.

"Hold on, Dingus." The bigger of his two companions put out his hand. "How about the conductor?"

"If he knows me," gritted Jesse, "it won't be for long."

"Better leave me go," urged Cole, knowing exactly what Jesse meant.

"I'm gone," said Jesse, shoving the baggageman ahead of him. "Foller along through the express car and wait up there for us."

He was back shortly, Bushnell and Conklin both with him. Cole looked at him. He did not seem so keyed up now. Still—

"How about the conductor?" he asked sharply.

"Never saw him before in my life," grinned Jesse.

"Thank the Lord for small favors," breathed Cole, producing the wheatsack from under his coat with patent relief. "Let's get on with it."

Bushnell opened the first safe, Cole emptying it in short order. He hefted the sack speculatively, grinned at Jesse. Old outlaw weighmaster that he was, he reckoned it a fair beginning. A man might be a thousand or two off, one way or the other, but there felt to be in the neighborhood of forty thousand dollars already in the bag, with the second safe left to go.

But the second safe did not go.

It was traveling locked all the way through, said Johnny Bushnell. Bushnell had been on the line twenty years. He was a Missouri boy. He would not try to horse *them*—that was certain.

Jesse scowled a minute, stepped over to Bob.

"Shag up in the cab and fetch an ax," he blinked. "Tell Clell and Ed to take it easy. We're going to be here the best part of the summer."

Bob was back at once, the fireman's coal pick swinging optimistically in his hands. Cole let him knock a few futile sparks off the steel box, then shouldered him aside. "Never send a boy about a man's business," he advised Jesse.

Under Cole's tremendous blows, a small hole was literally driven through the safe's top, but the big outlaw's huge paw would not begin to go through it. Jesse took off his coat, rolled up his right sleeve, tapped Cole on the shoulder.

"Never put a plow-horse to a pony's job," he grinned, and slid his small hand and wrist through the jagged opening. Stack by stack, he fished out the neatly bundled currency, toiling in strained silence as the precious minutes fled.

The July heat was stifling in the crowded car. The work hot and close, the hole in the safe a forcing, razor-edged squeeze even for Jesse's woman-small hand. When the last packet of bills was twisted through the opening, his forearm was coursing blood from wrist to elbow, his face streaming perspiration.

"By God," proclaimed Cole admiringly. "I never seen you sweat before!"

"By God," agreed Jesse pantingly, "you never seen me *try* before! Mister, that's tolerable warm work." He turned to Conklin. "Where's the water at, young feller?"

The baggageman pointed out the bucket. All three bandits drank heavily. His thirst slaked, Cole shouldered the sack and moved for the door. Jesse followed him. Bob started for the rear door and the vestibule into the first sleeper behind the express car.

"Where the hell you think you're going?" snarled Jesse. Cole glanced around, saw the quick blink of the pale eyes, knew the crazy-thin edge of Jesse's temper had sliced its vicious way free.

"Watch it!" he ordered Bob, sharply.

The youngster grinned off the warning. Hell, he knew Jess. And he knew Cole was forever mother-henning the little rooster. Coddling him. Fretting over him. Standing between him and the rest all the time, like maybe there wasn't anybody else in the bunch could handle him but big brother Cole. Well, the hell with that noise. . . .

"Aw shucks now, Jess." The grin spread. "I won't be a minute. I'm going to hunt me up a plug hat back yonder. I lost my super to Clell and a pair of aces last week. I'm needing a new one right bad."

"Damn you and your new super. Give Cole a hand with that Goddamn sack. We're getting out of here."

"Aw, c'mon now, Jess. You aint—"

"*Git out!*" Cole was roughing him toward the loading door. His fierce mutter continued, under his breath. "Don't never crowd him when he's blinking thataway. *Jesus, boy!*"

Outside the car, he tied the sack to his saddle, warned Bob to mount up and be quick about it. Jesse, last out and mounted, heeled his black back up to the express-car door. He laughed high and sudden, his peculiar temper as quickly quieted as it had flared.

"If either of you two boys see any of the Pinkertons," he called cheerfully, "tell them to come and get us. I reckon you won't need to tell them *where!*"

Ten minutes later the train crew, aided by an

excited score of passengers, cleared the last of the jumbled ties. Number Nine's whistle shrieked the all-aboard and the Lamine River was left behind.

The Rocky Cut robbery was on record—as of 10:43 P.M., July 7, 1876.

No official accounting of the loot has survived. Express companies are touchy with statistics of this sort. They mislead the cash-shipping customers, and raise hell with the insurance rates.

Years later, on a fine summer's afternoon in St. Joseph, Missouri, one of the parties of the second part tugged at his graying handlebars, squinted his pale blue eyes back down the long, long trail, and balanced history's books with a soft Clay County drawl.

"Eighty-eight thousand dollars," said Frank James.

# NIGHTFALL

# Chapter Ten

*Northfield*

Cole sat on the porch of his mother's farmhouse outside Lees Summit. He watched the evening breeze stir among the dead stalks of the August corn. He heard the first bullbat twitter and, looking up, saw the bird's blunt-headed form launch itself from a far fencepost and labor awkwardly for altitude against the cooling air. Across the barnyard an owl hooted sleepily, ruffled his plumage, thought briefly about the mice soon to be playing beneath the spill of the corn crib. With the thought he hooted again, dolefully, keeningly.

Cole moved uneasily, sighed heavily.

He and Bob and Jim had come in from Texas four days ago—or was it four years? They had come in at night, staking their horses out in the woodlot, not daring to stable them at the barn or show them in the open. They had hung to the house during the day, one of them always near the front window, watching the Lees Summit Road. Each evening they had emerged at twilight, sitting on the porch and talking the moon down. Then, following it, shortly, into the timber, there to bed down near their saddled mounts.

A year and a month had gone since Rocky Cut. With it, somehow, had gone their cut of the Lamine River loot. Gone, too, with that year and its misspent gain was something else. Something not to be replaced by another long ride and another armed robbery.

The big outlaw was thirty-one. Boyhood was far behind, lost forever in the haze which hid Old Hickory and Uncle Eben. Youth and the first, better part of the man-grown years had fallen away in swift turn. Ahead stretched God alone knew what.

God and Cole.

The little ranch in Texas? Him and Dingus? And his dream for the both of them living it out somewhere down yonder south of the Panhandle? Or of him being "Uncle Cole" to Dingus's young ones, and teaching them to set a hot-blood pony over a high pile of split rails, or to throw a Colt down on a cottontail before he cleared three jumps? Or mend a saddle, or trim a horse's frog out right and proper, or calk a shoe or fit a set of racing plates?

Just dreams. Sweet as the simple hopes that had built them up, empty as the bitter years that had torn them down. There would never be a ranch. There never could have been one. Not with Dingus, nor with his kind.

Cole knew that now.

He knew something else now, too. Something he had *not* known before—or, better, that he would not *let* himself know before. It was about him, Cole. And it unsettled a man. Unsettled him bad.

In the end, it was not just Dingus. It was you, too. In the end, you *were* Dingus. And he was you.

*You were of a kind.*

Somewhere back across the years there had been a place to stop. To take off the Colts, to hang the carbine up. To forget the rush of the night wind, the flicker of the campfire, the shrill cry of the rebel guerrilla, the spill and clink of the gold into the wheatsack. To lay aside the maps, the plans, the grins, the curses, the long, careful rides, the sudden thunder of the gunfire outside the banks. To unpile the ties from across the tracks. To turn away from the frightened screech of the wheel-locked locomotives, the grind and jar of the buckled couplings, the whine and ricochet of the galloping shots and the broken crash of the daycoach windows.

But a man could no longer see that far across those years. Where was that place now? When had it been ridden past? What hour, what min-

241

ute, what day would have been the right place to wheel on him and declare, "Dingus, I'm done! From here you ride it alone!"

Looking across the lonely rustle of the cornfield, a man knew the answer. There never had been such a day or hour or minute. Or such a place. For him and Dingus that time would come only with a posseman's or Pinkerton's bullet, and the place would be where they were when it struck them. As long as a man had it in him to be bad, had it way, deep in him, in his blood and his bones and his will, he could laugh and grin and crack jokes about it and be as breezy over it as he had a mind to.

When the sun went down and the night wind rustled in the cornstalks, he knew where he was.

Bob came out of the house just before the last daylight went. He sat down by Cole. Neither spoke. Presently, Jim came up through the dusk, walking from the direction of the timber, leading the horses.

"We'd best be going," he said. "Jess wanted us there by nine o'clock."

Cole nodded dully.

He got up, took his horse from Jim, climbed wearily into the saddle. Bob looked at him, then looked at Jim. The latter returned the look, and both brothers shrugged. They rode quickly out of the farmyard, north along the Lees Summit Road. Three hours later, with the pinpoint of the Samuels' window lamp pricking at them across the distant fields, Cole still had not spoken.

Turning for the Samuel barn, Bob, looking at him for the dozenth time, could stand it no longer.

"Cole, what the Sam Hill is eating you? You aint said a decent word since we left."

Cole came around with a start, squinting his wide gray eyes as though pulling his mind back from a long way off. "I dunno, boy," he said at last, his deep voice so low they barely caught it. "Maybe it's that I didn't say good-bye to Ma. I aint never done that before."

"Bushway!" laughed Jim. "Neither did I. You just got the fantods, man—that's all."

"Why sure!" grinned Bob in agreement. "I didn't say nothing to Ma, my own self. What the heck for? It aint like we wasn't coming back."

For once Cole failed to show the family good humor. He rode in silence almost to the barn. At the last minute he looked up at Bob.

"*Aint it, boy?*" he asked softly.


Twenty-four hours after the conference in the Samuel barn, the shadows of Cole's premonitions took form at Fort Osage Township in Jackson County, a night's easy ride from the Kearney farm. The substance of those shadows was divided by eight: Frank and Jesse James, Clell Miller, Charlie Pitts, Bill Chadwell, Bob and Jim Younger and Cole himself.

With no more than the briefest greetings, the eight horsemen swung north out of Fort Osage.

The days of planning, the hours of map-tracing and route-laying had all been done by Jesse, weeks before last night's gathering in his mother's barn. At the barn, he had given the others only the broad form of the venture, plus its general destination: "A bank job somewhere in Minnesota."

As he headed the gang north, guiding it carefully east of Kansas City, Lees Summit and Kearney, Jesse continued to keep his own counsel.

He had never worked out a job so thoroughly, nor had better reason to.

With the true instincts of the pack leader he had sensed as long ago as Muncie that the old gang was growing restive. And with the reasoning inherent to the born dictator, no matter how limited his subjects, he had known what must be done to insure his own survival. Only a major victory would provide the cement of self-preservation.

Minnesota would be that cement. This campaign, the victory. This last, great job, his masterpiece.

He knew where his real trouble lay, and with whom. It lay not with Frank, nor with the new boys, nor with Bob and Jim.

It lay with Cole.

The big outlaw wanted to quit. He had wanted to since before Adair. A man knew now that he should have let him. But August 16, 1876, was too late in the game for that. Jesse thought about the parable of the bad apple and the barrel. There was the real hell of it. It was not just Cole anymore. Frank and Jim had begun to side with the big devil, had begun to get harder and harder to talk into a job. And harder and harder to handle once they were on that job. It was why he had had to get new blood into the gang, to let in such as the likes of Charlie Pitts and Bill Chadwell, and to lean more and more upon them as things went along. A man did not like it but, when he could not hold on to his right hand any longer and felt his left slipping at the same time, he had no choice.

He looked back at his men now, sizing up them and his plans thoughtfully.

As usual with the major jobs, particularly where new men were involved, he had furnished the operating capital. No books were ever kept, the men drawing on him for whatever was needed of cash or equipment, and the advances were simply held out of their subsequent cuts. If there were no cuts, the pleasure was all Jesse's—and no questions ever asked. In the present case, no expense had been spared.

He had each of the boys superbly mounted, each well dressed and rehearsed for the role he would play along the route, each amply heeled with the pocket cash to back his part.

Bill and Charlie, the group's illiterates, were cattle buyers. The three Youngers, most affable at public relations, were railroad men. He and Frank, best spoken of the lot, were graduate civil engineers. Each man, no matter his role, carried a carbine slung to his saddle, each was additionally armed with two late-model revolvers. All wore long linen dusters of the anonymous type affected by the legitimate cross-country traveler-by-horseback.

The advance was as precisely scheduled as a railway timetable. North through Missouri, meandering eastward and then north again through Iowa. Once in Minnesota, boxing the horseback compass, circling west, riding north to St. Paul, east and then south to Red Wing and finally angling back west again into the selected area of southeastern Minnesota. Deliberately, no exact town or bank had been named. The selection would be made at the last minute. This time there would be no failures. He had seen to that. This time he would pick the day, the date, the victim, just twenty-four hours ahead of the strike.

Breaking his glance from his followers, Jesse kneed his black, picking up his gait to a lope.

He had it figured. His nod was one of pure professional satisfaction.

His crew was seven-eighths sound. His routes of approach and retreat were worked out in flawless detail. There was not a green hand nor a weak one riding behind him. He had a native guide who knew the enemy territory like Jesse knew Clay County: young Bill Chadwell, born and raised in south-eastern Minnesota, and knowing its every lake, creek, backroad hamlet, highway town, railroad line, unsettled section and abandoned farmhouse to the last vital detail.

Nodding again, he smiled the old, quick wolf-smile.

He had this one where it could not get away from him. He had nothing but old Cole to worry about and he could still handle that mutton-head when the time came. He always *had* handled him.

As to controlling Cole, perhaps Jesse was right.

As to the big Missourian being his only worry, he was wrong to the extent of one bustling little Minnesota city he had never heard of—a happy, prosperous, obscure center of farming and native industry on the banks of the Cannon River. It had been overlooked in the first grand sweep of the master plan, but not passed over by the hovering, gathering rush of a history now closing with unseen, deadly swiftness upon him.

Its name?

A humble, simple name. A name standing quietly along the banks of the Cannon for nearly fifty years, awaiting only the coming gunfire of the Man from Missouri to burn its ten letters into frontier legend for all time.

*Northfield.*

\* \* \*

They had been riding in Minnesota two weeks. Behind lay the waypoints of St. Peter, Lake Crystal, St. James, Garden City, Waterville and Madelia. Ahead lay Mankato and Cannon and Millersburg. And beyond them, Northfield.

Challenging fate, Jesse first selected not Northfield but Mankato for his triumph. Bill Chadwell had lived outside it. He knew the First National Bank there. It was rich as sin. He knew, too, a half dozen back-road ways out of the big bend of the Minnesota River in which the thriving town lay. The day was set, the date agreed upon.

Fate checked her own calendar against that of the Clay County bandit chief, smiled condescendingly, sat restfully back to wait.

On the stroke of nine, Saturday morning, September 2, five linen-dustered horsemen rode into Mankato.

They tied their horses in front of Simm's Restaurant, went in and enjoyed a leisurely breakfast. Returning to the sidewalk, they visited Anderson's Pharmacy and Luscombe's General Merchandise Store, making several trivial purchases of a type natural to respectable gentlemen traveling by horseback.

Shortly they found themselves at the bank.

Here their leader innocently entered to seek the change of a five-dollar bill. It was furnished him and he left the bank immediately. At the precise moment, grinning fate, waiting in the wings, sent an ex-Missouri resident toward the

248

bank door. The man stood aside for the traveling gentleman in the linen duster. As the horseman passed by him, the startled townsman took one popping-eyed look at him, turned his own face quickly away.

Subsequently, he went straight on through the bank, out its alley door, broke into a dead run for the sheriff's office. There he blurted news of some small sectional import to the latter. And he was very breathless about it all, too.

"Jesse James is in town!" he gasped. "He was just into the bank and went away. There were four others waiting for him."

*"Jesse James!"*

It was a far piece from Clay County, and every mile of it was mirrored in the sheriff's incredulous outburst.

"By Tophet, I know him! Know him by sight!" stammered the other. "I lived for years in Kearney and Lees Summit. I've seen him a dozen times. It's him, Sheriff, and it looks like him and his boys have got their eyes on the First National."

"Let's get to the bank—" The sheriff was already out the door. "They'll pull none of their damn tricks in this town!" he shouted.

The sheriff was right.

At the bank, he and a hidden posse waited the day away. Nothing happened. Jesse James and his men, if it was Jesse James, had disappeared as suddenly as they had materialized. All the following day, Sunday, the town remained alerted. That night, two of the men returned, drank quietly for four hours in a cross-river saloon, rode peacefully back away into the nowhere from whence they had come.

The sheriff advised his informer to have his eyes looked at, called it a bad day and went to bed.

At noon, Monday, the eight-man gang reentered the town. It was the dinner hour, carefully selected because at that time the bank population, staff and patron alike, would be at its daily low. The horsemen rode directly down Main Street, keeping their horses bunched, making no attempt to cover their presence. In the lead, Jesse sat his black, Clell Miller siding him. Behind them, Cole and Frank were lost in the body proper of the pack.

It was the first time in the memory of any of the gang that Cole had not had his bay at the side of Jesse's black. But it was the way Jess had wanted it and ordered it. Of them all, only Cole and Frank had exchanged blank looks over the arrangement.

Suddenly Jesse tensed, pale eyes sweeping forward.

Just beyond the bank, a crowd of about forty townfolk stood gathered along the sidewalk.

"What are those jaspers looking at?" said Clell tersely, his eyes only a second behind Jesse's.

"I dunno," muttered the latter. "We'll see soon enough."

They saw quicker than that. One of the men

in the crowd pointed suddenly. Jesse, following the line of the point, wound up looking at himself.

"By God, it's me," he snapped to Clell. "Some son of a bitch has spotted *me*."

"Damn. You sure, Jess?"

"Look at the bastards," grated Jesse.

Clell looked. The finger-pointer was gesturing and talking to the others. In turn, they were using their eyes, and not just on Jesse. The whole gang was getting a going-over.

"Damn it, what'll we do, Jess?"

"Ride straight on. Don't even look back at the sons of bitches. Make out like nothing's wrong. Pass it back to the boys."

Clell nodded, dropped his horse back.

While the crowd continued to stare, the gang kept going—straight out and away from Mankato, Minnesota. And straight out and away from fifty-five thousand dollars in the open vault of the Mankato First National Bank, which could have been theirs for the long-barreled request of a loaded Colt and waiting wheatsack.

The crowd on the sidewalk?

It was watching a construction crew working on a building out of sight of the gang's line of approach. The man who had pointed at Jesse was only calling attention to his superb black gelding, and the following regards and admiring comments of his fellow townfolk had been directed solely at the beautiful horseflesh which carried the rest of the Missourians.

The sheriff?

Tired out by two days of empty surveillance and convinced the James gang had never been nearer Minnesota than Adair, Iowa, he was soundly asleep in the good September sunshine in front of his office three blocks away.

He did not even have a deputy on duty at high noon of Monday, September 4.

The first stop out of Mankato was made that night, six hours and eighteen miles north. Jesse took one look at the town's name on the roadside sign, nodded to Clell, by now his constant traveling companion.

"Here's my hometown. It ought to do."

It was Jamesville, Minnesota.

As was their custom, the gang split up, entering the town in the pairings Jesse had ordered observed all along the line of march: he and Frank, the three Youngers, and Pitts, Chadwell and Clell Miller.

That night, he and Frank studied the map for three hours. If a decision was reached, it was not announced.

The following day they rode slowly, north and west, reaching the town of Cardova, another eighteen miles removed from Mankato. Here they rested their horses, swung wide of the town, turned yet more west and pushed on. Late that night, they arrived outside Millersburg.

They did not go at once into the town, but

made camp beside a wooded stream where there was good grass for the horses, heavy cover for their riders. They ate a cold saddlebag supper, prepared to sleep on the ground. It was September 5.

Shortly, by the guarded light of an Indian-small fire, the map came out again. This time Chadwell was called into the consulation with Frank. Cole, catching the latter's gaze across the fire, stared him down. Frank returned the look unhappily, chucked his head quickly toward Jesse, shrugged helplessly. Cole nodded, understanding.

Dingus, eyes watering, finger swift-pointing at the grimy map, was rising into his high-wild mood. Frank and Cole could sense it far ahead of the others. But Cole's nod to Frank meant only that he understood *him* and *his* position; not Dingus and *his*.

Somewhere north of yesterday, and south of tonight, he had lost Dingus. And somehow—crouching now with Frank and Chadwell over that map, there—he looked, suddenly, too far away ever for a man to find him again. Cole shook, as to a quick chill in the night wind. Setting his jaw, he looked long at Jesse. The ache in his throat came up dull and slow, and he could not swallow it away.

After an hour of low-voiced conversation, it was apparent to the big rider, where he watched and waited with the others just beyond the fire's dying perimeter, that an agreement had been reached.

And it had. Jesse nodded in final approval to Chadwell, waved the rest of them forward.

They came up, squatted quickly behind him, gaunt from three weeks of continuous riding, nerve-strung with the lack of sleep and the growing strain of Jesse's unwonted secrecy.

But the time of waiting was past—the master plan was ready for revelation.

His voice high, the old blink watering his red-rimmed eyes, Jesse gave it to them.

"This here town we're at is Millersburg. Angling up yonder here, ten miles, is Cannon City. Up north and east here, close to eleven miles, is Northfield and Dundas. The bank we're going to take is the First National. Bill tells me it's the richest in the south part of the state and that it's nothing for them to have a quarter of a million dollars on hand along about this time of fall. That's for paying off on the late harvests and tending to the payrolls of all them little river mills, most of which closes up for the winter soon."

He paused, letting them all study the map through the little silence, still not having named his town outright, but only giving them its bank.

"Now, tomorrow, along about noon, me and Charlie and Bob will move on through Millersburg without putting up. We'll stay the night at Cannon City. About four o'clock, Frank and the rest of you will ride on into Millersburg and put up at the hotel there. Frank will take you on from there the next day and give you the final layout tomorrow tonight. Any questions?"

Bob and Charlie Pitts, clearly flattered by the honor apportioned them, had none. Chadwell and Clell Miller apparently already knew the plan, or the best part of it, as did Frank. This left Jim and Cole looking at one another.

And Jesse looking at Cole.

The tall outlaw returned the look, quiet-eyed. He spat into the fire, stood up. His voice was as soft and easy as the movements of his big body.

"Who'd you say would ride on with you?"

"You heard me. Bob and Charlie."

"Mind saying why? Bob aint never fronted a big job before."

"It's the plan," said Jesse, eyes tightening.

The plan, thought Cole. God Almighty, always the plan. Since Pleasant Grove and Old Man Pettis's smokehouse, and as far back in his mind as a man could dig, it had forever been the plan. Just that. The plan. That simple and with no explanations. Dingus had a plan. If you wanted to throw in with it, all right. Otherwise—

"All right," he said. "It's the plan."

He knew it was not all right, and that it was not the plan. He knew it was something else. Something between him and Dingus that had never been there before. A man could feel it, taste it, smell it. And he could see it in the uncertain blink of Dingus's eyes.

*Dingus was afraid of him.*

"All right," echoed Jesse, not taking the blink off him. "Any more questions, *Cole?*"

"I reckon. If it aint too much to ask."

"Don't get funny with me, Goddamn it!"

Cole looked at him, something inside of him squeezing in hard and hurtful, like it had that years-gone day in the Widow Bowman's shack outside Lexington. He could almost feel again the desperate grip of the small hand on his arm, the rack and spasm of the torn lung rasping against his chest as he held him close.

"I aint never felt less funny in my life, Dingus," he said at last. "I reckon you know that, boy—"

"Now, don't give me none of that!"

He said it sharply, showing an edge of awkwardness in it, all at once feeling *something* across the fire between him and Cole. When the big lummox looked at a man like that, it made him think of the Little Blue and Mr. Peabody and that cussed Pleasant Grove School and a whole host of such like things which did not make any difference any more.

"Don't 'boy' me, Goddamn it," he finished angrily. "You got something to say, say it and be done!"

Cole stared him down until he had to drop his eyes. Cole nodded then, voice still soft.

"You mind telling us where we're going?"

Jesse swung his blink back up.

*"Northfield!"* he snapped defiantly. "That all right with you?"

"It aint mine to say, no more," murmured Cole, and turned away from him.

They came from the west. It was 2:00 P.M. and Northfield drowsed in the after-dinner quiet.

There were only three of them. If anyone noticed them, it was only because of the fine horses, two blood-bays and a lean, racebred black. They crossed the railroad tracks west of the bridge, the ironshod hooves of the horses clinking momentarily over the graveled road-bed. They were on the bridge, then, the hoof noises changing to the muffled ka-lunking of calked iron on worn wooden planking.

Directly, they were into Bridge Square, and still the horses walked, not hurrying, not nervous, but firm and chop-stepping under the steady hands that held them down.

Across the square lay Division Street, Northfield's main stem of business houses. On the southwest corner of Division Street, to their right, flanked by the mercantile establishments of Lee & Hitchcock and H. Scriver & Co., stood the First National Bank of Northfield. Straight ahead lay the hardware stores of J. S. Allen and A. E. Manning. To their left was Wheeler & Blackman's Drugstore.

Bringing his mount free of the square and turning him toward the bank, the man on the black made sweeping mental note of these stores and their locations. He nodded to his companions, turned the black in at the bank's hitching rail. Dismounting, the three tied their horses, walked deliberately away from the bank.

At Lee & Hitchcock's, they selected casual seats on the sidewalk dry-goods boxes provided for the purpose. One of them dug a bowie knife from beneath his linen duster, picked up a piece of wood, began to whittle and whistle as though he had ridden eight hundred miles for no other reason. The other two fell into a closemouthed conversation, their eyes darting constantly to the street that entered the square beyond the bank, and from the east.

Shortly, the smaller of the two stiffened.

"Yonder they come, Bob. Let's go."

Bob Younger looked up, saw Cole and Clell Miller slowly jogging their horses into Division Street from the east road. He nodded swiftly, passed the word to the third man. "Look sharp, Charlie. We're moving."

The whittler put away his knife, trailed off his monotonous whistle. "I'm right behind you," said Charlie Pitts. "Here goes nothing."

The three men walked quickly to the bank, entered it without looking again at the approaching horsemen.

Clell turned his mount in at the bank's hitching rail, tied him alongside the first three. He moved to the bank door, peered in, turned and waved to his companion. Cole waved back, swung off his tall bay in midstreet, began cuss-ing and tugging at a saddlegirth which was in perfectly good adjustment.

Clell stood squarely in front of the bank doors. There was no hurry in the way he unbuttoned the linen duster, hitched carelessly at the heavy Colts beneath it.

Jesse's Big Plan was running easy as gun-oil through a smooth-bore musket.

At least it was—outside the bank.

Inside the bank, the oil was hitting a few rust pits.

Hard at work, as Jesse and his two henchmen entered the building, were Joseph Lee Heywood, bookkeeper and acting cashier, A. E. Bunker, teller, and F. J. Wilcox, assistant bookkeeper. Heywood, new to his job and overanxious to please, moved unctuously from his desk to meet the strangers. His eager smile ended in a startled gasp.

The Colt passbooks had come out.

"Throw up your hands," said Jesse quietly. "And don't holler out. I've got forty men outside this bank. You're the cashier, aint you?"

Heywood denied it.

Jesse turned to Wilcox and Bunker in turn. Each shook his head.

Jesse nodded.

When he turned again to Heywood, he was beginning to blink. "I know a cashier when I see one," he said. "Open that Goddamn safe or I'll blow your head off." He did not say the last part of it—he snarled it.

"I can't open it," the cashier pleaded. "It's got a Barden Timelock on it."

Jesse stepped back, nodding to Pitts and Bob.

They seized Heywood, Pitts slashing him across the face with his pistol barrel, Bob hurling him bodily against the vault and jamming his Colt into his belly.

"You still got a Barden Timelock on that safe?" asked Jesse.

Heywood nodded stubbornly.

Pitts moved in, shoved his Colt an inch from his cheek. The powder blast tore open Heywood's face, ripped away his right ear.

"How about it?" said Jesse.

Heywood shook his lacerated head.

"Work on him," growled Jesse to Pitts. "Come on, Bob. Let's get the other two."

In fearful turn, Bunker and Wilcox had nothing to say. The bandits pistol-whipped them to their knees. The answer was the same. The safe was timelocked. "Keep working on yours," Jesse yelled to Pitts. "We'll git an answer somewheres, by God."

At the precise moment of his furious order to Pitts, inside the bank, fate was moving in on Jesse from along Division Street, outside it. And she was grinning a little as she moved, thinking perhaps of Jolly Wynmore.

Like Jolly, Henry M. Wheeler was also a nineteen-year-old college student. Home on summer vacation from Michigan University, at the moment Cole Younger swung off his bay to begin fussing with his saddlegirth, he was talking with J. S. Allen in front of the latter's hardware store. And, again like Jolly Wynmore, Henry Wheeler was quick of eye, wide of curiosity.

"Now, why the heck you suppose that man in the long duster is fooling so long with that strap? And what nerve, eh? Stopping right in the middle of Division. Say—" For the first time, he noticed Clell. "Look yonder. There's another of them standing by the bank door. Same coat and all. Now that *is* funny."

"Henry, my boy—" Allen had seen Jesse and Bob and Pitts ride up earlier—"there's more here than meets the eye. You set tight."

With the order, he moved down the street toward the bank. Coming up the sidewalk unhurriedly, he turned in at the bank as though to enter on business. Clell grabbed him, spun him into the wall, flashed a Colt into his stomach.

"Hold still and keep your Goddamn mouth shut," he ordered.

J. S. Allen was no college boy. He got a knee into Clell's groin, leaped away and back up the street. J. S. Allen had many talents, among them a fine bass voice. And the guts to use it.

"They're robbing the bank, boys! Get your guns! Get your guns!"

At the signal, the watching Wheeler was off across the square. He was a two-letter trackman at the state university and had the lungs to go with the legs that proved it.

"Robbery! Robbery at the bank! They're at the

bank! They're robbing the bank!"

In the center of the street, Cole watched the boy go. He had a clear, close shot at him and did not move to take it. There would never be a Jolly Wynmore for Cole Younger.

He swung up on his bay, deliberately blocking Clell's fire as the latter began to cut down on the fleeing youth. Wheeler was safely away in a matter of seconds and, in the confusion of his flight, Allen had made it back into his hardware store.

Business shortly grew brisker along Division Street.

Until this moment there had been only five outlaws on the scene. Now, in seeming answer to the gunfire, three more linen-dustered horsemen swung their mounts out of a side street and raced them for the bank.

As they did, Clell and Cole began wheeling their horses up and down Division Street, raking the storefronts with Colt slugs, the latter's huge voice bellowing belated advice to the dumbstruck civilians.

"Get in! Get in! Get off the street, Goddamn it!"

On the heels of his bass roar, Frank, Bill Chadwell and Jim Younger came up with a rush, adding the dreaded Missouri guerrilla yelps and their own revolver fire to the crash of the storefront glass and bedlam of citizen shouts already shattering the afternoon stillness of Northfield's main stem.

The walls of the First National Bank of Northfield were no more soundproof than were the cracking nerves of the three desperadoes within them.

Charlie Pitts wheeled, startled.

"Jesus Christ!" he shouted. "They're on to the boys outside!"

With the words, he slashed Heywood squarely across the eyes with his .44 barrel, knocking him senseless. The next instant he was leaping to join Bob and Jesse where they still held Bunker and Wilcox against the teller's counter.

At the sound of the outer gunfire, Jesse kicked the kneeling Wilcox in the genitals. With the bookkeeper spasming in agony, he turned to Bob. "This here bastard don't know nothing. How about yours?"

Bob seized Bunker, lifting him to his feet.

"All right, mister. Where's the money *outside* the safe? This here's the last time around, friend. Where's the cashier's till?"

Bunker gestured toward a cash drawer. Bob, producing Cole's wheatsack, ripped the drawer open. In it were less than a hundred dollars. He threw the pitiful flutter of bills into the sack, whirled, white-faced, on Bunker.

"There's more money! Where the hell is it? This aint the cashier's till, you bastard."

He leaped at the teller before he could answer.

"Get back down on your knees, Goddamn

263

you! Who told you to stand up?" The pistol barrel slashed and Bunker collapsed. Bob had him by the shirtfront before he hit the floor, the big Colt stabbing into his battered face. "Show me that till, you son of a bitch, or I'll kill you!"

Watching them, Jesse suddenly grimaced. "Leave go of the bastard. We'll find it ourselves."

They had no sooner turned from him than Bunker, hysterical with pain, leaped to his feet and ran for the rear door of the bank.

Pitts fired and missed, ran cursing after him. He fired again, down the outer alley. The bullet smashed through Bunker's shoulder but did not drop him. The bookkeeper staggered clear of the bank corner and around it to safety.

Pitts ran back through the bank, shouting wildly, "The game's up—he's got clean away!" At the front door he leaped back as a rifle slug smashed a pane and ricocheted into the vault ceiling. "Pull out!" he yelled at the motionless Jesse. "For God's sake, pull out, Jess. They're killing our boys outside!" With the yell, he ducked and ran through the door into the street, both Colts blasting.

"I'm gone, Jess." Bob's calm nod went to the still unmoving Jesse. "They'll have us treed in another ten seconds." He vaulted the teller's counter, slid out his second Colt, shot his way into the street, after Pitts.

Jesse came slowly around the counter, moving as though bewildered. He started for the door, stopped halfway, stared around him. He stood there, swaying unsteadily, eyes reddened, the salt water of blind rage running from them.

His voice came up in his throat like an animal's at bay, thick, wild, senseless, terrifying without formed words. At the base of the vault to his left, something stirred, caught at his vacant stare. It was Heywood.

Dazedly recovering consciousness, the cashier staggered drunkenly to his feet, weaved toward the door. Instantly, Jesse was behind him.

The single shot, powder-blasted from a range of inches, struck behind the cashier's right ear and exited above his left eye, blowing away his face. There were still no human words in the snarl, as his murderer shoved Heywood's falling body out of his path and ran, stumbling, for the door.

Outside, he stepped into a hell's heat of aroused-citizen fire.

Allen's Hardware was, by sanguinary fate, Northfield's principal gunstore. From the moment of his escape from Clell, the coolheaded merchant had begun issuing new rifles and boxed ammunition to his fellow townsmen. By the time Jesse reached the street, no less than thirty men were firing at his trapped followers.

And they had had ten precious minutes to pick firing points within the shelter of half a dozen strategic buildings.

Then, as Jesse burst out of the bank, the first Northfieldian fell. He was an unarmed, noncombatant laborer, and was literally torn apart

265

by bandit bullets as he ran for cover. His sense-less execution was the spark that blew up Northfield.

Enraged, one of his armed fellow townsmen ran out onto the sidewalk, blasted a shotgun charge at point-blank range into Clell Miller. Clell, now mounted up with Charlie Pitts, guarding Jesse's and Bob's horses, reeled in the saddle. The charge struck him full in the chest and face. Spraying blood, he fought blindly for leather, found the horn, stayed in the saddle. Jesse and Bob were now both clear of the bank, crouching behind their tied horses, fighting furiously at the knotted reins.

In the interim, death struck right and left among the raiders.

Bill Chadwell, riding between Frank and Jim Younger, took a .44-.40 Winchester through the heart. He slid out of the saddle so quietly his companions did not know he had been hit until his riderless horse galloped past and ahead of them.

Clell Miller, still streaming blood from the pock-blast of the birdshot, kicked his horse away from the bank's hitchrail, abandoning Bob and Jesse to the closing crowd. A Civil War Spencer boomed from the window of Allen's Hardware. The .50-caliber ball passed through both lungs, severing an artery. Clell struck the dirt of Division Street, "flopped around like a crazy chicken and died right there in front of the bank."

Frank took a .38 Smith and Wesson through the right calf. Cole was weaving in the saddle, shot in shoulder and thigh with heavy-caliber rifle balls. Both were still mounted when Jesse, at last freeing his black from the rail, hammered toward them.

At the hitching rack, Bob, desperately wounded, right arm shattered from wrist to elbow by two Spencer slugs, his horse shot dead in his tracks, shouted after his leader.

"Wait up, Jess, wait up! They got my horse!"

His plea drew only heavier fire from the advancing citizen snipers. Crouching, he drew his left-hand Colt and ran back into the shelter of the bank entrance.

Across from the bank now, Pitts and Jim Younger raced up to join Cole and Frank, Pitts unwounded, Jim sacked in the saddle from a belly-to-back shot, just missing his left kidney. An instant later, Jesse slid his neighing black in among them.

"It's no use, boys!" he screamed. "We got to get out. They'll kill us all."

"All right, which way?" shouted Frank.

"The way we come. It's the only one we know. West, over the bridge. Back to Millersburg."

Watching him, seeing the white paste of his face beneath the running eyes, hearing the hysterical shrill in his breaking voice, Cole felt his expression go dead blank. He drove his bay forward, shouldering him into the black. As he did, the last of the thin thread stretching across

the boyhood years to Pleasant Grove, and beyond, snapped.

"Hold up, Dingus," he said flatly. "How about
Bob?"

"The hell with Bob!" The hysteria rose in
pitch. "He's done for, bad hit. We caint get to
him. There aint no horse for him, no how!"

Cole reined the bay, back, stared at him.

"*You bastard*," he said quietly.

He drove the bay away from them, then,
straight toward the bank, standing in the stirrups, roaring to his brother, "Run out, Bob, run
out!"

He was hit twice more through the body before he slid his mount up to the bank. They saw
his big back twist and buck to the slugs as they
tore into him. And they saw him reach the staggering Bob, seize him and swing him up behind
him.

The powerful bay, lurching under the nearly
four hundred pounds, drove back across Division Street toward the bunched riders. He was
too slow. Another rifle slug cut into Cole, his
fifth in as many minutes. Still, he would not fall.
He was upright in the saddle when he brought
the bay up.

"All right," he grunted to the white-faced
Jesse. "*Now* let's get out. Bob's got his horse."

# Chapter Eleven

*Madelia*

They rode south, keeping to the main road, knowing no other, each of their racing minds turning hopelessly on the same, single thought.

The one thing which could have happened to the master plan, the one thing Jesse had failed miserably to foresee and figure against, had happened.

*Bill Chadwell was gone.*

The one man upon whom their leader's whole involved complex of planned retreat had so foolishly depended lay staring-eyed dead in the dust of Division Street. And dead with him lay the last, best chance of any man among them leaving Minnesota alive.

The thought hammered at them constantly, never leaving them from the first minute, never letting them rest, setting their jaws, slitting their dust-reddened eyes, chaining their tongues, driving them onward in heavily building silence.

They were in a strange land. All roads looked alike. It was a deadly, flat land, thickly timbered, cross-cut by a dozen small streams, blind-trapped with a hundred uncharted lakes. No least elevation was to be gained from which to route a course or determine the proximity of pursuit, front or rear. Posse behind, ambush ahead. Armed farmer to the right, enraged villager to the left. Angle east, angle west, double back north, or thunder on south. Who was left to say, now? Who among them any longer knew right from left, or north from south? Or road from road?

*Chadwell*, thought Cole. Chadwell knew. Dingus's precious little Bill Chadwell, *he knew*. But Chadwell was dead!

The big outlaw laughed aloud. The strange sound swung the frightened eyes of the others toward him. He laughed again, full into their startled faces. They looked away. None of them asked why he laughed. None of them cared to ask. Or dared to.

The village of Dundas, three miles south of Northfield, loomed ahead. They rode through it, their horses five abreast, their carbines naked in the afternoon sun, the blood-soaked Bob mounted double behind his towering brother. A few people stared curiously. No one challenged them. Incredible luck had foreridden the fleeing bandits.

The news of Northfield was already chattering the Dundas telegraph key. But the key chattered alone. The telegrapher was away, absent from his board on a half-hour errand!

In Millersburg, reached at 4:00 P.M., the preposterous luck held. The regular telegrapher was at home, sick in bed. His assistant had locked the key open, gone down to the Little Cannon River to try for a fat autumn wall-eye or frying-pan bass.

More curious gaped; more good citizens stared. And, again, no more. Not a hand was raised, not a question called.

South of Millersburg now. One mile. Two. Nearly five. No sign of pursuit. And the incalculable luck of the damned was still holding.

Younger met one farmer and relieved him of a fine horse. A second mounted native was encountered and lightened of the load of his saddle. Bob Younger was mounted again.

For the first time since leaving Northfield, there were sound horses all around.

Twilight came quickly on. Ahead lay twelve hours of darkness. Twelve hours which, with any reasonable continuance of their unbelievable luck, could take them fifty miles and more toward freedom. Tired muscles relaxed, jawlines eased. A little talk began.

But luck was done with them.

Six miles from Millersburg, Bob Younger's

borrowed saddle parted its girth. The tall youth fell heavily in the darkness, crushing his injured arm beneath him. He remembered the bursting shock of the pain, and nothing more.

Cole took him in his arms, like a great, blood-smeared child, carrying him unconscious before him as he rode. A mile later, a turn of the Madelia Road was missed in the darkness. Two A.M. found them in a trackless tangle of second-growth pine. No moonlight penetrated the matted timber. The only sounds they heard were those of the suck and pull of their horses' feet floundering to move ahead through the pothole bogland their riders had blundered them into. Within the hour, the fine drizzle which had been falling since dusk built into a driving rain. The air turned suddenly frost-cold.

Man and mount had had enough.

The men fell from their saddles into the muck and the mud of the swampgrass, not moving from where they dropped. The horses stood where their sodden reins fell, hipshot, hollow-flanked, rumps to the hammering slant of the rain. The storm closed in then, the rain sluicing down, the wind crying aloud in its buffeting rise. Soon even the bulking forms of the horses grew indistinct, shortly were blotted out altogether.

It was 3:00 A.M., Friday, September 8. The Great Northfield Raid was twelve hours old. Jesse and his men had ridden an incredible sixty-five miles since thundering out of Division

Street and across the Cannon River Bridge, the last forty miles of it at a staggering hand-gallop through the pitch-blind dark!

And the pothole swamp where their shivering mounts now stood over them, awaiting the first dripping gray of coming daylight?

It lay exactly *fourteen* crowflight miles south of Northfield, Minnesota.

By nightfall of the 7th, two hundred men were in the field against the gang, with more swarming out by the hour. And the complexion of the pursuers was altering swiftly from the disorganized crowd of embattled townfolk and shotgun-armed farmers which had taken up the chase in the immediate hours of the robbery.

The police chiefs of Minneapolis and St. Paul, accompanied by squads of their cities' detectives, were en route to the scene by train. Every county sheriff in southeastern Minnesota was out, backed by his regular deputies and scores of sworn-in civilians. From St. Paul, Omaha and Chicago the Pinkerton operatives poured in. Robert Pinkerton took personal command, with brother William coordinating the campaign from the Chicago headquarters.

The gang had been positively identified within an hour of the robbery, as soon as the telegraph key clicked southward to Mankato. The Mankato sheriff woke up with a belated start, realized what he had slept through, wired the St. Paul police the illuminating details of his dereliction of duty the morning of the 2nd.

273

The startling dispatch ran the telegraph wires of southern Minnesota like wildfire.

"It's the James gang. The James and the Youngers. Track them down. Shoot on sight. Block the roads. They must not escape. Minnesota must not become Missouri."

With the end of the second day, September 8, there were no less than five hundred armed peace officers and enlisted civilians combing the back roads and timbered crosslands for the fleeing bandits. And by the end of that day, pickets were posted at all bridges, known river-fordings, county roads, state highways, back trails and cowpaths in a sprawling semicircle roughly twenty miles south of Northfield, and stretching fifty miles east and west. Missouri was sealed off.

But was it?

Since the last report from outside Millersburg, the gang had vanished without a trace.

Then, suddenly, at noon of the 8th, came a report from a picket post on the Little Cannon River, outside Watersville. Earlier that morning, the bandits had approached the ford. The pickets had fired, the bandits fled back into the woods. Apparently, they were badly frightened. The pickets charged into the timber after them—which was clearly what they had been meant to do. The gang doubled easily back around them and crossed the abandoned ford unmolested.

These farmers had something to learn about

treeing the wily Missouri coon. And the bandits were across their first Rubicon, the Little Cannon. The picket line had been broken through before it was well set up.

But the enemy was learning.

The Northfield area was cleared out and a new line set up, fifty miles to the south and nearly a hundred miles long from point to point.

Then the electric news again.

Late Friday afternoon, the fugitives had invaded a farmhouse north of German Lake, had taken fresh horses at pistol point, pounded on their way. Instantly, a score of posses closed on the area. They had them now. This time they *were* sealed off. They knew where they had been within the hour. It would be impossible for six horsemen to break through the German Lake surround. Night fell before the trap could be sprung. Confidently, the pursuers bivouacked in barn and farmhouse throughout the quarantined area.

Thirty-six hours of rain, an incessant fall since Thursday evening, would have every road and trail an impassable morass for men on horseback before dawn of the 9th. Throughout the region, the streams were on the rise, more becoming unfordable with each downpouring hour. Come daylight, the chase would be over.

At least, so reckoned the excited posse leaders stationed that night at German Lake.

They reckoned without Jesse James.

*    *    *

The outlaw camp was in a tangled, brackish lowland, six miles east of German Lake. It was a far and lonely cry from what his followers had come to expect of Jesse's charmed leadership.

No cheery campfire, here. No rough guffaws and back-house jokes over the division of the loot. No fresh, highly trained Missouri horses munching their rolled oats on the picket line, waiting to carry their dashing riders airily away from the slow mounts of a half-partisan posse of fellow relatives. No booming laughs from Cole. No dry-blinked, acid humor from Jesse. No scholarly bit from the Bard of Avon or pointed inspiration of quoted scripture from Frank.

Here was no canopy of warm southern stars, no couch of pungent, dry-wool horseblanket, no well-remembered road stretching comfortably across the certainty of tomorrow, into the blessed safety of Clay County and the Little Blue.

This was Minnesota not Missouri.

The horseblankets hung from the gaunt bushes, leaking more rain than they shed. Beneath them, cold, sick, wet to the shaking bone, crouched the six survivors. Bob was out of his head with the fever and pain of his shattered arm. Cole hunched over him, muttering and growling like the wounded grizzly he was, fighting off the torture of his own wounds as he mothered his raving brother. Beyond them, close enough to touch in the darkness, huddled Frank, Jim and Charlie Pitts. Beneath another bush, ten feet away, alone and invisible through the sheeting rain, Jesse stared out into the blackness.

Presently, he arose, felt his way, tree trunk by tree trunk, to the tethered horses.

His clasp knife slashed quickly in the gloom, severing the reins of the first mount. Above the pelting drip of their blankets, the others heard his snarled "Hee-hay-yahh! Hee-yahhh!" and the answering smack of muddy hooves and startled neighs crashing away through the showering foliage.

"What the Goddamn hell!" rasped Cole, blundering to his feet.

"It's the horses!" blurted Charlie Pitts. "The crazy idjut's cutting the horses loose. Jess! Jess! For Christ' sake, Jess—!"

"Shut your damn mouth." Jesse's form loomed through the downpour, shouldered in under the horseblankets.

"Jess, what in the name of hell you think you're doing?" It was Pitts again, still incredulous.

"I said, shut up. We're getting out of here."

"But the horses! God Amighty, man!" Now it was Jim Younger, towering over him, eyes blazing. "You lost your Goddamn mind or something?"

"It aint my 'Goddamn mind' I'm thinking of, mister. *It's my lousy life.*"

The flat way he said it, the sudden dropping of the high-voiced snarl into the low, tight growl, carried to Cole through the darkness. He caught Jim's shoulder, forcing him back down.

"Set down," he said. "Leave him get on with it." And then, softly: "Dingus always has a plan."

Cole, like the others, even more than they, perhaps, sensed the disaster Northfield had brought upon them. In the extremity of its black hour, he drew for the last time to Jesse's side.

His plea to the others was a voice out of the past, an echoing, hollow voice, perhaps, and late in the night. But it sounded the shadow of a faith which had endured from Old Man Pettis's corn patch to Muncie's mailbags. Somehow the others sensed it, realized that in the darkness the wounded giant had come again to stand beside his leader. Feeling it, they took strength from it, and from Cole. They obeyed him instinctively, waited for Jesse to speak.

He let them wait a long time.

When he talked at last, it was the old Jesse: quick, fast-worded, absolutely sure of himself and of his plan.

"They figure they've got us treed." he began. "That we caint run no more. Well, they figure right. We caint *run* no more. But by God, we can *walk*!"

He paused, dramatically, then swept on.

"You remember what they used to call 'Old Jack's' boys during the war?" The reference was to Stonewall Jackson and his famed Shenandoah Valley infantry brigade. His listeners understood it, nodded dully.

"Foot cavalry!" rapped Jesse. "That's what, by God. He'd take them boys sometimes thirty miles in a night, and they'd go where horse troops couldn't begin to. The bluebellies never got onto it.

"Well, we got bluebellies after us, here. They got nothing but horsemen on their side and they aint looking for nothing but horsemen on ours. We'll just walk out on them—that's all. By God, we can do it and I mean to do it. Once through them, on foot, we can grab new horses somewheres and be long gone. We aint no more than one good night's ride from the Ioway line right now. And Shank's mare will start us over it. I'm done talking and I'm pulling out, now. Afoot."

As Jesse had gone along, Cole's gray eyes had narrowed. When he had finished, he had a single question, one he had asked before.

"How about Bob?" he said. "He caint walk to keep up with the rest of us."

Jesse turned on him, his plan having already foreseen that query. "I left three of the horses tied. I *figured* you to take Jim and Bob and pull out on me. Help yourselves."

"You figured wrong," said Cole. "We're sticking with you, Ding. You walk, we walk."

"Damn it, Cole. Bob will slow us down. I mean to march far. It's our only chance."

"Jim and me will see he don't slow you down," nodded Cole.

"You'd best see he don't," was all Jesse said. "Let's go."

Cole leaned down in the darkness. "Bob, you hear what we said?"

"Yeah—"

"You game to give her a whirl?"

"Help me up—"

"Jim. Get him on the other side."

"All right, I got him."

"You set, Bob?"

"I'm set," the youngster gritted.

"Let's go," Cole said softly to Jesse. "*And don't forget who's behind you.*"

They marched all of Friday night, hid away the daylight hours of Saturday on a tiny swamp isle. With dark they moved again, plowing the night away through the calf-deep mire of the lowlands. Sunday there was another, interminable, fireless camp, so close to the hamlet of the Marysburg they could hear the church bells tolling the sun down.

Darkness again at last. They stumbled on.

Shortly before ten o'clock they blundered on an outlying hencoop. They caught three of the chickens before the baying of the farmer's dog sent them back into the endless swamp. The fowl were torn bodily in half, devoured raw— the first food in forty-eight hours. Bob could not make it, vomiting on his second mouthful. Cole ate Bob's share on top of his own, forcing the slimy, raw flesh down, locking his jaw to keep it there. His strength *had* to be fed.

They went on, homing more certainly now that a half-hour hole in the scudding clouds had shown them the north star, briefly.

At 2:00 A.M., three miles north of Mankato, they reached an abandoned farmhouse. Human flesh could stand no more. They had been on the retreat four days and three nights, were still less than fifty miles from Northfield. But the last thirty of those had been covered in fifteen hours, on foot, with no food other than the sickening flesh of three summer-molted Dominicker hens. Stonewall Jackson would have been proud.

But safety was still a far bell, beckoning in the distance from a reef of disaster.

The torrential rains sluiced on.

You can still hear about that rain in Northfield. Beginning on the night of the robbery, it fell steadily for twelve consecutive days. By the time Joose and his men reached the Mankato farmhouse, every tributary stream in southern Minnesota was out of its banks. They were cut off at last, not by any cordon of human pursuers, but by an impassable posse of swollen creeks and flooded lowlands.

The halt was called.

All day Monday, Monday night, and Tuesday until dusk, they stayed inside the house. Charlie Pitts and Frank James forayed out late Tuesday night, returned with five more chickens. This time a small fire was risked. Bob had to eat.

Cole tore out the living room partition with his bare hands, kindled the blaze in the center of the front parlor floor. The molding horseblankets were hung across the paneless windows, their owners sleeping uncovered on the pine floor. There was no dissent. By now the light of a fire meant more to the inner man than did the warmth of a wet blanket to the outer.

The last of the chicken was rationed out and recooked at dusk, Wednesday. The bones were cracked and marrow sucked to the wingtip, the shanks and scaly feet eaten to the toenail. They awaited full night, strengthened by the food and the sheltered respite from the incessant rain. After an hour, Jesse said he was "going out on a scout," and that "some action would be taken on his return." He then talked guardedly to Frank for five minutes, and left.

They waited his return with mixed feelings.

Frank had not said ten words since leaving Northfield. Pitts and Jim Younger had been equally glum. Bob was still irrational with fever and none in the dreary room but knew he had traveled his last mile.

Cole, the indomitable, still stood head and shoulders the tallest of them all.

Since saying he would walk with Jesse, he had done just that. If a man stumbled in the dark, it was Cole who helped him up, who slapped his muddy buttocks and grinned him on. If a path was lost in the rain and Jesse hesitated in the lead, it was Cole who moved up beside him, pointing the way. "Left, Ding, she appears to open out thataway." Or, "Take the right fork. She bears southwest and that's our line." And, again, "Straight ahead, Dingus. That's Missouri wind a-blowing, boy! Caint you smell it? We aint far to go now."

No, it was not Bob alone that the big outlaw had carried those last miles. He had carried them all.

But as they waited now their thoughts were not on Cole. Nor on what lay behind.

They were on Jesse and what lay ahead.

Where was he? What was he doing out there in the rain? Why had he *really* left? What was keeping him?

Even as they wondered, Jesse returned.

He said he had gone down to the farm where Frank and Charlie had got the chickens. He had had no trouble finding it from Frank's directions. Down there, he had stalked the farmer to the barn, meaning to take him from behind and force him to bring them up some food, and some bandages for Jim and Cole and Bob. But as he was about to make his move, a posse had ridden into the barnyard. The men were from Mankato. What they had to say stopped any idea of jumping the farmer. Jesse had been so close he had heard every word.

The German Lake surround had just closed in on the three tied horses they had left behind.

The word now was that Jesse and his men had walked out of the trap, had a long, four-day start, were undoubtedly out of the state and safely on their way to Missouri by this time.

The Pinkertons and a few odd posses of die-hard local deputies were still on the lookout for them, but the big bulk of the more than one thousand men who had been in the field as of Sunday night had given up and gone home. There had been more, but Jesse had not waited to hear it. He had already heard more than any of them could ever have hoped for.

"Boys!" he concluded, eyes flicking savagely. "We've got one chance now. *One chance*!"

"Damn if it don't look like we aint," breathed Pitts. "Looks like if we can get horses now, we're as good as home. You spot any down yonder? Frank said something about a nice pair of grays—"

Jesse shot a sidelong glare at his brother. "Frank's off his head," he shrugged, recovering quickly. "Them grays wasn't no good. The posse took them along, anyways. They was their horses and was left there by them, Saturday. Besides," he paused, blinking irritably, "I aint talking about horses. You hear?"

"What are you talking about, Dingus?"

Cole put the question quietly, not liking the way Jesse's eyes were working, nor the corners of his mouth pulling in.

"You know what I'm talking about," he said. "*It's Bob*."

284

Cole shot his glance to the corner where his brother lay half-consciously dozing. "What about Bob?" he said. "And keep it down. He's most asleep."

"We caint make it toting him."

Jesse said it flatly. Seeing the look in Cole's eyes, he struggled lamely to qualify it.

"We done already wasted four days on him, Cole. We could have been in Adair by this time. He's got to stay here. We can send some farmer back to pick him up, once we're clean away. He'll be all right here. We can leave him some water and all the blankets."

Cole let him finish it, trying to see his side of it, knowing, too, that the others must be thinking the same thing, or close to it.

"All right," he said at last. "You all go on. But I caint do it. I caint leave him here, bad hurt and by himself. You go along—that's only fair. Me and Jim will stick with Bob and bring him along as best as we can. We'll try to stay with you, near as we can manage. But we aint leav ing him "

"You got to," rasped Jesse. "One way or the other. We caint have him tagging along no more."

"What the hell do you mean, *one way or the other*?"

Cole stood up slowly.

"Just what I said," snapped Jesse. "He stays right here. Dead or alive."

The big outlaw shook his head, his voice

never varying its level monotony. "You don't mean that, Dingus. You don't mean you'd actually do that. To put a bullet in a man that's backed you since he was a boy."

"Comes to my life or his," said Jesse evenly, "you Goddamn well lay I mean it."

Cole stepped back. The flicking slide of his right hand caught them all off guard. The big Colt glinted dully in the dying light.

"Jesse, get out."

None of them had ever heard him use the name before. They stood waiting now, not believing what their eyes saw, nor accepting what their ears heard.

*"Get out before I kill you."*

Jesse's guns were holstered at his sides. He still had his Winchester in his hands from the scouting of the farm. He made no move for the Colts, did not lift the carbine.

"Turn around," said Cole, "and walk out."

Jesse looked at Frank.

"Frank—?"

"I'm coming," Frank said and stood up.

"Anybody else?"

It was Cole's turn now, his eyes never leaving Jesse. Nobody answered, nobody moved.

"Once you're through that door," he said, "don't never let me see you again."

Jesse turned for the door. Frank hesitated, stepping toward Cole. "Bud, for God's sake what are you doing? Wait a minute now, all of you. We can still—"

286

"Get out, Buck. You go with him. It's your job now. You can read up on it in the Book of Genesis. Four: Nine," he added softly.

"*Am I my brother's keeper?*" murmured Frank.

Cole nodded, waiting. Frank looked at him. He did not drop his eyes as Jesse had. "I'm sorry, Cole. I reckon you know that."

"I reckon."

Frank looked away from him, to Jesse, waiting at the door. Just before he turned to follow him he nodded, low-voiced, to Cole, "*All that a man hath, will he give for his life.*"

Watching them go, Cole returned the quotation, hard-faced. If Frank heard it, he did not look back. He was, indeed, his brother's keeper, and his brother was already gone.

It was the last Cole Younger ever saw of Jesse James.

He stood staring after him a long time. At last he said it, very softly and to himself:

"I ought to have killed him. I ought to have killed him a long, *long* time ago—"


A hundred yards from the farmhouse, the brush closed behind Frank and Jesse. As it did, the latter whirled on his older brother, eyes blinking furiously.

"You damn ninny, you near fixed it for sure!"

"Fixed what? What are you talking about?" Frank stammered his genuine bewilderment.

"The grays, you damn idjut. You told them about the grays!"

"What if I did, Jess? What are you getting at?" Frank's puzzlement held for another brief moment. Even as it did, he had his answer in the cold spread of Jesse's grin. "Jess! For the luvva God, you weren't lying about them grays?"

"Don't preach to me, Frank. Save it for Cole. There's two horses and there's you and me. It's why I come back from the barn at all—to tell you that we was going out, just the two of us. Cole only made it easy—that's all."

Frank nodded. There was no more room for words. Nothing more to be said. Jesse had said it all. The latter, not even waiting for his brother's nod, had already turned and started through the brush again. Frank followed him. Jesse always had a plan. You could take it or leave it.

The rain, sheeting down with renewed sullenness, hid them from view within seconds. An hour later they were five miles away, guiding the stolen mounts due west. Seventy-two hours later they had crossed the South Dakota line and were free.

There is no documentation existing for the seven days of inner hell which must have followed for the Cole and the others. The trail picks up exactly one week after Jesse's defection, at a point outside the remembered village of Madelia. Four facts are known concerning those seven days.

The hue and cry after the Northfield fugitives, which had almost died down following the discovery of their tied horses at German Lake, burst into full clamor again with the news of the theft of the two gray horses near Mankato and the subsequent, successful dash of those two grays and their riders through a picket-line post on the Crystal Lake Road west of the latter town.

The four outlaws remaining in the abandoned Mankato farmhouse left that refuge some time during the morning of Thursday, September 14th, within hours after Jesse and Frank had fled it.

Early the following Thursday morning, September 21, they were sighted crossing the dairy pasture of the Suborn farm, near Madelia, by the farmer-owner's seventeen-year-old son, Oscar.

Madelia is a bare twenty-five miles southeast of Mankato.

Twenty-five miles in seven days and nights! Twenty-five miles through a land as strange to them as the outer surfaces of the moon. Averaging but a little better than three miles in each twenty-four hours, and this over a region again swarming with the hornets' nest of official posses and rural pickets stirred up by Jesse's desertion. Yet they were not once seen until that fatal morning outside Madelia!

Then, following Oscar Suborn's reported sighting of the fugitives, posses from Madelia and nearby St. James surrounded the farm. Other posses moved quickly in from the east and south. Four hours after the first alarm, two hundred men were converging on Hanska Slough, the latest reported sighting of the fleeing outlaws.

Hanska Slough was in reality a backed-up side channel of the Watonwan River. Below the slough the channel spread out in a shallow, breast-deep swamp pond called Hanska Lake. Below the pond, the channel proper of the Watonwan.

First cry of fox was raised by the posse of Madelia's Sheriff Glispin. Prying along the west shore of Lake Hanska, he suddenly saw the fugitives struggling along through the mudflats about twenty yards out from his own, the west, bank of the lake. He waved his men to take cover in the reeds, cautiously studied the four outlaws.

All of them were unkempt and filthy, with heavy, rain-wet beards. Their clothes were shredded and ripped and the sheriff at once noted the absence of the famous linen dusters. The largest of the bandits, apparently their leader, was walking in front of the others, leaning heavily on a crutch-like stick. The two following the first man were nearly as large as he. One of them appeared badly wounded, for the other was supporting him bodily. Glispin now rose up out of the reeds and shouted the order to halt. He might as well have ordered the rain to cease falling. The bandits, waved on by the big man in the lead, ran for the shelter of a low mudbank. They got safely behind it, and the silence which ensued was more unnerving than any gunfire. Sheriff Glispin took the opportunity to reevaluate his position.

His posse was small, only five men. The mudflats were naked, offering no cover for an approach toward the waiting outlaws. The time for the kill, the Madelia officer at once decided, was not yet. His low orders to his men were as quick as they were wise: "Pull back, boys. We'd better wait for some of the others to come up."

In his terse, later explanation of the retreat, Glispin only remarked, "They were all mighty desperate-looking men, though the fourth one wasn't near as big as the others."

The Madelia sheriff might well have added that it was a chore beyond the capacities of most men to be as big as a Younger.

With the Madelia posse hesitating to close in, Cole led his followers in the only direction open to them—straight away from the west bank, out across the lake itself. Somehow, they made the crossing, wading, slipping, floundering, flailing through the deeper holes, but always keeping their precious Colts arm-high above the brackish waters. Quite apparently, in the closing desperation of the chase, the Missourians had abandoned their saddle-guns, preferring, in the final analysis, the classic handgun to the cumbersome carbine: "Todd's terrible revolver fighters" to the bitter end!

The horses of Glispin's possemen would not take the water, and hurriedly the sheriff ordered his followers south to the ford at the outlet of the pond. Here he led them across the Watonwan and at a hard gallop up the east shore. As they rode, he shouted them excitedly on, having deduced from the direction of the outlaws their big leader's east-bank objective: a herd of pastured saddlehorses grazing in a lakeside field.

It was a race of fresh horsemen against the failing time and strength of four exhausted men on foot, three of whom were desperately wounded. Glispin won it by a narrow margin, cutting between Cole and the pastured horses, just as the latter led his staggering band out of the water and up the east-bank mudflats.

Again the sheriff's cry to halt and surrender rang out.

The Missourians, caught on the naked flats, replied in the only tongue left them. It was a ragged, thin volley. But Cole's third shot raked the ribs of Glispin's horse. The stricken animal reared, throwing its rider. In the resulting confusion, the outlaws got back into the reeds of the lakeside, working through this cover down toward the outlet and shallow crossing of the Watonwan.

They reached the ford safely and across its

narrow channel beheld a sight of princely wealth: the hunting camp of a group of St. Paul sportsmen.

And in that camp, not a hundred yards from where they stood, were the hunters' four picketed saddlemounts—under leather, full-bridled, ready to ride!

Had Frank been at that moment on the east bank of the Watonwan, rather than with Jesse a miserable, safe hundred miles across the border of Dakota Territory, he might have quoted Richard III with touching point. As it was, the shrinking kingdom of Cole's Missourians was up for instant trade, Richard or no Richard.

"*Four horses*!" croaked the big outlaw hollowly, and plunged into the Watonwan.

Behind him came Jim and Charlie Pitts, dragging the cursing, weeping Bob between them. "Go on, go on!" sobbed the youngster. "For Christ's sake leave me be and get out yourselves. I caint ride, anyways!"

"Easy, boy," muttered Jim. "We'll make it now. See yonder, there! Cole's almost acrost!"

The wounded youth raised his head. Looked. Saw, Struggled desperately on. Cole *was* almost across!

But the gunfire up the lake had aroused the St. Paul hunters. When they saw the bearded, scarecrow apparitions rise up from the reeds across the river and plow toward them through its shallow channel, they acted in unquestioning accord. Cole had not yet reached the west bank before the camp was as innocent of hunter as it was of hunter's horse.

And Cole had not stood upon that west bank thirty seconds before his haggard glance told him that, with his crossing of the Watonwan, the Clay County Fox had brought his ragged pack to its last earth.

*They were trapped.*

The ground upon which they stood formed a five-acre triangle of wild grapevine, willow, box elder and plum. The triangle was based, behind them, by the head of Lake Hanska. To their right, it was sided by an impassable, thirty-foot bluff, to their left by the channel of the Watonwan.

The end came with merciful quickness.

Within minutes after the bandits entered the trap; the bluff-tops were crawling with possemen. Across the Watonwan, other scores of manhunters suddenly appeared. Their trap was boxed.

Cole came to bay in a heavy copse of grapevine and willow near the tip of the triangle. Here at least they had some protection from the field of fire afforded their enemies by the bluff above. And they could, with their own fire, cover the wide base of the triangle upriver from them.

He helped the others make a crude couch for Bob, turned with them to crouch and peer through the vines, waiting for the rest of it.

The waiting was singularly short. Its brevity was a tribute to the nerve and determination of a county sheriff whose name is known today only in Madelia, Minnesota.

Glispin could have waited for starvation to do his work for him. Instead, he selected six picked riflemen and closed in at once, on foot.

The skirmish line advanced across the base of the triangle in full view of the hidden outlaws.

At two hundred feet, the posse spotted a movement in the vines ahead. They hesitated and Cole's gun roared. Seven carbines crashed in reply. Pitts began firing now, and Jim. A fourth Colt crashed, and the possemen knew the wounded Bob Younger had somehow forced himself up and into the battle. Glispin's skirmish line moved straight in, braving the scattered revolver fire, answering it with ordered rifle volleys of their own. At point-blank range, later taped off as thirty feet, they fired their last rounds.

All sound had ceased within the grape thicket.

Then a vine moved suddenly.

From beneath it writhed the body of a man. He rolled to his knees, struggled to his feet, stood facing them. He was a mass of fresh blood but the big Colt still dangled from his left hand. His right hand was strapped in a dirty sling across his chest, and the blood on that hand was old and black and fly-encrusted.

"I surrender," whispered Bob Younger. "They're all down but me."

"Drop your gun, then," ordered Glispin.

The big fingers loosened. The gun slid from them. It struck a rock in falling, bounced into the sodden leaf-mold, lay there, still and dully gleaming under the raindrip of the thicket.

Bob followed it down, falling heavily as the posse moved forward.

"Keep your guns cocked, men," said Sheriff Glispin, and stepped over the motionless body of the young outlaw. Behind him, his possemen moved gingerly around the body, keeping their eyes on Glispin. They followed him into the thicket, fingers inside trigger guards, jaws hardset, carbine muzzles nervously probing the silent vines. All sensed the shadow of tension and fear falling ahead of that last, interminable moment. None sensed the deeper, longer shadow standing beyond it.

An era had died with the dropping of Bob Younger's gun.

What Glispin's men found in that Watonwan River thicket, as well as a priceless, last glimpse of Cole Younger at his grinning best, was supplied within the following grim minutes.

Inside the grapevine fortress Charlie Pitts lay dead, five bullets having done the job that several hundred had failed to do at Northfield. Bob Younger had a fresh, deep chest wound, in addition to the shattered wrist and right elbow sustained in the First National Bank ambush. Jim Younger, like Pitts, was carrying five rifle slugs, the last one of which had smashed his jaw and the whole lower half of his face into a shapeless pulp. Cole, the only one of the four still conscious, was bleeding from eleven separate wounds, at least six of which he had received within the past ten minutes.

In the words of an emotional James-Younger historian, "Thomas Coleman Younger, who looked like a bishop and fought like a bengal tiger, lay upon the ground soaked with the rainfall and with his own blood—and smiled as he saw approaching him Colonel Vought, proprietor of the Flander's House hotel in Madelia, where Cole and his brothers had stayed overnight previous to the Northfield Raid."

What the good colonel heard, as he stood staring down at his recent, well-remembered guest, may not belong in Cousin John Bartlett's collection of deathless quotations. It certainly belongs in any proper memory of the unquenchable head of the Younger clan.

Rearing himself up on his left elbow, Cole managed to sweep off his black hat with his mangled right hand. And managed, somehow, to do it with a flourish to match the white-faced smile that came with it.

"Good morning, landlord," grinned the big outlaw. "You'll excuse me for not getting up, but I've taken on quite a bit of weight since last we met, and do not feel so well."

Then, still grinning, and just before he
slumped, face forward, into the boot-churned
mud:

"How are *you*, sir—?"

The morning of the 23rd found the Youngers
held under heavy guard in their hospital-prison
rooms in Madelia's Flander's House, whence
Glispin had transported them by wagonbed following their capture on the Watonwan. Cole
and Jim shared one room and a single bed. Bob,
considered nearer death than either of his older
brothers, had been granted a room to himself.
The only person admitted to see them, other
than the several compassionate churchwomen
of Madelia who were acting as their clock-
around nurses, was a city reporter from the St.
Paul *Pioneer Press*.

Cole's only response to the latter's questions
was to ask him to express publicly the brothers'
thanks to the citizens of Madelia who had
treated them with such kindness. He added
simply that he was greatly surprised at the treat-
ment, and mighty grateful for it.

Jim, his multiple-fractured jaw horribly swollen and infected, could not speak. When offered
pencil and paper and asked to make any statement he might wish to reach the public, the second brother only shook his head and "turned
his poor, mutilated face to the wall."

Bob, though assumed to be dying, and perhaps because he agreed with the assumption,

talked with more freedom. Thanking the *Pioneer Press* man for a proffered cigar, he apologized for his shackled hands, asked politely for "the loan of a match."

With the panetella lit, he inhaled deeply of its fragrant smoke and calmly stated the terms in which he would ask posterity to remember him and his brothers.

To begin with, he nodded soberly, he and Cole and Jim were all grown men. They knew their situation perfectly well and were ready to abide its clear consequences. Naturally, they all regretted their situation, but they had chosen their own way of life and were not complaining about it.

He would not discuss the murder of Heywood, the Northfield cashier, beyond saying that the witnesses undoubtedly knew which of the bandits had shot him. Neither would he talk about the disappearance of Frank and Jesse James, nor admit they had ever been along in the first place. In the same line, he refused to identify any of his other outlaw companions. He was reluctant to say anything much about his own previous life, or the adventures of the gang prior to Northfield. About Northfield he spoke in detail, dwelling at particular length on the stark sufferings of the escape march.

He concluded by taking the full blame for the capture of his companions. Their loyal insistence on remaining with him had in his opinion cost them a freedom they could otherwise quite easily have won.

There the interview ended. The St. Paul reporter provided his own grim postscript to it:

"Sheriff Glispin will proceed to Faribault by way of Mankato, leaving here at 5:45 A.M. The body of the dead robber (Pitts) goes on the same train to be embalmed. The trip will be hard on these wounded men particularly the one shot in the jaw. He suffers much. The doctor here objected this morning to moving them but the men are plucky and said they will go along all right."

Under Minnesota law of the day, a confessed murderer could not be hanged. Cole, Jim and Bob, in turn, pleaded guilty to the principal charge: accessory to the murder of J. L. Heywood, cashier of the First National Bank of Northfield, Minnesota. Judge Samuel Lord sentenced them all to life imprisonment in the state penitentiary at Stillwater.

Just before the trial, and afterward, all three relented and spoke freely of their past crimes and present regrets. Each continued to insist in his grave, quiet way, however, that he and his brothers were victims of a troubled time and had been largely "drove to" their lives of crime. At no time did any of them, from the moment of his capture to the day of his death, admit the identities of the other five men who had been with them on the Northfield raid. They had come to the end of their road. They willingly admitted it had been a bad one. Past that, there were no further apologies, no added details or explanations.

The best farewell of the Youngers was spoken outside the walls of the Stillwater Prison, as they all stood before its waiting gate breathing deep of the last freedom's air and gazing, far-eyed, across the heads of the small crowd which had gathered to see them admitted.

It was Cole who spoke its major theme, young Bob who delivered its soft amen.

A Madelia lady, one of those who had nursed Cole through the hours of suffering at the Flander's House, broke forward impulsively in the final moment to tell him how glad and grateful she was that the brothers had fallen into her town's Christian hands and that they had all been so well taken care of.

Cole, his handsome face thin-drawn from the weeks of courtroom testimony and the unhealed torture of his wounds, still had one smile left. "I am grateful, too, ma'am," he said. "But I caint say that we deserve it—"

He paused, his eyes finding the horizon again, the slow smile fading. "Circumstances, ma'am, sometimes make men what they are. If it had not been for the war, I might have been something. As it is, I am only what I am."

And then, this wonderful valedictory from Bob, standing at his older brother's side, speaking softly to the thoughtful lady from Madelia, his eyes and inner memories as far away as Cole's:

*"We are rough men, ma'am, and are used to rough ways."*

# Chapter Twelve

*St. Joe*

Though it was to be delayed across a span of five sinister years, Jesse's end came as certainly as had Cole's—and with a poesy of justice, no olden minstrel ever sang truer words than these:

> The dirty little coward
> Who shot Mr. Howard,
> Has laid poor Jesse in his grave . . .

But in September of 1879, the forgotten Clay County bard who penned this most enduring of Dingus's epitaphs had not yet "gazed in silent tears into that lonesome box of pine," and the body of his bearded hero was yet many a long, hard month from growing cold, yet many a weary, hunted mile from the storied "little white house on the hill" in old St. Joe.

What of those three years since the gates of the Stillwater Prison had closed behind the last of the Youngers? Again, the long, silence, the gaping blind spot in the trail, this time stretching unbroken for three years and a month, to the day. The honeycombed warren of the borderground's earth had opened once more, had swallowed Frank and Jesse without a sound, or a single sight, or a solitary telltale track.

It is known that some time in the month following the Northfield raid Jesse and his Bible-quoting brother passed through Missouri. In the passing they collected their wives and children, their entire combined families leaving the home state "in the dead of the night and in a single, rickety covered wagon driven from Kansas City by their stepbrother, John Samuel."

Tradition has Jesse hiding in the wagon with the women and children while Frank outrode the perilous journey by saddlehorse. No man from Missouri likes to question his homeland's native legends. But it takes a little faith in local lore, together with a lot of innocence of Jesse's inherent wolfishness of character, to picture him cowering in a wagonful of women and children.

It is a safe assumption that where Frank's horse stepped during that flight, no matter how warily or far in the lead, he was stepping in the tracks of Jesse's black.

# Death Of A Legend

The files of the Pinkertons today disclose the amazing geography of that three-year hegira which began that dark night in Kansas City. During its wide-flung course, Frank and Jesse, always with their wives and children now, lived successively in Kentucky, Tennessee, California, Texas and Missouri. Jesse consistently used the name of Howard; Frank, the family surname of Woodson. So complete was Jesse's peculiarly faceless anonymity that at one point in the Pinkertons' unremitting pursuit of him "he entered and rode his own horse in the Nashville Races, with the fairgrounds alive with Pinkerton detectives and local law officers."

For all his crimes and the worldwide notoriety they had brought him, he was still a man without a face to his relentless trackers. The only picture ever made of him remained the one which "hung in the locket around his poor mother's neck."

It is not entirely beside the delightful point, for one who would remember the real Jesse, to recall that he not only entered and rode his own famous black in the Nashville Derby—*he won it*!

But if the point is, in its twisted Jamesian way, delightful, it is equally and by the same token singular.

It is the last recorded bit of Jesse's iron-veined sense of humor. Beyond this one small, pale-eyed smile, the trail turns exceeding grim.

With the passing of the third year, the considerable loot of the Rocky Cut robbery ran low. The pressure from the Pinkertons, successfully defied while the family funds were in relative abundance and could afford unrestricted bribery and safe passage across the land, mounted with sudden intensity. In September, 1879, three years to the month from the disaster at Northfield, a telegram went from Kansas City to the Chicago headquarters of William Pinkerton, now replacing his famous father as head of the agency. It was unsigned and consisted of five unqualified words: "HE IS BACK IN MISSOURI."

A thousand-word deposition over Jesse's own signature could not have told William Pinkerton more.

By now he knew his man and he knew his methods. Thirteen years on the trail drew instantly into spotlight focus. The beam fell mercilessly upon Clay and Jackson counties. Its operators held it there, silently, watchfully, still waiting with that enormous patience which was Pinkerton's, and with that deadly faith, which was also his, of the trained manhunter in the main creed of his dogged calling: *The criminal will always return to the scene of the crime*.

In the late twilight of October 7, 1879, Jesse "returned."

The scene was Blue Cut on the Chicago & Alton Railroad near Glendale, Jackson County, Missouri. There were six men in the gang. The old guerrilla method was employed.

The horses thundered into Glendale on the dead run. The rebel yells echoed, the Colts roared, the window glass crashed and fell. The employees at the depot were pistol-whipped, herded into and locked in the baggage room. The train was flagged down, boarded. William Grimes, the express messenger, sought valiantly and in vain to hide the thirty-five thousand dollars in his charge. He was beaten senseless and left for dead. The escape was as complete and successful as had been the assault. There was no attempt to "take the coaches."

At once, the Pinkertons pounced.

Witnesses by the score were dredged out of the Clay and Jackson county back country. Fearful testimony was given and taken in secret. The old immunity was broken and within twenty-four hours the Chicago office released a bulletin naming the new gang: Jesse James, Ed Miller, Wood Hite, Bill Ryan, Dick Liddell, Tucker Basham.

Searching that miserable roster, Frank James might have muttered, "Samuel. One: Twenty-seven. *'How are the mighty fallen!'* "

Where, indeed, were the magic names of old? The night-riding rebel faithful of Todd and Anderson and Quantrill? Where were Cole and Jim and Bob? And Jim Cummins, Clell Miller, Big George Shepherd and fierce-eyed brother Oll? Where, indeed, was Frank James himself?

The answers echo hollowly. Only the names respond. The men are gone.

But sorry crew or not, thirty-five thousand dollars in very real money were missing. And missing with that money, shadowy and swift as ever the old, glorious band was, were Jesse and his new recruits.

For months the border was quiet. Then a sudden, smoldering flare sprang to life.

Big George Shepherd, comrade of the "Bloody Bill" Anderson days, was released from the Missouri State Penitentiary. A legend came back to life, a forgotten era reincarnate, Big George strode briefly and shadow-tall across the darkening stage.

His last statement on entering prison had been to Yankee Bligh, the Pinkerton detective who had trailed and jailed him, following the Russelville robbery. "I don't know any of the men who were with me," Big George had insisted, in the best thieves'-honor tradition.

But the gray-walled years had changed Big George's mind.

On his release, he went straight to the office of the Kansas City marshal. That astute officer, listening to his proposition, furnished him with a fake newspaper clipping purporting to relate how Shepherd, unswerving in his allegiance to his noble bandit pals of yore, had become the object of a widespread manhunt by the very officials he was working with. With this sorry bait, Big George is supposed to have sought out his former outlaw comrades.

Weeks later, he returned to Kansas City and the headlines blared his triumph.

JESSE JAMES IS DEAD!

Shepherd's story was simple.

Jesse and the boys had welcomed him heartily. At the opportune moment, he had got Jesse to one side, alone, and shot him.

For William Pinkerton the tale was *too* simple. Bulldog-wise, he demanded a body. None was forthcoming. The Pinkerton office refused the ex-guerrilla's claims, giving wide publicity to their clear discrepancies. For some time the official Pinkerton viewpoint was given broad public acceptance in Missouri. Those people *knew* Jesse James. You did not just walk out and take *Dingus* with any old newspaper yarn.

But then the months rolled on. There was no more Jesse. No more new gang. No more train-boardings. Public opinion wavered.

Cuss it all, maybe old George had got him. Maybe he had shot Dingus, after all. You had to admit George had been a member in good standing as of the Russelville, Kentucky, job. And that he had taken his medicine for that job without squawking on Dingus or Frank or any of the others. By damn, maybe Jesse had been glad to see old George. Maybe he had welcomed him into the new gang, just the way Big George told it. Maybe Jesse James *was* dead.

William Pinkerton shook his big head and thought otherwise.

Keeping his own counsel, he went back to his watching and waiting. As he did, 1880 wore away. Then 1881 eased past January, crawled through February, started, and only started, into March.

In the first week of that month the gang, with Frank back at Jesse's side, struck like lightning and far afield: at a stagecoach outside Muscle Shoals, Alabama!

It was a feint, only.

On July 10 the first of the real blows fell: on the Davis & Sexton Bank in Riverton, Iowa—to a net result of five thousand dollars and a spot-clean getaway.

But now the Pinkertons had their man back in the glare of the searchlight. All-points bulletins were dispatched into the five key states of Iowa, Missouri, Kentucky, Tennessee and Texas. In these bulletins Pinkerton tersely warned his operatives:

Missouri, the home state, is no longer safe for the gang. Its backwoods hideouts are all under twenty-four-hour Agency surveillance. Its local peace officers are at last alert under an anti-James administration. Jesse James is on a last, desperate raid to make a final, king's ransom killing and perhaps quit the outlaw trail forever. . . .

Five days after the wired warning, history fulfilled William Pinkerton's final prophecy.

Jesse began the forecast killing.

# Death Of A Legend

The engineer grumbled, jerking the throttle closed and throwing the sand and steam to the drivers. He had been late getting out of Kansas City, and the Chicago, Rock Island & Pacific's Train No. 23 was running twenty minutes back of schedule into Cameron station, sixty-four miles out of K.C.

Train No. 23 was running into something a little more sinister than a late schedule at Cameron station.

Three husky, bearded men made their way into her smoker as she pulled out for Gallatin, another sixty miles up the line. They were rough-looking men, their smoker-mates remembered, wearing black broadcloth suits of back-country cut, dirty riding boots and wide, dusty black hats. They spoke quickly among themselves in low, guarded tones, pulled their hats over their faces, slumped back in their seats and "went promptly to sleep."

It is to be assumed, from what followed, that this honest slumber was broken now and again by the half-lidded gleam of a professional eye scanning the smoker's assortment of plug hats from beneath those dusty, pulled-down hat-brims—and that on the part of one set of those eyes, at least, the covert regard was shuttered by a chronically sore-lidded blink.

At 10:01, No. 23 pulled into Gallatin, sat coughing nervously for five minutes, chuffed hurriedly on toward Winston, eleven miles ahead. It was 10:29 P.M., July 15, 1881, when she rolled into the Winston depot. The engineer had made up fourteen minutes, was feeling considerably better. He began to unburden himself, along those relieved lines, to his fireman.

While he was thus happily engaged, four other events of at least comparable importance were taking place behind him, in and about the body proper of train No. 23.

One of the bearded travelers in the smoker was coming half awake and was, his curious fellow passengers remarked, sleepily waving a large white handkerchief back and forth across his window to the apparently deserted platform of the Winston depot.

The smoker's conductor was swinging to the depot platform, chatting with the station agent a moment, swinging back aboard, reentering his smoker car and beginning, "with an affable smile," to collect his tickets and stick their tabs into the hatbands of his new passengers.

Two men were sliding out of the shadows north of the depot, running to the baggage car's handrail, swarming up it to the roof of the car, crawling stealthily along it toward the fireman's tender and the engineer's cab.

The three bearded slumberers in the smoker were leaping suddenly to their feet, jerking out Single Action Colt's revolvers, blasting a round of warning shots over their fellow passengers' startled heads, and shouting the old, familiar order:

312

"All right, get them up! Get them up! Don't nobody move or you'll get your heads blown off!"

With the order, their leader fired three shots at the oil lamp at the far end of the smoker. The lamp shattered. On the signal of its crash, the Great Winston Train Robbery was under way.

The conductor ran toward Jesse, who stood under the second, nearer lamp of the smoker, crying, "Don't break the other! Don't break that one you're by. We don't want a fire in here!"

As he came up to Jesse, the full light of the remaining lamp fell on his face, and for the first time the bandit leader had a clear, close look at No. 23's smoker-car conductor.

The former's eyes widened with sudden fury, the latter's with stark fear.

Over his shoulder, Jesse snarled to Frank and Wood Hite. "You remember this son of a bitch, boys? Look at the bastard, Frank. Look at him *good*!"

"Westphal! Good Lord, it's Billy Westphal!"

Frank's gasp of recognition seconded Jesse's snarled question. And was seconded in thundering turn by the explosions of Jesse's Colts.

He fired with both guns, into the conductor's groin. The trainman staggered back, turned and stumbled groaningly down the aisle toward the rear door. Jesse followed him, not hurrying, not trying to stop him, but pumping another deliberate shot into his back every three steps of the way.

Somehow, the dying man reached the vestibule door. Jesse stood back, out of his way, letting him fumble the door open, fall down the smoker's outer steps to the depot platform. Following only as far as the last step, he shot him four more times as he lay writhing on the pine planking.

Back in the smoker he simply nodded to Frank and Wood. *"He'll take no more trains into Kearney."*

Seven years before, conductor William Westphal had been in charge of the special Hannibal & St. Joe train which had crossed the Missouri to sidetrack at Kearney the night of the Samuel farmhouse bombing!

It is not known how Jesse remembered him after all those bitter years. And there is only tradition to tell us that he *did*. Or that Frank was even in the smoker with him *when* he did.

But that he killed him, and did it with "nine bullets, none fired at a range greater than ten feet, and five of them from behind," is the inhuman fact, based on eyewitness affidavits of fifteen fellow passengers, and upon the inquest findings still on file in the Daviess County coroner's office.

In her lean black book, fate was closing out the account of Jesse W. James. At the hour of the Winston robbery, there remained to his dark credit in her grim ledger only three mistakes to be made.

The moment William Westphal died, these three were less by one.

The Winston robbery was a miserable failure.

Jesse had possessed information that the combination express-baggage car was carrying upward of twenty-five thousand dollars. His informant had forgotten to state that the twenty-five thousand would be in the form of non-negotiable (via bandit wheatsack and saddlehorn, at least) fifteen-pound ingots of mint silver! Outside of the bullion there were only six hundred dollars in the United Express Company's safe.

And the affair in the smoker had been miserably mismanaged.

Another passenger, unstrung by Westphal's murder, had tried to run out of the car and the cursing bandit leader had cut him down in brutal turn. Frank and Wood Hite, stampeded by the double murder, had backed out of the car, abandoning the raging Jesse. At the same time, alarmed by the shooting in the smoker, the conductors in the train's only other cars, two coaches and a sleeper, had bolted their doors and put out all of their aisle-lights. Then, during the following assault on the express car, the engineer—his guards called off to aid in the fruitless sack of the express-company safe—had quickly extinguished his cab lamps and headlight, plunging the entire train into darkness.

Cursing their frustration, the bandit crew had run for their horses, a disorganized, inept, bungling facsimile of the once mighty James gang. They had not had time to steal a single watch or lift one passenger's pocket-change. The high cost of outlaw living was not dropping a penny, but the price of murder was going down. Splitting the six hundred dollars with his four accomplices, Jesse paid himself sixty dollars apiece for his two homicides.

A life for a life, and cheap at the price.

For that hundred and twenty dollars, Jesse bought his own death warrant.

Governor Thomas Crittenden, who in 1881 had just come into Missouri's executive mansion, signed the lethal paper. Crittenden had campaigned for the governorship and won it smashingly on an unprecedentedly simple platform: *The solemn determination to overthrow and to destroy the outlawry in this state whose head and front is the James gang.*

Missouri law forbade the offering of more than three hundred dollars in reward money. When the news of Winston and Westphal's murder reached the state house, Governor Crittenden forgot the law. He summoned a secret conclave of railroad-company heads to Jefferson City. On July 28, one week after the Winston robbery, he called in the press and released the terms of the warrant Jesse had drawn with his own pistols:

A reward of $5,000 for the capture of Frank and Jesse James and $5,000 for the conviction of each is hereby posted. It is understood that the railroads will supply the funds. . . .

For the first time in fifteen years a *real* price had been put on Jesse's head. In simple terms, since conviction was certain, it meant that his captors would stand to pocket ten thousand hard dollars.

Judas Iscariot had hired out for thirty pieces of silver.

For five years to the day after the citizens of Northfield had begun to lower it along Division Street, the last-act curtain rang down on the stage career of Jesse James.

Enemies were now everywhere. Pinkertons swarmed over the state. Local peace officers, fired by financial ambition, were at last on the hungry prowl. Private citizens, ex-guerrillas, sometime outlaw comrades of yore, all alike pricked pecuniary ears and took the golden trail. The governor's ten thousand pieces of silver stared at the hunted men from every cabin door in western Missouri.

While the huntsmen prowled the orchestra pit, Jesse came out of the wings.

Will Henry

Curtain time was 8 P.M. of the evening of September 7, 1881. The stage was twice-familiar to the veteran cast—Blue Cut near Glendale, Missouri.

Act One was redundant.

The pile of cross-ties athwart the rails of the Chicago & Alton roadbed. The scream of the whistle, the lock of the drivers. The rough, bearded men leaping aboard the slowing cars. The engineer covered and escorted to the express car by the nervously blinking star of the piece.

But Act Two had been rewritten by the leading man himself.

In the deviation, Jesse withdrew the second of his remaining mistakes from fate's dwindling account-book. For the first time in the history of the play, and for a reason known only to its author, Jesse introduced the members of the cast to its unwilling audience.

With a flourish of his pistols, the bearded hero bowed to the engineer and the express messenger.

"Allow me to introduce myself," he drawled. "I'm Jesse James."

Then, without waiting for the applause:

"This is my brother, Frank James. The one with the big grin and the bad front teeth is my dear cousin, Wood Hite. That's Cousin Clarence Hite with him. This is Dick Liddell, Ed Miller, and Charlie Ford. I don't believe I caught your gentlemen's names—?"

What possessed Jesse in this moment of peculiar rashness can scarcely be imagined. Nothing could have been less typical of him. What would bring a man who had made a lifelong fetish of hiding his face and name, and who had for fifteen years demanded and got a fantastic loyalty from his followers as to their own or their fellow robbers' identities, to suddenly make a stage-play of this sort is still hard to understand.

The only key was furnished many years later by the self-effacing Jim Cummins. Speaking to a *Kansas City Times* reporter in answer to the question, quiet Jim looked back across the years and said:

"After Northfield, Jess was never the same. He got a little crazy, I think. Me and most of the others from the old bunch got a little leery of him after that. You couldn't trust him no more and we fought shy of him." Then, after a long pause, the final soft drawl:

"We always figured he never got over running out on Cole. Cole was really the smart one, you know. Nobody else could ever handle Jesse after he was gone. We all thought a heap of Old Cole. He was the best of the lot."

But whatever possessed him in the opening moments of the second Blue Cut robbery, and whatever the key to it, Jesse quickly recovered. With his introductions made, he returned to standard form for Act Three.

The safe was cleaned out, the passengers

fleeced, the wheatsack tied and the getaway made on smooth schedule. But it was a lean fall for highway harvests. Total gleanings from the second Glendale cutting amounted to only two thousand dollars in cash and jewelry.

The voluntary identification of the gang's members was on the telegraph wires within twenty minutes of the robbery. By daybreak, Missouri was teeming with blood-money badgetoters.

By dint of immediate split-up and all-night, wild riding, the gang got across the state and safely away. By nightfall of the 18th they were over the Tennessee line. They reached the hideout at the home of Frank James outside Nashville the next day.

Here they held together for three days. Then the disintegration began. It had been building hourly since Jesse's erratic naming of his fellows in the Chicago & Alton express car. When Frank returned from a scout into Nashville and reported that William Pinkerton himself was in the city, the long-delayed disaffection set in.

Charlie Ford was the first to go, disappearing without saying good-bye, some time during the night of the 22nd. Clarence and Wood Hite followed him twenty-four hours later. Dick Liddell was the next to depart. In leaving, he told Jesse that the Hites had gone to the family hideout in Kentucky and that Ford was heading for his Ray County, Missouri, farm. Ed Miller, brother of the dead Clell, stuck it out until that night, then announced that he, too, was cutting his stick.

Jesse looked at him a long time, finally nodded.

"Wait up," he said. "I'm coming with you."

Even in his last den the Clay County wolf had a plan. He had already let too many of the pack get away. Running loose as they were, their howling was bound to be heard sooner or later. This last one of them to leave had better be followed. It was the least a man could do. No use leaving Ed take to the woods alone. Or get off by himself where he could start to yapping.

For Frank, he had a parting piece of advice, one that rang a singular note of dark prophecy.

"You'd best stick here, Buck. Things are going to pop up yonder. I'll get in touch with you."

He and Ed crossed into Missouri that same night, bound for the Samuel place in Clay County. Somewhere short of their destination, Jesse murdered Ed Miller.

The known facts are few. Early on the morning of the 25th, a farmer who knew Jesse well saw him riding south of Norborne, Carroll County, "with a companion on a brown horse." Later that same day, the farmer heard a man's body had been found in some blackberry bushes north of Norborne. He rode over and had a look. It was the man on the brown horse.

Meantime, other murderers were afoot.

The morning of his arrival in Ray County, Charlie Ford held hurried council with his

# Will Henry

young brother, Bob, a sometime hanger-on of the James gang. Within the hour, Bob saddled up and rode away—straight for the governor's mansion in Jefferson City. Here the business was short, if far from sweet. Yes, his Excellency did guarantee the ten thousand dollars for the boys. He guaranteed it—no matter his proclamation was not clear on the point—for *either* Frank or Jesse. And yes, the guarantee *did* stand at *Dead or Alive*.

Bob Ford was back at his brother's farm by nightfall.

A few days later, he and Charlie were in Kansas City, where "Mr. Howard" had joined his wife and children in a rented house. Charlie stayed with Jesse and his family for several days. Bob rode back to the Ford farm almost at once.

In Kansas City, the sojourn was brief. Within the month Jesse accompanied Charlie Ford to the Ray County farm. Here they were in time to learn that Wood Hite had come in from Kentucky some days earlier. They did not get to talk to Cousin Wood, however. The previous night, Liddell and Bob Ford, fearful that Hite had gone over to the law, had murdered him in the farmhouse living room, Bob delivering the *coup de grace* with a "single shot through the head."

This was not, of course, the story Cousin Jesse got. And Liddell, seeing the narrow blink with which Jesse received the lie, reached a sound conclusion. When the latter suggested that "he take a little ride with him and Charlie," Liddell hastily declined.

In his subsequent confession, he put the refusal succinctly. "They tried to get me to go with them," he stated, "but I declined to go. I mistrusted Jesse by that time and believed he wanted to kill me. When he had come up from Nashville leading Ed Miller's brown horse and told us Ed had been took sick and he didn't think he would get well very soon, we all knew what had happened. So I refused to go with him and Charlie and they left."

The year turned. Jesse flitted through the mid-Missouri backwoods like a ghost, now sleeping a night at the Samuel place, now lurking a nervous week with his wife in Kansas City, now returning for a few days with the Fords. Finally, he removed his family to St. Joseph, renting the ill-fated "little white house on the hill."

Mr. Howard had made his last move.

January passed, March drew to a close. And through every hour of their crawling passage the Fords, through a third brother, Elias "Cap" Ford, were in touch with Jackson County's Sheriff Timberlake. Timberlake, in turn, kept his posse on a twenty-four-hour standby alert and held a special train in Kansas City, "under full steam and prepared to roll on ten minutes' notice."

The trap was ready, and straining at its springs. On March 29, the last ounce of treacherous weight was gingerly placed on its sensitive pan.

Dick Liddell, who had surrendered to Timberlake on a promise of clemency from Governor Crittenden, signed a fourteen-page confession. In it he named dates, places and faces for every job the gang had pulled since Northfield.

Liddell's "coming in" had been well guarded by the authorities. It was not until his confession hit the front page of the *Kansas City Times* on April 2 that his former colleagues had any idea where he had gone and what he had done.

Even then, the news was overnight in reaching St. Joe. Jesse's first hint of it was when he stepped out on the front stoop of the Howard home to pick up his copy of the *St. Joseph Gazette* the morning of April 3.

Behind him in the "little white house" at the historic moment were his mother, his wife and two children, and Bob and Charlie Ford. In his statement at the inquest, Bob Ford related that Jesse walked into the living room from the porch, holding the paper, unfolded.

"He stopped just inside the door," he continues, "opened the paper and looked at it. He gave a little start and then just stood there staring over the top of the paper at us and blinking like he always did when upset."

Ford's next line was unquestionably the correct translation of that last, pale-eyed blink.

"I knew then I had placed my head in the

lion's mouth," he says fearfully. "How could I safely remove it?"

It was just after 8 A.M. the morning of April 3 when he asked himself the question. A few moments later, fate answered it for him.

For the first time in sixteen years, Jesse took off his guns.

Fate was waiting. It was the third mistake. His account was overdrawn. Quietly, the black book closed. Its last page bore the purple cancellation stamp of the fabled telegram dispatched to Governor Crittenden and Sheriff Timberlake at 8:27 A.M.

"I HAVE KILLED JESSE JAMES. ST. JOSEPH. BOB FORD."

The news struck a stunned Missouri to her editorial knees. On the front pages of every paper within the state, the voice of a heartbroken people was heard. "JESSE BY JEHOVAH," solemnly announced the *St. Joseph Gazette*. "THE KING IS DEAD!" cried the *Osceola Democrat*. "JUDGMENT FOR JESSE," tolled the *Evening News*, "THE NOTORIOUS BANDIT AT LAST MEETS HIS FATE AND DIES WITH HIS BOOTS ON!"

The *Kansas City Journal* said it best. Her banner was the heartbeat of a homeland, faithful even unto death.

"GOOD-BYE JESSE!"

The coroner's inquest was held at 3:00 P.M., in the old circuit courtroom of St. Joseph's Buchanan County courthouse. Present were Mrs. Zerelda Samuel, Mrs. Zerelda James, and

Dick Liddell and Bob and Charlie Ford, the latter "all heavily armed."

The brief rest is best and most brutally told in the testimonies of the two principal witnesses: Robert and Charles Ford. The latter was the first under cross-examination.

". . . Well, now, will you explain how it was you came to kill him?"

"Well, we had come in from the barn where we had been feeding and currying the horses, and Jesse complained of being warm and pulled off his coat and threw it on the bed and opened the door and said that he guessed he would pull off his gun-belt as some person might see it. Then he went to brush off some pictures, and when he turned his back I gave my brother the wink and we both pulled our pistols but he, my brother, was the quickest and fired first. I had my finger on the trigger and was just going to fire but I saw his shot was a death shot and did not fire. He heard us cock our pistols and turned his head. The ball struck him in the back of the head and he fell. Then we went out and got our hats, and we went and telegraphed Sheriff Timberlake what we had done. . . ."

Robert Ford was then called, and followed his older brother on the witness stand. It is remem-

bered that he gave his evidence in a "clear, firm
voice and did not once falter."

". . . And did the governor then tell you anything about a reward?"

"He said ten thousand dollars had been
offered for Jesse or Frank dead or alive. I
then entered into arrangements with Timberlake. I afterward told Charlie of the conversation I had with the officers and told
him I would like to go with him. He said if
I was willing to go, all right. We started that
night, and went up to Mrs. Samuel's and
put the horses up. Jesse's stepbrother, John
Samuel, was wounded and they were expecting him to die. There were some
friends of the family there whom Jesse did
not wish to see him, so we stayed in the
barn all night until they left, and that was
pretty near daylight, and we stayed in the
house all next day, and that night we
started away. That was on Thursday night;
Friday night we stayed at his brother-in-
law's. We left Mrs. Samuel and went about
three miles into the woods for fear the officers would surprise us at her house. We
started from the woods and came up to another of his brother-in-law's and got supper
there and started from there here."

"This was last week?"

"Yes. We came at once to St. Joseph and then talked over the matter again, and how we would kill him."

"What did you tell Jesse you were with him for?"

"I told him I was going with him."

"Had you any plans made at the time to rob any particular bank?"

"He had spoken of several but had made no particular selection."

"Well, now, will you give us the particulars of the killing and what time it occurred?"

"After breakfast, between eight and nine o'clock this morning, he, my brother and myself were in the room. He pulled off his pistols and got up on a chair to dust off some picture frames and I drew my pistol and shot him."

"How close were you to him?"

"About six feet away."

"How close was the hand which held the pistol?"

"About four feet I should think."

"Did he say anything?"

"He started to turn his head but didn't say a word."

"Do you know anyone that can identify him?"

"Yes, sir, Sheriff Timberlake can when he comes. He was with him during the war."

For three days the witnesses came forward, each in his somber turn declaring his association with the bandit chief, swearing to the identity of the bearded corpse. Mrs. Zerelda Samuel was the last witness called. Her broken testimony concluded the inquest over all that was mortal of Jesse Woodson James.

"I live in Clay County and am the mother of Jesse James. Oh, my poor boy. I have seen the body since my arrival and have recognized it as that of my son, Jesse. The lady by my side is my daughter-in-law and the children hers. He was a kind husband and son. . . ."

Nothing remained but the inevitable post-script returned by the coroner's jury twenty-eight minutes after filing out: that the body of the deceased was that of Jesse W. James and that he came to his death by a wound in the back of his head, caused by a pistol shot fired intentionally by the hand of Robert Ford.

Thus, officially, closed the Last Act. The house lights went down. The play was over.

The body was taken by train to Kearney. For twenty-four hours the coffin stood open in the lobby of the Kearney House, the town's single hotel. All day long the pushing crowds filed past the casket, fighting and shoving for a look at the famous outlaw. By nightfall, untold hundreds had gazed upon the fabulous face of Jesse James. Perhaps in the entire gaping multitude there were a lone, hard-eyed handful of bearded, rough-clothed strangers who knew it well, and nodded silently to one another.

Even in the last, still-cold hour, Jesse James was only a name. He had no face.

Funeral services were held at the Kearney Baptist Church. The text was taken from the Book of Job, xii, 8: *Man that is born of woman is of few days and full of trouble.* . . .

At 4:00 P.M., the cortege wound slowly across the graying hills toward the Samuel farmhouse. Once more, Zerelda Mimms stood in a farmyard beneath a tree and watched them bring her lover home.

But this was not a catalpa tree, and not her

father's farmyard. And this was no nineteen-year-old cousin for whom she waited now. Sixteen weary years had fled. The day was late, the sun low.

By its last light, the coffin was lowered into the grave at the foot of the lone coffee-bean tree fronting the Samuel place. The clods showered hollowly down, the shovels shaped the final moundings of the heavy earth. The men went away, still-faced. Their women stayed to weep.

Presently, Mrs. Samuel shivered to the evening breeze. She drew her dark shawl closer, moved away toward the house and toward the beckoning warmth of its yellow lamplight. Zerelda Mimms was alone with the shadows and the crushed flowers and the faint marble legend of the man for whom she had waited a thousand lonely nights:

JESSE W. JAMES

DIED APRIL 3, 1882

AGED 34 YEARS, 6 MONTHS, 28 DAYS

MURDERED BY A TRAITOR AND A COWARD

WHOSE NAME IS NOT WORTHY TO APPEAR

HERE.

When the moon came, she was still there. Still waiting for Jesse.

Somewhere, far out in the ghostland of the crowding hardwood forest, away and across the silent Clay County hills, a lonesome hound bayed keeningly and long.

*Was it Old Hickory?*

# ABOUT THE AUTHOR

WILL HENRY was born and grew up in Missouri, where he attended Kansas City Junior College. Upon leaving school, he lived and worked throughout the Western states, acquiring the background of personal experience reflected later in the realism of his books. Presently residing in California, he writes for motion pictures and television, as well as continuing his research into frontier lore and legend, which are the basis for his unique blend of history and fiction. Four of his novels have been purchased for motion picture production, and several have won top literary awards, including four of the coveted Spur Awards of the Western Writers of America. Mr. Henry's most recent books include: *The Bear Paw Horses, From Where The Sun Now Stands, The Fourth Horseman, Chiricahua* and *The Raiders*.

# MAX BRAND

## RIDERS OF THE SILENCES

**"Brand is a topnotcher!"**
*—New York Times*

He sweeps down from the north like a cold blast of death. His name is Red Pierre, and he is bent on drawing blood. The locals say the man he hunts can't be beaten. But six years of riding with a wolf pack have left Red Pierre with a burning hate and a steady trigger finger. Now he is going to get the bushwhacker who shot his father. And if his six-guns can't put the yellowbelly six feet under, he'll go after his gutless enemy with his bare hands.

\_3838-2                                          $4.50 US/$5.50 CAN

# WILDERNESS
## The epic struggle for survival
## in America's untamed West.